And so there grew great
Wherein the beast was e
But man was less and le
Alfred, Lord Tennyson,

Whoso pulleth out this sword of this stone and anvil, is rightwise king born of all England.
Thomas Malory, Le Morte d'Arthur

Nay, I may not so, for I have promised to do the battle to the uttermost by the faith of my body, while me lasteth the life, and therefore I had liefer to die with honour than to live with shame; and if it were possible for me to die an hundred times, I had liefer to die so oft than yield me to thee; for though I lack weapon, I shall lack no worship, and if thou slay me weaponless that shall be thy shame.
Arthur to Sir Accolon, Thomas Malory, Le Morte d'Arthur

On a lonely sword leaned he,
Like Arthur on Excalibur
In the battle by the sea.
G. K. Chesterton, The Ballad of the White Horse

Other books in the Padwolf 13 Series:

APOCALYPSE 13 Edited by Diane Raetz
MERMAIDS 13 Edited by John L. French
FANTASTIC FUTURES 13 Edited by Robert E Waters & James R Stratton
LUCKY 13 Edited by Edward J. McFadden III

Other Padwolf books by John L. French & Patrick Thomas
RITES OF PASSAGE: *a DMA casefile of Agent Karver & Bianca Jones*
FROM THE SHADOWS/BULLETS & BRIMESTONE *a Mystic Investigators omnibus {forthcoming}*

Other Padwolf books by John L. French

PAST SINS
BAD COP NO DONUT [editor]
THE NIGHTMARE STRIKES
THE GREY MONK: SOULS ON FIRE
THE DEVIL OF HARBOR CITY (coming soon)

Bianca Jones series
HERE BE MONSTERS
MONSTERS AMONG US

Other Padwolf books by Patrick Thomas
AS THE GEARS TURN: *Tales of Steamworld* - EXILE & ENTRANCE
NEW BLOOD Edited by Diane Raetz & Patrick Thomas

THE MURPHY'S LORE™ SERIES
TALES FROM BULFINCHE'S PUB - FOOLS' DAY
THROUGH THE DRINKING GLASS - SHADOW OF THE WOLF
REDEMPTION ROAD - BARTENDER OF THE GODS

THE MURPHY'S LORE AFTER HOURS™ UNIVERSE
NIGHTCAPS - EMPTY GRAVES
FAIRY WITH A GUN - FAIRY RIDES THE LIGHTNING
DEAD TO RITES: *The DMA Casefiles of Agent Karver™*
LORE & DYSORDER: *The Hell's Detective™ Mysteries*
BY DARKNESS CURSED: *a Hexcraft™ collection*
BY INVOCATION ONLY: *a Hexcraft™ novel*
GREATEST HITS: *a Soul For Hire™ collection*

MURPHY'S LORE STARTENDERS™
STARTENDERS - CONSTELLATION PRIZE

DEAR CTHULHU™ Series
HAVE A DARK DAY - GOOD ADVICE FOR BAD PEOPLE
CTHULHU KNOWS BEST - WHAT WOULD CTHULHU DO?
CTHULHU HAPPENS

CELEBRATING THE SPIRIT OF ARTHUR AND HIS KNIGHTS

edited by
John L. French and Patrick Thomas

PADWOLF PUBLISHING INC.
WWW.PADWOLF.COM

CA MLEOT 13: *Celebrating the spirit of Arthur and His Knights*
Edited by John L. French & Patrick Thomas

Cover Art © Daniel R. Horne

Cover design Roy Mauritsen

ISBN 13 digit 9781890096779, 10 digit 1-890096-77-6

Thomas Malory defined knighthood as living one's life for the greater good, placing character above riches, and concern for others above personal wealth.

Malory's knights vowed to refute sexism in all its guises; to be fair to all, faithful in love, and loyal in friendship.

To all those who live as Malory wished his knights to do, to those who strive to do the right thing without thought of reward or recognition, this book is dedicated.

As long as knights such as you still live among us, Camelot has not yet fallen.

The Quests

The Knight's Tale

Michael A. Black & Dave Case

The story of King Arthur, Camelot, and the Knights and the Round Table has evolved through the years into many incarnations. As the seeds of mythology are said to have been planted with reality, this story follows in kind. Step back into the time of kings and knights, sovereignty and honor, and the legends to come.

He dropped the helmet first, and then unstrapped the breastplate. Not knowing how far he'd traveled in the darkness, fatigue and the pain of his injuries finally caused him to tumble from his mount. The trained war horse stayed by his side waiting for his master to rise, but Lancelot lay on the uneven ground, the wet mud seeping through the links of his chainmail. The blood continued to flow from the wound, but the pain was nothing compared to the dreams.

The demons had visited upon him the night before the duel, and he had fallen on his own sword. As he felt himself slipping into the netherworld, overcome by fatigue and pain, he prayed they would not return. But if they did, he still grasped his sword.

The dispute between Sir Gawain and him had been both taxing and bloody, but he had fought to defend the reputation and honor of the Queen. Gawain's spurious insinuation had breached the limits of royal deference. Normally, Lancelot could have bested his fellow knight with ease, but he'd gone into the contest with an open wound on his side which laced each movement with a searing pain. The scarlet ribbon of his own blood had begun to leak through his chain mail even before the initial joust. He had taken particular care to pack it with dry strips of cloth to prevent any unseemly stains prior to the initial foray. After it started, any conspicuous blood would, he had reasoned, be relegated to the assumption that it had been sustained in the combat.

A cold rain pelted him and Lancelot rolled over, face down upon the muddy ground. Hoof-churned soil and filthy water lapped upon his face and he struggled to lift himself. His powerful body shook with effort, but failed to gain his release from the sodden earth. Twice more he attempted to sit up, finally managing to place his arm partially under his cheek to prevent his submersion into the expanding puddle. The moonlight seemed to filter through the tops of the leafy canopy. Or was it the rising sun? He did not know, nor did he care. Lancelot, knight of the realm, first guardian of King Arthur, had fulfilled his mission, serving the King and defending the Queen's honor. If that was to be his last measure as a knight, then so be it. He was exhausted now, and he would rest… Closing his eyes, he knew not what waited for him on the other side of slumber as the darkness descended.

A black void…

Voices…

Were they part of his dream?

No, these voices were disparate, intrusive. A man … A woman … Guinevere?

Not the queen. A young girl.

"But, Father—"

"No. This is a man, not one of your rescued forest creatures." This voice was older, authoritative.

Lancelot kept his eyes closed, and surreptitiously flexed his muscles, testing whether or not he was bound.

"You should have left him where he fell," the male voice said.

"But he would have died."

"And if the Duke discovers a strange knight amongst us, what then, Daughter? Need I remind you of the temerity of the Duke's wrath?"

Lancelot felt unencumbered by any shackles, but where was his sword? And his armor? The last thing he remembered was riding off, in pain, from the battle with Gawain, lest his own injuries be discovered. He had to find out where he was.

Opening his eyes, he took in the surroundings. It was a hut made of stone and straw, the walls packed with mud. Embers glowed in a stone hearth on the far side of the room, radiating heat and funneling the smoke out a crude piping made of more stones. He turned his head and saw the man and the girl and no one else. The man wore a threadbare tunic. The girl's garment was equally ragged and worn. A profusion of dark hair descended on either side of an angelic face. She was young and just reaching the full ripening stage of womanhood.

She turned toward him and her eyes widened. Twin pools of amber held his gaze, soft, and unlike Guinevere's, but striking just the same.

"Where am I?" Lancelot asked. His own voice sounded cracked and harsh.

The man turned and a frown twisted his countenance as the girl rushed to Lancelot. Her hands dipped to the side of the pile of woven blankets upon which he lay, and she came up with a damp cloth which she used to dab his face and wet his lips.

"You've been hurt," she said, her voice a soothing whisper. "You must rest." She turned to the man. "Father, to turn him out will surely kill him. He must stay here until he has regained his strength. Please. I beg of you."

The man's scowl twisted his visage further, and then he nodded.

Moving to the door, he paused before peeling back the waxed cloth which separated the inside of the hut from the outside. "A fortnight, dear daughter. No more than that. And pray that the Duke's men do not come early to collect our taxes."

Lancelot watched as the man thrust aside the hanging curtain and stormed off.

"Where am I?" he asked again. "And who are you?"

"I am called Elaine," she said, quickly covering him with the worn blanket. "You are in the province of Corbin."

"And who is this duke your father spoke of?"

"Duke Pelles." The color drained from her face.

"Pelles?" The name sounded foreign on his tongue.

"But you must not ask of him." Her lips drew into a tight line. "He is a very powerful man. And ruthless. Now you must rest. Overcome the fever that burns within you."

Lancelot started to speak but suddenly felt weak. His vision fogged, and he was engulfed by a wave of heat, but at the same time he felt so cold he began to shiver.

"Sleep," she said. "You must rest."

Fairies and dragons danced through his mind ... Comely nymphs waded in the cool water of a pond, laughing and smiling as he strode forward, only to see the fairies coalesce into a huge dragon. The dragon's mouth opened wide releasing a torrent of fiery dragon's spew that engulfed him.

Heat... His body was on fire, and then it was suddenly cold. His teeth chattered and he began shaking. A soft warmth moved against him.

Her flesh pressed to his, the softness of her supple body, warming him, cooling him, exciting him. His groin stirred and he looked at the vision before him.

"Guinevere?" he asked.

Through the haze of fever, he saw her smile.

Yes, yes, he thought. But no, they should not. The King...

He felt her finger tracing over his chest, his stomach, his hips…

Lower.

"Guinevere?" he asked again.

A finger touched his lips, silencing him.

It was all right … everything was all right.

The dragon's hot breath vanished and the cooling touch of the nymphs engulfed him. Waves of pleasure washed over him, immersing his body in the soothing warmth of a blue lake. Serenity soon followed.

Lancelot awoke in the semi-darkness of the now familiar hut to find the girl's naked body pressed against his. Startled, he sat up and thrust off the coverings of blankets, feeling the pain in his side. This movement stirred her to consciousness and her brown eyes looked up at him.

"How do you feel?" she asked, the back of her hand pressed against his forehead.

He felt the cool air against his skin and realized he was naked. "What has happened here?"

"You had the fever," she said. "The fire was not enough to keep you warm. I used my own body."

Lancelot's eyes swept over her: the swell of her breasts, the curve of her hip ... She was a comely lass and indeed a woman.

"Did we…?" He let the sentence die in his throat. The scarlet blush that crept up her neck was answer enough.

Lancelot felt a rush of shame. He had betrayed his true love, Guinevere, but not surely knowingly, not intentionally. Theirs was an unrequited love. So seeking solace with this girl, in the time of his unknowing, could hardly be something to be regretted, could it?

She touched the crusty scab on his side. "Tis healing nicely. I have been applying special herbs and the roots of the ginger plant."

He felt the wound as well. It did feel almost healed.

Her fingers moved upward, snaking around his thick neck and urging him downward into her waiting embrace.

He resisted for only a moment, then his calloused hands began to roam over her, caressing her charms.

For the next few days they frolicked together, running through the wooded glens, wading in the warm waters of the stream, occasionally hiding in a cave or hollowed tree as Elaine's father searched for them, calling out to her that he needed help in the field.

"You must come out," his frustrated voice bellowed while they hid scant yards away in the tall shrubs. "The Duke's men will come tomorrow to collect the tax and there is much work to be done."

With only silence answering, the old man wandered off, his head bowed.

Lancelot felt a rush of guilt. Would not a true knight be of better service to assist the old man in his husbandry? Still, he found the fetching beauty of Elaine irresistible.

"The duke again?" He asked. "You must tell me of him."

Elaine's pretty face pulled taut, her eyes seeking the ground.

"He's a very evil man," she said. "He rules the province, and his men come every month, even in the lean times, to extract their booty. They take what they want."

"What do they take? Your crops?"

She nodded, then looked downward again. "Among other things."

"Other things?"

She looked down once more. "Have you not noticed how few young people we have in our village?"

He lifted her chin until her eyes met his gaze.

"Did this not strike you as strange?" she asked.

Before he could answer, she continued. "The Duke takes whatever and whomever he pleases. He takes the young men to serve as his serfs and work within the walls of his castle. They are sometimes forced into the Duke's militia, taught to fight, and added to his legion of ruffians." She paused. "The girls, he takes to be his wenches. When he tires of them, they scrub the floors and are passed to his men-at-arms."

"How long has this tyrant ruled?"

"For as long as I can remember." Her throat tightened visibly. "They took my younger brother three months ago. I would have been taken as well, save for my father managing to hide me in the woods each time."

"How old is your brother?"

"He is but ten and six years." Tears welled up in her eyes. "I so fear for him."

That such a situation could exist so close to Camelot distressed Lancelot. His residual guilt came galloping back regarding his conduct with this young woman. Frolicking had no place in knighthood, especially when there were injustices to set right.

They heard screams emanating from the village, accompanied by men shouting and harsh laughter.

"Tis the Duke's men," Elaine said. "They have come early."

They began running toward the village. A group of five men, three still on horseback, swaggered in the center of the huts, laughing, taunting... One of them seized Elaine's father by the hair and forced him to his knees. The ursine ruffian drew a long dagger from his boot and held it to the old man's throat.

"And where is that sweet daughter of yours?" the ruffian asked. "Tales of her ripeness have caught the Duke's attention. He wishes to sample her wiles."

"Never," the old man said, his hands gripping the other man's gauntleted wrist. "You take our food, our youth. Have you no decency?"

"You dare question the sovereign decree of your Duke?" The ruffian pressed the point of the blade against the old man's cheek, drawing it downward and leaving a crimson thread. "I think I'll cut off one of your ears so you'll be reminded to listen more attentively."

Lancelot was almost upon them now. He and Elaine stopped by the corner of a nearby hut.

"Where is my sword?" he asked, knowing he had no time to don his armor.

"Tis in yonder hut," she said.

"Fetch it for me," he said.

He watched her slip away, and then surveyed the brutal scene in front of him. The ruffian's laughter was accompanied by the grinning leers and chuckles of his compatriots.

"Do it, Newberry," one of the men on horseback shouted. "Cut off the pig's ear."

"And make him eat it," another said. "I'll bet it's as tough as a sow's bum."

As their chuckling continued, Newberry grabbed the old man's ear and set his blade upon it.

Lancelot knew he could wait no longer. He stepped from between the huts and strode toward the group.

"Release him now," he said.

The ruffian paused with his cutting and looked toward Lancelot. A simper spread over his face, exposing a gap-toothed cavern.

"What have we here? The man's dagger dropped to his side. "From where did you come?"

"Release that man or feel my wrath," Lancelot said. His arms hung at the ready. Perhaps only the length of a scant rod separated them.

"*Your* wrath?" Newberry said. He shoved Elaine's father to the ground and brought his fingers up to scratch the blond stubble on his portly cheek. The movement left a reddish streak of the old man's blood. "Methinks another lesson is in order here." Moving quickly for a man his size, the big ruffian reached with his free hand and thrust the dagger with his other.

Lancelot parried the blow, grasping the hand that held the knife, and then quickly turning the blade inward, toward the overstuffed belly of the ruffian. The metal thrust upward into the softness, spilling a torrent of blood onto the dry earth. Lancelot twisted the man's wrist, ensuring the blade would do maximum damage.

Newberry's face sagged and he released his hold on the knife, both hands going to his expansive gut. He fell to his knees, the flow of crimson now cascading downward, accompanied by a serpentine loop of entrails.

Lancelot withdrew the dagger and stepped forward, using a slashing motion that almost severed the head of the next closest man-at-arms. As the ruffian fell, one of the men on horseback surged forward, withdrawing a sword from its sheath.

Lancelot danced to the side of the charging steed and stabbed downward, piercing the rider's left thigh with the blade of the dagger. Dropping his sword, the rider screamed in pain, still atop his horse as it galloped off.

Two more riders remained. Both of them withdrew their swords and charged forward. Once again stepping to the side, Lancelot flipped the dagger upward, caught it by the tip, and hurled it toward one of the men on horseback as he passed.

The blade caught the man in the back of the neck and he slumped over, dropping his sword as his horse continued to run in terror.

The final horseman reined his animal around and glanced back at Lancelot. A smile crept over the mounted ruffian's face at seeing Lancelot devoid of weapons. He kicked into the horse's flanks and lurched toward him. Lancelot doubted his sidestep would work yet again, and waited. His only chance was to try to duck under the descending blade and perhaps trip the animal.

Then the unexpected happened.

Elaine ran from one of the huts holding his long sword. The horseback ruffian's eyes diverted momentarily to her, and he swiveled the steed toward her.

The horse plowed into her, but as Elaine fell to the ground she managed to fling the sword upward. It rotated in the air, the sun glinting off its steely blade, and Lancelot simultaneously grabbed the horse's snout with his left hand and caught the spinning sword with his right.

Pulling the animal's long snout away from the girl, he thrust his blade into the body cavity of the last ruffian. The man screamed as a gush of blood flew outward from his snarling mouth. The horse strode forward three more steps, away from the supine girl, and the rider fell from the saddle.

Lancelot turned, his sword at the ready, checking for any new threats, but saw none. The man with the leg wound was as nowhere to be seen. The others were dead or almost so. Lancelot plunged his sword into the earth and knelt next to Elaine. His fingers brushed errant hair from her face and she stirred to consciousness.

"Are you all right?" he asked.

She nodded.

He picked her up into his arms and stood, cradling her against his chest.

The angry voice of her father intruded. "What have you done?"

Lancelot stared at the man.

"You have brought the wrath of the Duke upon us now," the old man said, trying to staunch the flow of blood from his ear with a soiled rag. "He will surely wreak a terrible vengeance."

"It appears that his wrath was already upon you."

"You do not understand," the old man said. "The surviving rider will tell him of this, and he will send the Dark Destroyer to lay waste to our village."

"The Dark Destroyer?"

"His champion knight." The rag was saturated with blood now. "A demon in armor. The best in the land."

Without another word, Lancelot turned and carried Elaine into their hut.

"Must you go, my love?" Elaine asked as Lancelot scrubbed the mud off of his breastplate.

He ignored her question. "Where is my helmet? And my shield?"

"The helmet was covered with dirt," the girl said, turning her face toward the wall. He still saw the tracks of her tears winding their way down her smooth cheeks. "I sent two boys down to the stream to clean it."

Lancelot nodded and considered how far out of control he'd let this situation become. After taking a deep breath, he stepped toward her and placed his hands on her shoulders. She jerked at his touch, then placed her fingers over his. "Must you go? You could be killed."

"Aye, and the same holds true if I stay here. Only then, you and the rest of the villagers would be at risk as well." His fingers caressed her neck, gently squeezing, her skin feeling like silk beneath his touch. He wished he had the chance to make love to her one more time, but in his heart he knew that, too, had been a mistake. Had he sown the seeds of his own destruction?

"But the Dark Destroyer has a cadre of knights," she said. "He will not fight you alone."

"They have never faced a foe like me. One who is true of heart." He turned her face toward him and let his lips brush hers. "You must gather your father and the rest of the villagers. Flee into the woods until I come back for you."

She looked up at him. "And if you do not?"

Before he could answer, two boys rushed into the hut carrying Lancelot's helmet. It had been washed and shined until it gleamed like a silver beacon in the candlelight.

"Your helmet, Sir," one of the youths said.

Lancelot smiled and took the helmet from them, placing it under his arm. He turned back to Elaine. "So you were not able to recover my shield?"

She shook her head.

This bothered him. He must have dropped it back in Camelot, after the contest against Gawain. No shield, no lance, but at least he had his sword. And his horse.

"Your steed has been watered and saddled, Sir," the youth said. "He awaits."

Lancelot nodded and smiled, dismissing the two boys. He wished he had some tokens to give them, but he was bereft of anything of value. But then a thought struck him and he called to them to halt and took out the long dagger that he'd taken from the dead ruffian's belly. The blade was keenly sharp, and Lancelot pried off two small pieces of mesh from his chainmail undergarment. He invaginated the dagger and gave each boy a piece.

"Hold these dear," he said. "And remember they were given to you by a Knight of the Round Table. Be that it as it may that one day you both shall become knights." The eyes of the two urchins widened. "Present these pieces at Camelot and tell this tale to the King. If I am not present, tell him I promised you to be squires. He will see that it is done." He glanced at Elaine, then back to the boys. "Remember that a knight's heart is always pure and true. He must do what is honorable and right, even if it is not the easiest choice."

The two boys accepted the tokens and scurried out the door. Lancelot turned back to Elaine, who was smiling wistfully.

"They will treasure those pieces for the rest of their lives." She stepped forward and embraced him, but he could feel nothing through the heavy buttress of his plate armor. "Nor will I ever forget you."

Lancelot placed a quick kiss on her upturned lips and walked through the portal to the outside. The entire village stood in rudimentary formation holding an array of chopping and raking tools. The two boys held his steed, whose coat gleamed.

Elaine's father broke ranks and walked up to Lancelot.

"I spoke foolishly before," the old man said. "We have lived under the yoke of the Duke's tyranny long enough. We shall accompany you and fight to the death." The old man's lip jutted out in defiance even as a new line of blood leaked from his wound.

Lancelot placed a hand on the old man's shoulder.

"Let me do the fighting," he said. "Be ready to flee into the woods should I fall. Save your people."

The old man said nothing, his face a mask of determination.

Lancelot stepped away and walked to his horse. The two boys placed a stool next to the animal to assist his ascent, but Lancelot merely smiled, grabbed the horn of his saddle, and swung his body upon the horse's back.

"A true knight needs no assistance," he said. Then he surveyed their faces. Elaine still had not come out of the hut. "I ride for all of you."

With that, he slipped on his helmet and pounded his armored fist against his chest in a farewell salute. The two urchins ran up and offered him a long staff, fashioned from a fallen sapling. The end had been meticulously trimmed to make a hooded handle, while the other end bore a crudely fashioned point.

Hardly a proper lance for a Knight of the Round Table, he thought. But one that I shall carry with pride.

Onward to meet the Dark Destroyer.

He had not gone very far when he heard the approach of several horses. The road leading out of the woods wound through a grove of trees and then opened into a large, open field. Across the glen, he saw a group of knights, fifteen of them. They looked to be an unimpressive bunch, save for the enormous knight at the rear, who was clad in ebony armor and atop a coal black steed. A set of a deer's twisted antlers had been affixed to his helmet.

Behind them, a fancy carriage pulled by two horses, was stopped on the hill. The black-armored knight rode up next to the carriage and seemed to confer with the occupant, then rode back to rejoin his forces.

The Dark Destroyer, no doubt, Lancelot thought. He paused at the edge of the wood and adjusted his grip on his make-shift lance. It was time to meet his foes. And for his foes to meet him.

Suddenly Lancelot heard a stirring in the foliage behind him. He reined his horse around and saw the collected villagers, their farming implements in hand, assembling.

Elaine's father looked up at Lancelot and smiled with a grim resolve. He nodded.

Lancelot returned the nod and turned his mount around to face the enemy.

He urged his steed forward and rode to the center of the field. Several of the ersatz knights pointed and looked back to their leader. He gave them a silencing command and their ranks parted as he rode forward alone.

Lancelot scrutinized the man. He was large of frame, and exuded confidence as he rode. The armor had obviously been colored by smoke and fire and was polished to a high sheen. His stout lance was long and also colored black. The bejeweled handle of his broadsword gleamed in the late afternoon sunlight. He halted his steed a small distance from Lancelot and lifted the visor of his helmet.

White teeth gleamed from within a dark face inside the helmet.

A Moor, Lancelot thought. *The Dark Destroyer.*

The other knight had been assessing him as well. Finally, the Destroyer spoke, his voice deep and full of authority.

"You are the rogue who killed the Duke's tax collectors?"

"I am," Lancelot said. "And you are the ruffian in armor who, in the guise of a knight, terrorizes the poor and unarmed at the behest of this so-called Duke?"

The Moor's teeth flashed their whiteness again.

"I am known as the Dark Destroyer, and a true knight. How are you so called?"

"I am Lancelot of the Lake, Knight of the Round Table, champion of King Arthur, and defender of the innocent."

"Is that so?" The Moor chuckled. "A vaunted knight of the Round Table without a shield or proper lance? Methinks not."

"Both were lost in my battle," Lancelot said. "Neither of which I will need to dispatch you and this ragtag band of brigands."

The Destroyer paused and scrutinized the collected villagers on the edge of the woods. After a smirk, his gaze returned to Lancelot. "However, you carry yourself well and with honor. As a fellow knight, I extend to you that courtesy of taking your leave, despite your lack of proper accouterments. Ride away now, or be fodder for the carrion as a companion of the foul earth."

"And what of the villagers? Will they be afforded the same courtesy?"

"We both know that they must be made to pay for the transgression of killing the Duke's tax collectors." He paused. "Worry not, good Sir Knight. Not all will be put to the sword. There are fields to work, walls to be manned, and cocks to be attended."

Lancelot said nothing, thinking of Elaine and her father.

"Well?" the Moor said, canting his head slightly. "Which will it be? Safe passage through my gauntlet, or death."

"We both know the answer to your question, Sir Dark Destroyer." Lancelot raised his voice so all could hear him. "Have you the courage to meet me in a contest of champions, here, in yonder field?"

The Moor's head lolled back in laughter. "I most certainly shall," he said. "If you prove worthy."

Lancelot watched as the Dark Destroyer reined his horse around and rode back to his group of men. As he passed them, he lifted his arm high above his head, and then dropped it. The group of knights drove their steeds forward, each raising his lance as their mount broke into a full gallop.

The odds are against me, Lancelot thought. *But these are no doubt men devoid of honor.* He brought his own pitiful lance to bear and rode to meet them.

One knight drove his horse hardest, arriving ahead of the rest. The knight brandished his lance so high that Lancelot was able to catch the end with his sapling weapon and parry the intended blow. He lashed out with his gloved hand as he passed the other rider, knocking the man to the earth. A second foe was quickly upon him, and Lancelot shifted the sapling to the other side, smashing the approaching knight's helmet. This man tumbled from his saddle as well. The third armored ruffian tried to evade the sapling lance but was struck between breastplate and neck. He slumped forward and Lancelot pushed him from his horse.

The sapling lance had splintered with the contact and Lancelot was left with little more than a stub, but he deftly swung it like a mace and felled two other opponents.

Five were unhorsed, but eleven remained. A burning sensation crept up Lancelot's left side, and he knew his wound had reopened. The warmth of his own blood seeped outward and soaked through his garments beneath his chain mail. Lancelot needed to keep the knowledge of his injury from his enemies. Two more knights charged him, one on each side. He managed to use the sapling club for one more strike before he was unhorsed by the second lance. And even as he was launched backward from his saddle, he thought, if only I'd had my shield.

He landed on the ground in time to see the advancing hooves of the opponent's steed galloping forward. Lancelot was able to roll from the beast's path and then pushed himself to his feet. As he drew his sword, he felt the blistering agony ripple from his old wound.

Each movement exacerbated the searing pain, but he knew he dare not stop. Thrusting the blade of his broadsword upward as another rider passed, Lancelot saw the man scream and drop his weapons. He brought his blade up in time to deflect another blow, but the sky seemed to darken as so many riders closed around him. A blow smashed into his shoulder… Another crashed against the side of his helmet. All light vanished for an instant as a swarm of blackness sought to eclipse him. He found himself on one knee, still holding his sword.

The closest ruffian laughed and another yelled, "I want his sword. You can keep his breastplate."

"And I want his wench," another yelled, swinging a mace downward.

Lancelot managed to parry that blow, but all seemed lost. A troubling vision of Elaine being ravaged by these fiends gave him strength to try to rise. Suddenly the edge of the deadly circle broke open as the villagers surged forward, hacking and chopping with their long tools. Two of the riders were pushed from their horses. The other mercenaries began raining down blows on the pedestrian villagers. Several fell, their heads split open and bloody. The untrained villagers continued to fight, but it was obvious they would not last long.

Lancelot pushed out of the encirclement of doom. As he did so, one of the ruffians galloped toward him, lifting his axe to deliver a crushing death blow.

Lancelot whirled and lifted his sword, fearing all was lost, but then another steed dashed past him, this one carrying a true knight in shining metal. Lancelot recognized the armor.

Sir Percival!

Percival's lance struck the armored ruffian squarely in the chest. The man bounced off his horse and Percival swung around to spear two more of the opponents. Another true knight rode past swinging a mace on a chain. It was Sir Hector. The spiked ball lashed out, felling one of Lancelot's opponents after another. The villagers backed away and began to cheer. Lancelot's heart was bursting with excitement. Truly the pure of heart would be delivered from the unjust.

Percival returned with Lancelot's horse in tow. He reigned his animal to a halt in front of Lancelot and lifted his visor.

"Your steed, good sir," he said, handing the reins downward with a wry grin.

Lancelot lifted his visor to return the grin and swung himself aboard the horse.

"We've been searching for you since your combat with Gawain," Percival said.

"I'm glad you found me." Surveying the scene, he saw Sir Hector chasing the remaining ruffians while the Dark Destroyer gazed on from his perch next to the carriage.

"May I borrow your lance, Sir Knight?" Lancelot asked.

Percival started to hand the weapon to him but stopped. "You're wounded. Let Hector or me dispatch him."

Lancelot shook his head and held out his hand.

"This is my fight."

Percival gave him the lance. "Would you have my shield, as well?"

Lancelot said nothing. He pointed the lance toward the Dark Destroyer and began a quick gallop across the open expanse toward the black night. The Dark Destroyer rode to meet the challenge.

The two met in the middle of the field, Lancelot deftly blocking the Destroyer's thrusting lance with his own, but seeing the metal tip deflected off the other man's shield. They passed each other and both turned, ready for another run.

This time the Dark Destroyer timed his thrust more carefully, managing to catch Lancelot under the arm and knocked him from his saddle. Lancelot crashed to the ground, feeling the wind rush from his body. With the deftness of a cat, he rolled to his feet and drew his sword. The Dark Destroyer was already turning to do another attack on horseback. Lancelot stood ready, holding his sword, waiting. At precisely the right moment, as the Dark Destroyer bore down upon him, Lancelot stepped to the side and grabbed the other man's extended lance, driving it into the earth. The black armored knight was pushed backward, falling from his mount. He landed hard on the ground in a jangle of metal, but instead of rushing the fallen man and delivering a quick death blow, Lancelot merely stood there waiting.

There was no honor in dispatching a helpless foe. He allowed the Dark Destroyer to get to his feet and draw his broadsword

"That was a mistake you'll end up regretting," the Dark Destroyer muttered.

"I think not," Lancelot said and lifted his blade. The sun glinted off the fine metal, which was now stained with blood.

The Dark Destroyer advanced, lashing out, but Lancelot stepped out of the way, allowing the blade to slip by. With the pain searing his side, Lancelot knew he was weakening. He turned and met the Dark Destroyer's next thrust with a clanging of the metal of his broadsword. The two blades crashed again, sending a melody of soon-to-be death into the air.

Once more the Dark Destroyer attempted a telling blow, but this time Lancelot grasped the other man's wrist and struck an arcing strike to his opponent's leg. The Dark Destroyer jumped back and Lancelot brought his sword forward, the point piercing the vulnerable space between breastplate and groin. The Dark Destroyer grunted in pain and tried to retreat, but Lancelot grabbed one of the jutting antlers and brought more pressure to bear. The tip of his sword poked out of the other man's back. The Dark Destroyer made a gurgling sound as he fell to his side. Lancelot watched the Dark Destroyer writhe on the ground for several seconds as a torrent of blood leaked from under his armor. Weakly, the felled knight held up his hand in salute to the victor.

The clumping of horse's hooves sounded and Lancelot looked up to see Sir Hector escorting the plush carriage back to the scene of the battle. The edge of the woods was suddenly alive with the villagers, who marched forward. The carriage pulled to a stop and the driver hopped down from his perch with a terrified look. He tried to run but was restrained by several villagers. Elaine and her father were at the forefront.

Lancelot strode forward and ripped open the door of the carriage. A corpulent man cowered on the floor, holding his hands covering his face. Lancelot reached in and pulled him through the opening. He landed with a plop on the ground.

"Please," he said, his voice trembling like a shaking vine in a righteous wind. "Do not hurt me."

Lancelot pressed the tip of his sword against the cowering man's belly. "Is this the Duke?"

Elaine's father nodded.

Lancelot knew he had to set this ungainly situation right. The knight used the Duke's doublet to clean the gore from his sword. Then he stood and spoke so that all could hear. "Duke Pelles has hereby relinquished all of his lands, monies, and authority."

The Duke lifted his head; his countenance registered shock. Before he could shake his head, Lancelot fixed him with a fierce look and prodded him with the sword. "Is that not correct?"

"Oh, yes, yes," the Duke said. "So long as you do not harm me."

"No harm will befall you, varlet," Lancelot said, leaning down so that their faces were a scant hand's width apart. "But you shall spend the rest of your days within the confinement of a dungeon, to pay for your oppression of these good people."

"But who will lead them?" the Duke said. "They are like sheep. Who will care for them?"

"Duke Pelles shall lead them." Lancelot said.

Faces in the crowd showed confusion. Lancelot straightened up and motioned for Elaine's father to step forward. "From this day forth, you shall be known as Duke Pelles, the ruler of this land of Corbin." He motioned for the old man to kneel, then Lancelot took his sword and placed it on the old man's shoulder. "By my authority as a Knight of the Round Table, vested upon me by King Arthur, I name you Duke Pelles, ruler of this realm of Corbin."

A hush fell over the people.

The old man nodded, the tears flowing from his eyes. "Now I can free my sons and the others from bondage."

Lancelot glanced to Elaine, who stood as still as a statue, watching his every move. He leaned close to the old man and whispered, "Rule wisely, or I shall return."

"So I shall," the new Duke Pelles said. "Thanks to you, Sir Knight."

Several days later the three Knights of the Round Table rode through the gate of the newly populated castle of Corbin on the road back to Camelot.

"As I told you last night," Percival said. "Merlin has foreseen a great war on the horizon. Arthur will need his most valiant knight."

Lancelot said nothing.

Suddenly he saw a young woman running toward them, her dark hair flouncing in the wind.

Elaine.

She stopped in front of them and handed a bouquet of wildflowers up to Lancelot. Their eyes met for but a moment, and then she was off, running back through the gates.

"It seems you were busy prior to our arrival," Percival said, looking at the bouquet. "The Dark Destroyer was not your only conquest."

Lancelot held the flowers to his face, savoring the sweetness of their scent.

What might have been, he thought, *if only Guinevere had not captured my heart.*

He gazed wistfully toward the gates, but did not see her.

"Methinks the knight's tale does not always have a happy ending," Percival said, smiling as he looked from the flowers to the fleeing girl.

"Onward to Camelot," Lancelot said. "For the King."

And for the Queen, he added silently.

The three knights began a quick gallop down the road. Lancelot held the bouquet of flowers until he was well out of sight of the castle, and then dropped them on the roadside, one by one.

KNIGHT OF THE GREEN

A New Knights of the Round Table story

John G. Hartness

The yellow school bus groaned its way up the steep incline and pulled into the gravel parking lot. Gwen Dimont looked out the window at all the green surrounding the vehicle and suppressed a shudder. This was so far out of her element as to not even be on the same periodic table. She was a city girl, through and through. Charlotte wasn't huge, but it at least gave her the comfort of concrete under her feet and a healthy coating of smog in her lungs. She was sure that this field trip was going to end with her eaten by a bear, or at least with a horrendous case of poison ivy. Could you die from poison ivy? If anyone could manage, she could. That would be the perfect capper on her craptastic morning.

First Lance called up and bailed on this Bataan Death March of field trips, claiming some garbage about an exam in his trig class. Gwen took trig last year, so she couldn't even tell if he was lying. Then Rex shows up at the bus with no permission slip, and his dad on some BS trip to Chicago for work or something, so she was stuck without her boys on this stupid ride. It wouldn't have been so bad if everybody else in her history class didn't hate her because she was smarter than them. Or for the other thing. Anyway, people are stupid, her boys had abandoned her, so now she was going to die in *Deliverance* country with a bunch of stupid high school kids. This was not the glamorous death she had envisioned for herself. Unless the bus blew up in the next ten seconds and took them all out at once. That would be sensational enough. She really hoped her mom wouldn't use the picture from the yearbook for her memorial service.

"Come on, Murden, why are we all the way out here in the middle of nowhere," Liam Crawford called from the back of the bus. As much of a goon as Crawford was, Gwen actually agreed with him for once.

"We are out here to experience history on the ground, my boys, where it happened," Mr. Murden said with a broad grin. His long white hair was pulled back in an uncharacteristic ponytail, and he wore a polo shirt and a pair of khaki cargo shorts, the least formal attire the students had ever seen him wear. The bus driver opened the door and Murden bounded down the stairs, his huge floppy hat bouncing atop his head and his skinny stork legs reflecting enough light to blind then all. The ridiculous-looking teacher clapped his hands and called up to the bus.

"Get your lunches and eat quickly, students. We have thirty minutes for lunch, then we are hiking to the battlefield. Our guide will be here promptly at one!"

Gwen got up and stomped to the front of the bus, joining the throng of students. Of course, Liam's buddy and partner in crime Scott Golbert was right behind her.

"Hey Gwen," Scott breathed on her neck. "How's it hanging?" He chuckled at her, his voice low and dirty.

Gwen reached behind her without looking and grabbed Scott's crotch. She felt the boy suck in a huge breath at the sudden agony in his testicles.

"I dunno, Scotty," she said, not turning her head. "Feels like it's hanging about three inches. Now fuck off."

She let go of his nuts and he sagged against the seat in front of him. Gwen hazarded a glance back as she turned to descend the steps at the front of the bus and was happy to see Scott sitting in a seat, a sickly green cast across his features. *Good,* she thought. *Those gorillas have been making my life hell for two years. It's time I started dishing out a little payback.*

She jerked to a halt as she came face to chest with Mr. Murden at the bottom of the steps.

"Do you think that is appropriate behavior for a young lady of your stature, Miss Dimont?" Murden's voice rumbled over her.

She looked up, but the anger she expected to see on his face wasn't there. Instead, he looked…disappointed. That was worse, of course. Adults always knew how to twist the knife. And Murden had been around a hell of a lot longer than any other adult she knew, so he had plenty of practice.

Gwen hung her head. "No sir, probably not. But I'm not going to apologize," she added before Murden even made the ludicrous suggestion. "I'm tired of putting up with crap from Scott and Liam and all those close-minded goons. I don't have to anymore, and I won't. Period."

Murden sighed and shook his head. "I do hope that you will come to a better understanding of the Code before you do something you'll regret."

"Don't worry, boss. I promise not to regret anything."

She shot him a grin and skipped all the way to the picnic table set up with box lunches. She grabbed a veggie sub and took a seat apart from the other students. No point setting herself up for abuse. If Lance and Max weren't going to be there, she might as well just eat alone. Gwen pulled out her phone and opened the e-reader app. The new Jim Butcher book was out, and she'd made sure to download it before leaving home. A few moments later she was immersed in the world of Harry Dresden and his talking skull Bob.

"What'cha doing?" the small voice jolted Gwen from the world of dark wizards and noble, if flawed, heroes.

She turned to see a small boy kneeling on the bench across from her, his elbows on the table. He was a cute kid, she thought, with his straw-blond hair and blue eyes. He smiled at her and waved, dimples appearing in his cheeks when she looked at him.

"Hi there," Gwen said. "I'm reading."

"My mommy reads to me every night before I go to sleep," the boy said. Gwen guessed he was about five or six from the looks of him.

"Do you like her reading to you?"

"Yeah. She reads big books. I can read. But not big books. I can only read little books."

"That's okay. Someday, you'll be able to read big books, too."

"You're pretty."

Gwen felt a rush of warmth to her face, and she ducked her head to hide her watering eyes. "Thank you. You're a very handsome young man."

"I like your hair. It's funny."

Gwen smiled, and looked up at the boy. He pointed to her pigtails, long dark hair with vibrant streaks of pink and blue intertwined throughout. Her smile faded as she heard footsteps crunch on the gravel behind her.

"Beat it, kid," a deep voice came from over Gwen's shoulder. She recognized the voice as Jared Forman, the third in her mental Unholy Trinity of eleventh-grade assclowns. The little boy got down from the bench and ran off to a pretty blonde woman, who swept him up in a big spinning hug. Gwen watched him go with a little regret. She certainly had a better chat with the kindergartener than she would have with Jared and his pals. Sure enough, Liam and Scott came around either side of Gwen and sat on the bench opposite her. Jared sat down beside her, way further inside her personal space than she'd normally allow, but the short picnic table didn't give her any room to scoot away. Besides, she was tired of running from these dicks.

"What's up, G?" Jared said, reaching over and plucking an apple slice from the zip-lock bag on the table in front of Gwen. "You don't mind sharing a little dessert, do ya?"

"Not at all, Jared. Just like we used to do in elementary school.

Wasn't it Ms. Howell that taught us all to share in second grade?"

She hoped by reminding Jared that they'd literally known each other since first grade that he might back off a little, at least for a day. School wasn't easy on her best days, but away from her safety net of teachers she could count on to cover her, and friends she could vent to when it got to be too much, the field trip was way harder on Gwen than most days.

"Yeah, those were the good ol' days, G. Back when you knew what was what. You know, line up to go to the bathroom, boys on one side of the hall, girls on the other. Freeze tag at recess, boys against girls. It was all easy then, wasn't it?"

"Not for everybody, Jared," Gwen said in a rare moment of honesty with the jock. *Fuck it,* she thought, *let's see if we can make this a teachable moment.* "I knew I was different even in second grade. I just didn't have a word for it. I knew I wasn't like you. Or Scott. Or Lance. Or any of the boys. I knew that something didn't match. Didn't fit. But I was a kid, and I didn't know the words for what I was feeling."

Scott looked at Jared, and for a second, maybe two, she thought she saw a hint of the little boy she used to play on the swings with back at Winterfield Elementary. Then he opened his mouth, and everything went downhill from there.

"What you were feeling, *Gareth,* is that you're a freak. Because you are. You're just a freaky little sexual deviant that oughta be locked away from normal people, and never be allowed around little kids. What were you doing with that little boy? Telling him it was okay to wear dresses? Play with dolls?"

"Worse, Scotty. I was telling him it was okay to *read*. You've heard of that, right? Not that you've ever done it. By the way, how are your balls?"

"How are yours, *Gareth*? They shouldn't even let freaks like you go to school. You oughta be locked up."

"You gonna lock me up, Scotty-boy?" Gwen stood and stepped back from the table. "Come on, asshole. Let's let the whole class see you get your ass beat by a girl. Again."

"I'd feel bad about breaking your face if you were a real girl, bitch. But come on, let's do this."

Scott got up and came over to Gwen, getting chest-to-chest with her. Gwen was almost tall enough to look him in the eye, but her slight frame gave up significant weight.

"Scott..." Jared

"Nah, bro. I'm tired of *Gareth* here acting like a girl when he wants to be a girl, but acting like a dude when he wants to scrap. You want to throw down with me? Bring it. But I'm not going to fight like you're a girl. I'm gonna beat your ass just like I did back in seventh grade gym class."

Gwen gave him a little smile, and reached for the power she knew bubbled just below the surface of her life. She could feel it, the power of the Knights of the Round Table that coursed through her, Rex, Lance, and Kyle. The ability to get stronger, faster, more skilled when they needed to go into combat. She felt the power, the soul of Sir Gawain, the Knight of legend, but...something was wrong. She couldn't reach it. She couldn't touch the power. Something was blocking her, and now Scott was about to break her face.

"Is there a problem here?" Mr. Murden's voice cut across the picnic area like thunder, all low and rumble through the still air.

Scott took a quick step back and sat down hard as the bench hit him right behind the knees. "Nope, nothing at all, Mr. Murden. *Gwen* was just sharing *her* apples with me and the boys. *She's* super-nice that way, you know."

"I am aware that Miss Dimont is very nice, Mr. Golbert. I am also aware that it is time to begin our ascent into history. So if the four of you would please dispose of your garbage in the appropriate receptacles and join the rest of the class, we shall depart post haste."

Murden gave them a steady look that brooked no disagreement, then turned and walked to where the rest of the class was gathered, watching.

"I guess we'll finish this conversation later, *Gareth*," Scott said, stomping off after the teacher's stork legs.

Gwen gathered the last scraps of her lunch and shoved everything into the brown paper sack she'd carried on the bus with her. The whole time she cleaned up after herself, her mind whirled. *Why couldn't I get stronger? Can I only become Sir Gawain when we're all together? Or maybe just when Rex is around? Am I* not *a knight without Arthur? What the hell?* With no answers forthcoming from the universe, Gwen tossed her trash in the green barrel by the table, slung her backpack over one shoulder, and joined the rest of the class.

Mr. Murden stood at the trailhead, delivering a lecture about the importance of the Battle of Kings Mountain to the colonials' cause in the Revolutionary War. Gwen smiled to herself, knowing that while Murden had technically lived through the American Revolution, he was as dependent on the history books as the class he taught, since he'd been asleep in a tree for the whole thing. Not to mention the centuries on either side of it.

Murden's former life as Merlin, archdruid of England and chief advisor to King Arthur was useful for a lot of things, but his firsthand knowledge of American History was pretty lacking.

"Now, please welcome Mr. Richard Gualtieri, our guide for the next portion of the tour."

Mr. Murden stepped aside, and a guy that looked more like a suburban dad than a historian stepped up, a broad grin splitting his round face.

"Good morning," he said. "My name is Rick Gualtieri, and I'm a ranger in the U.S. Park Service. Yes, I am, in fact, Ranger Rick." He looked around, as if expecting a laugh, then pulled out a red bandanna and mopped a few beads of sweat from his gleaming bald head. "Anyway," he went on. "Today we're going to hike up this trail about half a mile, then we'll get to the actual location of the battle, and you'll be able to see why the conditions very much favored the colonists, who were familiar with hunting and trapping in these hills. The redcoats, or British Army, were much more accustomed to fighting on at least somewhat level ground, where large groups of men charged at each other over huge fields, supported by swift cavalry and thundering munitions."

Ranger Rick started walking up the inclined trail backward, never looking behind himself or paying any attention to where he put his feet. He just kept up a steady stream of monologue as he led the students up the graveled walkway and into the dense woods. Gwen hung back a little, giving the rest of the class a little separation as Mr. Murden dropped back to join her.

"Is everything all right, Miss Dimont?" Murden asked.

"Yeah, I guess," Gwen replied. "Todd and those jerks were just giving me the normal crap. You know, I'm a freak, I'm not a real girl, I shouldn't be allowed to live like a girl, all that shit. Oops, sorry."

"I suppose we can excuse the language as long as the rest of the class is beyond earshot," Murden said, a kindly smile stretching across his narrow face. He glanced ahead of them, where Gwen's fellow students followed Ranger Rick's beaming face and khaki cargo shorts further up the mountain. "But that isn't all that's bothering you, is it? You deal with their close-minded opinions every day, and while their treatment of you is often reprehensible, I have seldom seen it trouble you to this degree."

Gwen sighed, trying to figure out how to put into words what was bugging her. "Yeah, there's something else. When I was getting ready to fight Scott, I was ready to kick his ass once and for all. And now that I can turn into Sir Gawain at will, I finally have the power to. But when I went to change, I couldn't. I could still feel the Gawain-Gwen there, but it's like she was just out of reach. Like something was blocking me."

"Did Scott instigate the fight?" Murden asked, his blue eyes sharp under the bushy white brows.

"Of course he did!" Gwen's voice rose, and she quickly dropped her volume as a couple of the students near the tail of the procession glanced back. "I mean, he came over and started calling me names, and saying stuff like he always does. He totally started it."

"I don't doubt that he was the first to begin the confrontation, but did he choose to initiate the actual fight?"

Now Murden's eyes seemed to bore into her very soul, and Gwen could see why Merlin was often credited with having even more magic than he actually did. With that gaze on you, the truth seemed to be the only thing you *could* speak.

"Well…no," she admitted. "I mean, he started with the shit-talking and harassment, and I finally had enough, so I was going to get all Green Knight on his ass and teach him a lesson."

"But you couldn't," Murden said.

"Yeah. I couldn't. What the hell? Can I only be Gawain when Rex is around to be Arthur? Is it like a Wonder Twins thing?"

Murden's brow knit at her cartoon reference, but he shook his head. "I have no idea what a Wonder Twin is, but the explanation is much simpler. The power of the Round Table is not lightly granted, and it does not allow itself to be lightly used. Perhaps your intentions were not worthy of a knight."

Gwen stopped cold, her hands on her hips. "Come on! I'm not allowed to defend myself? I thought knights were all about defending the innocent!"

"They—*you* are," Murden said with a slight smile. "But were you actually defending an innocent in this situation? Or were you seeking retribution?"

Gwen didn't speak for a long time. She just stood there in the middle of the trail, looking up into her teacher's now-kind eyes.

"So what am I supposed to do?" she finally asked, tears welling in her eyes. "Am I supposed to just take it? Ignore it? Be the bigger person? I'm *tired* of being the bigger person, Merlin! It fucking hurts, the shit they say to me. *About* me. You don't know what it's like, trying to just live like everybody else, when the first thing people think when they meet you is 'what's in her pants?' Do you know how goddamn exhausting it is, to explain who you are every single day?" Gwen turned away, dashing away a runaway tear with the back of her hand.

Murden put a hand on her shoulder, and when she turned back to him she saw moisture rimming the old man's eyes. "No, my dear, I do not. I cannot understand. I can only tell you that I am sorry that people are not better, and I can hope that someday they will be. But I can tell you this," his jaw set and his voice became firm. "A Knight of the Round Table, in my time or today, does not begin fights for their own retribution. She does not seek revenge, but justice. She does not attack for herself, but defends the innocent. No matter what Scott has said to you, he did not deserve to be beaten, perhaps severely injured, by a trained warrior such as Gawain. He may well deserve a thrashing from Gwendolyn Dimont, but *not* with the assistance of a Knight. I believe that is why you were not allowed to transform."

"Because I wasn't good enough," Gwen didn't bother to try and keep the bitterness from her voice.

"Because your motives were not chivalrous. Had Scott and his friends attacked you with more than words, you likely could have transformed to defend yourself. Had they sought to harm another, you could have acted in that person's defense. But to escalate a war of words into a battle of blade against flesh? That is not the way of a Knight."

"Then the way of a Knight sucks. Because Scott definitely deserves an ass-kicking."

Gwen stuck her chin out, everything in her posture screaming defiance. But if Murden pressed her, she might have to admit that there was a little bit of doubt in her mind.

"I have no doubt that is true," Murden said, a smile touching his lips. "But wouldn't it be all the sweeter coming from you than from Gawain?"

Gwen opened her mouth to respond, but a scream stopped her cold.

Her head whipped around, looking for the source of the cry. The cry for help came again, down one of the side trails to a "scenic overlook." Gwen and Murden sprinted down the narrow graveled path, coming to a halt at a wide flat area surrounded by wooden guardrails. A frantic blond woman stood at the edge, alternately looking down and whipping her head around as if looking for help.

"Oh thank God," she panted as they arrived. "Tommy ducked under the railing, and now he's gone!"

Murden stepped to the panicked woman and took her by the

shoulders. "What do you mean, he's gone? Has someone fallen over the edge?"

"My baby!" The woman wailed. "He just slid right over!"

The woman collapsed, falling to her knees in the dirt and sobbing against Murden's shoulder. Gwen didn't want to look, didn't want to see the broken form of a child at the bottom of the fifty-foot drop, but she forced herself to slowly walk to the split rail fence that was more a suggestion than anything else. She peered over, leaning a little further out than she really felt safe doing, trying to see any hint that the child was still safe.

The edge of the drop-off was ragged, and she could see the rounded patch of mud where it collapsed under the child's weight. There was a rounded section of fresh muddy dirt revealed where his little rump had hit the edge and slid down. A soft sound drifted up to Gwen's ears and she forced herself to lean out further. There, on a ledge a little less than ten feet down, lay the little boy she'd talked to at the picnic tables. The one who said her hair was funny. He was conscious, but looked disoriented, like maybe the fall knocked the wind out of him.

"Don't move, Tommy!" Gwen shouted. "We're coming to get you! Just stay right where you are and don't move a muscle!"

Gwen pulled back over the guard rail and turned to Murden.

"He's alive. There's a ledge a few feet from the edge. It looks like he slid down and got the wind knocked out of him. He might be hurt, but he's moving."

Murden nodded at her, helping the mother to her feet. Gwen's heart broke as she saw the hope bloom in the woman's eyes, and knew she had to do something. Without any further thought, she vaulted the railing, lay down on her belly, and wrapped her hands around the post holding the decorative fence up. Gwen slid her body around, letting first her feet, then her whole body dangle over the side of the overlook. She closed her eyes, held her breath, and dropped.

Her sneakers slapped into the stone outcropping a few feet down, and she knelt beside the little boy. He looked up at her, tears welling in his eyes. "My arm hurts. It hurts real bad."

She looked at the child's arm, twisted at an unnatural angle, and knew it was broken.

"Ouch," Gwen said. "That looks like it really hurts. You're being super-brave down here. You didn't move at all, just like I asked you to. That's really good. Can you be really still for another minute while I figure out how to get us back up to your mommy?"

Tommy nodded, and Gwen turned to assess their situation. It wasn't great, although they seemed to be in no immediate danger. The shelf of rock they stood upon jutted about three feet out from the edge of the cliff, and was about eight feet wide. So there was plenty of room for the trim girl and the little boy, but not enough for anyone else. They could likely just wait right there until the rangers rappelled down to rescue them, as long as she could keep Tommy still and quiet.

"My back hurts, too," the boy said, rolling over onto his side. *So much for waiting*, Gwen thought. There was a six-inch tree branch sticking out of the child's torso. If he didn't get medical attention, and fast, he wasn't going to make it off that mountain.

"Mr. M.?" Gwen called up to her teacher.

"Yes, Miss Dimont?" Murden's head appeared over the guard rail, a scowl on his face. "Your actions this morning have been exceptionally imprudent, but I believe this particular decision may in fact be one for the record books."

"We kinda need to wait a little while for the scolding, if that's okay. Tommy has a broken arm, and he fell on a branch. It stuck him in the side, and I really need to get him back up to you. *Now*. Any ideas?"

Murden's head disappeared, then popped back a few seconds later. "I have nothing here that will aid in such an endeavor. Tommy's mother is calling the park rangers, who can be here soon with climbing and rescue apparatus. She says that she is a nurse, so perhaps she can be of assistance."

"She really doesn't need to see this, I don't think," Gwen called up. "Crap," she muttered, shaking her head. "I need…I need a rope, or something. Anything! It's barely eight feet, but it might as well be a mile. I'm just not strong…wait. *I'm* not strong enough. But I know someone who is. Mr. Murden!" She called up.

The teacher's face, which had vanished from the edge, reappeared. "Yes. Gwen?"

"Do you think you could pull me up if I got close enough? I can't carry Tommy and climb, I won't have enough hands."

Another head appeared next to Murden's at the guard rail. It was Jared, and he looked a little green as he glanced past the narrow ledge at the drop behind her. "Wow, G. You really got yourself in a good one this time, didn't you?"

"I don't have time for your shit, Jared. There's a little boy down here, and he's hurt."

"I know," Jared replied. "That's why I'm here. Remember when we used to play basketball in middle school?"

"Yeah, why?"

"Your vertical leap was the bomb. It's 'cause you're so skinny. Well, that's about to come in real handy."

Jared's head disappeared, then popped back over the edge, this time under the guardrail. He was obviously lying on his stomach to get closer to her. He held out an odd bundle of straps, then dropped them down to her. The straps, Gwen could now see, were leather belts fastened together to make a rope. The belts fell down the cliff face a few feet, but still dangled a couple of feet above Gwen's head.

"You gotta jump up and grab the belts. I'll pull you up," Jared said.

"Can you pull me?" Gwen asked. "I'm not as skinny as I look. And I'll be carrying a kid with me."

"Scott's here, and with him and Mr. Murden, we can totally haul your narrow butt up a few feet. You just gotta *hold on.*" He gave her a hard look, and she nodded.

Gwen knelt beside Tommy and said, "Okay, buddy. You've been super-brave, and really tough so far. Just one more thing, and I'll get you back up there with your mom and she can get your arm all fixed up. Okay?" Tommy nodded, and Gwen said. "I'm going to need you to hug me real tight around my chest, okay?"

Tommy got up, walked over to her, and wrapped his good arm around her neck. Gwen took her own belt out of the first three loops on her jeans, then threaded it through Tommy's belt loops and fastened it back to itself, tying the boy to her. She could only hope that the loops would hold if the child's grip couldn't.

"Okay," said, crouching down to spring upward. But with the added weight of the child, she could only hop a few inches, nowhere near high enough to reach the makeshift rope dangling over her head. She tried again, and got higher, but still nowhere near the end of the lower belt.

"Come on, Gwen!" Jared shouted. "I thought you were some badass ninja chick or something. Weren't you going to kick Scott's ass all by yourself half an hour ago?"

I wasn't, but not all by myself, Gwen thought, reaching out with her mind, through the mists of time, feeling the power of Sir Gawain, the Green Knight, course through her muscles and bones. She wasn't alone. She never had to be alone again. She had all her brother Knights, and all the power of Camelot to draw upon. Gwen leapt again, and her legs, charged with the strength of someone used to riding for miles in full armor then spending a day in battle, flexed stronger than she had ever felt them. She wrapped her suddenly strong grip around the leather strap, and held on.

"I got it!" she shouted. "Pull us up." She looked down into Tommy's teary eyes and whispered, "It's okay, buddy. You're being super-brave and in just a minute you'll be up there with your mommy again."

Four huge tugs later and her right arm and shoulder broke the plane of the ground. Jared let go of the leather belts and wrapped both hands around her wrist. "I got you, Gwen. I got you." He slid backward on his rump and Gwen scrabbled up the cliff with her legs, rolling over to shield Tommy as much as she could.

The second she was fully on solid ground, she reached down and unfastened her belt, setting the little boy free to clamber over her and run to his mother as fast as his stubby legs would carry him. Ranger Rick was already there with a big, red first aid kit, and Gwen could hear the siren as an ambulance pulled into the parking lot below. She lay flat on her back, looking up at the blue sky, feeling the strength of Gawain and the Round Table flow out of her, leaving her exhausted.

"Damn, Gwen. That was crazy," Jared said, sitting cross-legged beside her.

"Yeah, remind me not to do that again."

"It was really brave, though."

"Thanks for pulling me up."

"What else was I supposed to do, leave you there? Then who'd give me apple slices at lunch?" Gwen reached out and lightly punched him in the leg.

They stayed there catching their breath for a moment, then Jared spoke again. "I'm sorry."

"Okay."

"I just don't understand it, and it makes me a dick."

"Okay."

"I'll try to do better. And I'll make Scott be less of a dick, too."

Gwen laughed. "Don't make promises you can't keep, Jared."

Jared chuckled. "Okay, I'll *try* to make Scott be less of a dick."

They both laughed, and clambered to their feet as Mr. Murden walked over to them. "Are you injured, Miss Dimont?"

"No, sir."

"Good. That was very brave, and also very stupid. Please try to learn the difference between the two. Now, I believe we were only beginning our tour." He turned and walked off to the rest of the class, Gwen and Jared in tow. Scott walked up as they came to the main group of students. "Good job, Jared. Saved the kid, and the freak. You oughta get a merit badge or something."

Jared didn't say a word, just looked at his best friend for a long moment, then kneed Scott in the balls and walked right on past. Gwen covered her mouth with a hand to hide the smile, and felt a familiar *click* in her head, in the part of her that touched the magic of the Round Table. She looked at Jared, her mouth agape, and saw him limned in a white light, as if an aura surrounded him. It looked like Camelot had found another Knight. She smiled as she walked up the trail. Poor Jared had no idea what he was getting into…

The Bionic Mermaid vs. The Lady of the Lakes

Hildy Silverman

The stern voice of Commander Summer James, head of enforcement for the United Nations and Oceans Security Council, crackled in Thessalonike's earpiece. "You are being recalled to active duty."

Thessa sucked deep ocean water through her gills and released it slowly, in the mer equivalent of a deep sigh. "Commander, my bereavement leave isn't over until next week."

"The recall isn't for next week. You're needed *now*." James' tone shifted from glacial to merely icy. "I realize your loss was particularly traumatic."

Yes, thought Thessa. *Many would consider having to execute your own brother to end his murderous rampage somewhat traumatic.*

"Nevertheless, we have a situation that threatens our entire nation," Thessa imagined James's eyes rolling as she added, "and yes, that includes its waters."

The commander understood her priorities well. But before Thessa could respond, an agonized wail echoed through the deep ocean crevasse. She glared a warning at its utterer.

James's groan in her earpiece was unmistakably aggrieved. "*Thessa.* What are you…"

"Understood," she said hastily. It was best for both that James not ask so she didn't have to tell. "I can be back at headquarters by thirteen-hundred. Is that acceptable?"

James waited a couple of heartbeats to respond, and Thessa imagined her deciding whether to pursue the matter. "Acceptable. Just see to it that your… personal business is nailed down tight before then."

"Yes, Commander," said Thessa. The corners of her mouth twitched in amusement. In another life, the practical James would have made an acceptable mer. "That will not be an issue."

James muttered something she didn't quite catch and severed the communication.

Thessa returned her full attention to her personal business, who regarded her through red-veined, swollen eyes. "I am afraid I must end our time together sooner than expected," she said with genuine regret. "Duty calls."

"Th-Thessalonike, please. J-just end me. I beg you, by Poseidon!" yammered Laurus, the mad mer scientist known colloquially as the Sea Witch. To Thessa, though, she was nothing but the monster whose experiments had turned her beloved little brother, Aegeon, into the stuff of nightmares. Blood seeped steadily from the many wounds Thessa had inflicted during the weeks she'd kept the Witch shackled to the side of this deep-water chasm, yet beyond an initial foray not even sharks dared approach. They recognized a greater predator had already claimed this particular prize.

Thessa swept strands of orchid hair away from her eyes while considering her options. She could turn what was left of Laurus over to the Court of Triton for prosecution, but it was unlikely they would go against her parents' decree that their surgically-altered daughter was dead and deign to grant her an audience. She could slice Laurus's throat and end the matter neatly. Or…

"You may find this amusing," said Thessa. "Do you know what item of etiquette both we and surface-dwellers have in common?"

"Pl…please…"

"We agree it is wrong to waste food. Besides, patience should be rewarded, don't you think?" Thessa tilted her head back and released a broad, sonar-level summons.

"Y-you don't know." Laurus strained against her chains. "There are things… I have more information that your s-surface superiors would value! I had so m-many clients." She widened her eyes until they nearly bugged out of their sockets. "Like, like… the Lady! She has plans…"

"I would *love* to stay and continue beating all your secrets out of you," said Thessa as large shadows gathered above them. "But I believe you have given me enough leads to follow up on until I take my final float." She offered a mocking bow. "Rot in pieces, witch."

Thessa swam up through the black waters of the chasm, her bionic tail propelling her past the gathering sharks so quickly they barely reacted to her passing. Or, perhaps it was because they were too focused on the sizeable, blood-basted treat awaiting them below.

Laurus's screams echoed in Thessa's ears as she glided to the surface. "I love you, Aegeon," she murmured, and began her long swim back to U.N.O.S.C. headquarters.

***

Thessa sat in the briefing room watching as Commander James displayed video snippets of speeches given by various surface-dwellers. Each proclaimed a different set of priorities, but repeated one common theme:

"When I am in charge, I will end the entitlements that are draining good, hard-working citizens of their earnings. As the chosen leader of these United States..."

"If you follow me, your truly chosen savior, I promise I'll return us to our former glory as Jesus's favored nation..."

"Tired of Beltway insiders who promise everything and deliver nothing? Then follow me, the first candidate chosen in modern times to lead..."

James put down the remote and turned up the overhead light. "At last count, we have surveilled twenty-three of these people, all from different walks of life, representing different genders, political leanings, religions, and careers - none of which included politics before now. The main thing they have in common is a claim to have been," James fashioned air quotes with her index fingers, "*chosen* to lead the United States."

"Your people are scheduled to elect a new president within this year," Thessa said. "Considering the actions of your current one, any one of these would probably be an improvement."

"Over a man whose main qualifications were his good looks and string of starring roles in action films?" James snorted. "I can see why you might think so. However, we believe that if any of these people takes his place, things will indeed get worse for the United States - dramatically so."

"But will it be worse for the waters under U.S. oversight? Hard to imagine, given the erosion of our treaties under the current administration." Thessa shrugged. "Regardless, I am not understanding how this is a U.N.O.S.C. concern."

James ran her blunt-cut fingernails through closely-cropped gray hair. "The situation is that not only are these candidates claiming to have been chosen by someone or something, they are *acting* as if they have been. As in, they've made it clear in their rhetoric that they're not merely running for election; they're preparing to seize power regardless of how the democratic process unfolds. What's more concerning is that each one is attracting large numbers of followers." James shook her head sharply. "No, that's too mild a description. They are rallying increasingly more fanatical, blindly devoted true believers, all enthusiastically proclaiming their willingness to fight, kill, and die for their particular champion."

Thessa frowned. Admittedly, she was no expert on how the surface-dwellers selected their rulers, but what James had described was typical among merkind. The most powerful ruled, and if necessary, led their followers into battle against any opposition.

"The U.N. at large is concerned we might be on the brink of a second Civil War, only this time with multiple, powerful factions poised to tear each other apart," said James. "If this country falls apart, the ensuing war would no doubt draw in other nations jockeying to back those they favor to win. It could destabilize the entire world."

Thessa nodded. "Then I can understand the United Nation's interest, but why bring U.N.O.S.C. in on this?" She gestured to indicate the otherwise deserted briefing room. "And why assign the mission to me? My people are disinclined to involve themselves with surface leaders, no matter how *chosen* one claims to be."

In response, James picked up her remote. Thessa returned her attention to the screen as it displayed a series of still images taken of different people standing next to or sitting in boats on inland bodies of water. "Here is Sussman, a former bank teller, chosen to shepherd the U.S. into a socialist paradise." *Click.* "This is Auschlander, an unemployed handyman who claims he will bring about a glorious return to a United States of only pure citizens - whatever the hell that means. *Click.* "And Winters here, a former IT specialist, has announced she was chosen to squash male domination and form the first Femigarchy. Now *she* might be onto something." James gave a one-shoulder shrug. "What do you see, agent?"

Thessa peered more intently at a blurry image onscreen. Realization tingled along her spine. "Each Chosen is beside a lake."

"And I was hoping you might have some insight as to why," said James. "Our investigation turned up several photos like these, mostly from the Chosens' social media properties, and all from shortly before each proclaimed their status and intentions. We suspect their lake visits are relevant even though they occurred in different locations." She clicked to a final image of a large man leaving a library, his face partially concealed by his sweatshirt's hood. "This one's on our radar based on his recent chatter in a dark web group, the Anti-Antifa. He's a local. So far, he hasn't visited a lake though."

"Mer do not only live in oceans," Thessa said, half to herself. "While the seas are our source, throughout generations many have migrated to lakes through intracoastal waterways." She drummed her pale orchid fingernails on the table. "Commander, when last I... ah, conversed with the Sea Witch, she mentioned something that did not seem meaningful at the time. However, in light of these images and the situation you describe..."

James leaned across the briefing room table and stared intently at Thessa. "Don't leave me in suspense, agent."

Thessa was reluctant to incriminate her kind, even peripheral members like the lake mer, before she had all the facts. "All I have are suspicions based on information from a notoriously unreliable source. I will need some time to investigate to be certain."

James scowled, but nodded. "Fine. Time is of the essence, though. The more slavish devotees these fanatics attract, the greater the threat they pose. If they start going after each other before the election, which frankly seems the most likely scenario so that the strongest remaining can battle for ultimate supremacy... let's just say our trigger-happy president won't hesitate to suspend the Constitution and impose martial law to rein them in."

"Understood, Commander." Thessa rose and saluted. "I am confident I can uncover the facts and find an effective solution with alacrity."

"I don't have to tell you how ugly this could get for the mer, should the current administration have their worst rhetoric confirmed - that your people will never be satisfied until you control the land as well as the water." James gazed meaningfully into Thessa's eyes.

Thessa took a deep breath and released it without looking away. *Which is why you have only assigned me to this mission, at least for now.* "I will be discreet."

James grunted a dismissal, and Thessa left the room. As she did, that final, blurry image remained seared in her mind - that of a surface-dweller standing on a lake's shore and reaching toward its center.

And, rising from the water, a pale silver hand hefted something long and thin that shimmered with reflected sunlight.

***

Thessa entered the intracoastal waterway connecting the ocean outside U.N.O.S.C. headquarters to multiple inland lakes. She navigated down a tributary, her bionic tail allowing her to travel at a rate the fastest speedboat captain would envy, into the closest body of water to the residence of the last human from James's presentation - one where a lake mer resided. When she reached its center, she released a sonar-based announcement that roughly translated to, "Cousin, you have a visitor. Greet me as is proper!"

When her polite request failed to result in a greeting within a reasonable period, she began surveilling along the lake's periphery.

Several hours passed before she spotted a large human male. He came out of the surrounding woods and made his way down the sloping embankment. He raised a hand to shade his eyes from the midday sun's glare as his gaze darted in all directions across the lake's surface.

Thessa crossed underwater to a rocky outcropping, and hovered so only her eyes were above the surface. A few minutes later, the black hair-draped face and shoulders of a silver-skinned mer broke the surface in front of the eager searcher. He jerked backward and nearly fell.

"Greetings, Chosen One." The lake mer glanced at the sun's position in the sky. "Thou art punctual. We take it thou art ready to accept thine destiny to lead the greatest country on Earth."

What nonsense is this? Thessa had lived among humans long enough to recognize cliché film dialog when she heard it. Besides, no mer would ever seriously refer to a surface nation with such reverence.

"Y-yup?" said the large man.

The lake mer sighed. "That was… unconvincing."

He flushed red and cleared his throat. "I mean yeah, damn right, I'm ready! I'm a'gonna straighten this country right up, lemme tell you."

A simper. "Much better." The lake mer raised her torso clear of the water and held something aloft that reflected the sunlight in a dappling pattern over the lake's surface. "Then kneel, Sir Bannon, and accept this boon like Arthur of legend from the Lady of the Lake!"

Bannon's mouth fell open. His gaze wandered from the mer's bare bosom to the sword as though unable to decide which had him more entranced.

Thessa took advantage of his delay to propel herself silently to just behind the lake mer. She tapped her on the shoulder.

The startled mer spun around, black hair concealing her face. "What from the depths!"

"Greetings, cousin." Thessa offered a shallow bow. "I am Thessalonike, an agent of the United Nations and Oceans Security Council."

The lake mer tossed her hair back over her shoulders, revealing a guarded expression. "I am Derketo. What do you seek?"

"That." She nodded to the sword still clenched in Derketo's right hand.

The lake mer immediately dropped her arm so the sword was underwater. "Whatever for?"

"Um, ladies?" Bannon was on his knees, leaning awkwardly over the lake, hands outstretched to receive the sword.

"You ignored my greeting. Now you pretend not to know why

U.N.O.S.C. would be interested in that sword." Thessa leaned closer and stared hard into Derketo's eyes. "Are you *absolutely* certain that feigning innocence is your best course of action?"

Derketo offered an exaggerated shrug. "This sword belongs to me and I am thus free to offer it to any mer or human I choose. This *is* a free country, is it not, Sir Bannon?" She looked over her shoulder at the hovering man, who nodded vigorously as he grasped the air like an overeager child anticipating a present.

Thessa shifted her gaze to the large male and said, "This matter no longer concerns you. Leave."

Bannon's hands curled into fists and remained clenched. He stood slowly and clumsily, thick eyebrows knotting like a pair of copulating caterpillars. "Just who in the hell do you think you are, fish lady?" he sneered. "This here sword was promised to me by divine right, and I'm not goin' no place with…"

Thessa slapped the water with her bionic tail, propelling herself ten feet above the lake. She executed a tight somersault mid-air and split her tail into legs on the way down before landing directly in front of Bannon. She grabbed him by his lapels and hauled his ruddy face down to hover just above her own. His eyes widened as he apparently grasped that regardless of his mass, she was the one to be feared.

"*Mister* Bannon," Thessa said very quietly and calmly. "If you do not walk away right now you will not walk anywhere. Ever. Again. Nod if you understand."

Judging by the way the whites now shown all around his dull blue irises, her message had been clearly received. He nodded rapidly and said, "Yessir. I mean, yes'm. I mean, I'm… I'll be headin' home now."

Thessa released him. He stumble-ran up the embankment, and disappeared into the woods beyond.

Derketo snorted.

Thessa returned her attention to her cousin in the lake just in time to see her plunge the sword into one of the large rocks behind which Thessa had hidden herself earlier, leaving a shower of sparks in its wake. Derketo positioned herself in front of it, and folded her arms, features contorted with contempt. "Ah, so *you* are the mangled one I've heard about. Still, there is power in this sword beyond any ocean mer's capabilities, monster or not."

Thessa bristled. Too many of her people mocked her condition, yet every time they called her mangled, mutilated, or deformed she felt as if the blades of the propeller that had severed her natural tail were slicing through her heart.

As though I chose to have this surface-dweller technology affixed to me! The bastard who replaced her birth tail never asked permission before making her a subject of experimentation. At least she had the comfort of knowing his sunken skeleton had long ago been picked clean for his offense.

Very deliberately, Thessa slid back into the water and converted her legs into the metallic, iridescent tail, her gaze never wavering from Derketo's. Maintaining a conversational tone, she said, "I could beat you into handing that sword over to me right now, but the truth is I need to know what you intended by giving it to that giant dullard. Also, why have you and your sisters been claiming to be the Lady, distributing swords, and lying to incompetent humans that they are chosen champions?" She spread her gills in a gesture of benign intent. "Cousin, all I require of you are these answers and that sword, and then I will be on my way."

One of the clearer differences between her people and the lake mer was a lack of gills, as the latter had evolved to surface whenever they needed oxygen. Therefore, Thessa couldn't use the flattening of gills to spot Derketo's intent to refuse cooperation. Still, it became clear enough from her obstinate expression, along with her jaw muscles bunching visibly.

Fool. Still, if this was the game Derketo was determined to play... "Then I will be taking that sword to headquarters now." Thessa swam closer to the lake mer. "And you, cousin."

"You are welcome to try. *Cousin.*" Derketo's voice dripped contempt. "You forget, you are in *my* water now. I am not a mere human easily intimidated by an arrogant ocean mer, let alone one that is a freak!"

Commander James was always going on about interrogation techniques - *something about sticks and root vegetables, and when one was more effective to use than the other.*

Thessa decided it was time for the stick.

She sped forward and slammed directly into Derketo before the latter had an instant to react. Pinning her arms to her sides, Thessa dove, driving them both down through the brackish waters until Derketo struck the rocky bottom deep below. Her breath bubbled out, and she immediately began struggling to slide free. Thessa used the gyros in her tailfins to hold herself, and by extension Derketo, firmly against the lake's bottom. Derketo's eyes bulged as she thrashed her tail in panic.

"Be still!" Thessa pulled her forward and then slammed her back hard against the lake's floor, driving the last breath from Derketo's straining lungs. "You want to breathe again? You will do so while answering my questions. Honestly, this time."

Recognizing that she was outmatched, Derketo stopped flailing uselessly. She splayed her webbed fingers in a gesture of submission.

Thessa hauled Derketo back to the surface. As the lake mer gasped in warm, sticky air, Thessa released her. "Let us try this again. There is only one sword I know of that can be used to force others to submit to the wielder, and only one lake mer in possession of it. That sword you sheathed in the rock is as false as the title you claimed as your own"

"Y-yes," panted Derketo. "The original was crafted of rarest caliburnium, and used to anoint a surface-dweller as a champion of merkind."

"That happened generations ago," said Thessa. "It has become the stuff of legend among both our peoples." For good reason, too. When the legendary mer of that particular European lake attempted to forge an alliance in the land that would eventually become Great Britain, the barbarian king she chose wound up being cuckolded by his wife, alienating his allies, and leading a doomed quest for a fancy cup.

"*The* Lady," murmured Thessa. "But this time there are several surface-dwellers proclaiming themselves as Chosen, using multiple swords to compel obeisance. How can that be when there was only ever a single caliburnium sword?"

Derketo's expression became smug. "You do not think *she* could have forged more than the one, given generations to do so?"

Thessa fought to keep her expression neutral as she considered the implications of Derketo's reveal. The Lady of the Lake mer, Mnemosyne, was ancient by any standard. Powerful, too, to the point rumors of her abilities had reached similar mythological proportions to those that had surrounded Laurus, the Sea Witch. Most attributed her power and longevity to ages spent in a lake under which the first vein of caliburnium was discovered, believing she had absorbed the element's mysterious properties. Mnemosyne eventually depleted the vein to forge her legendary sword, but had apparently retained enough inside her to wield unchallenged authority over the world's lake mer for ages.

"It is said that sword had the magic to compel absolute loyalty to the one who wields it," Thessa said, mostly to herself.

Derketo snorted. "*Magic*. Don't be ridiculous. Next you will say you believe the Sea Witch is an actual supernatural being!"

Thessa chose to ignore the barb. "Caliburnium is an extremely rare element. Supposedly, the only remaining veins run so deep within ancient, underwater volcanoes they cannot be mined." Realization struck: *Unless, of course, an evil but undeniably brilliant mer scientist and engineer figured out a way around that.*

It all comes back to that damned witch. Thessa mentally tail-slapped herself. *Perhaps I should have let her linger a bit longer after all.*

Aloud, she said, "Mnemosyne went to Laurus for assistance reproducing the sword, didn't she?"

"That I don't know," said Derketo.

Thessa thrashed her tail.

She quickly added, "I swear it, cousin! All I do know is that our Lady set out a few years ago to reach this country. By the time she made her presence known and began visiting us," Derketo shrugged, "she had multiple swords and orders to distribute them to seemingly random humans."

"She must have met up with Laurus during her travels." Thessa rubbed her chin. "The Sea Witch may have been mad, but she certainly earned her reputation for doing the impossible."

"May have *been*?" When Thessa simply stared back in silent acknowledgement, the lake mer shuddered. "I have told you all I know. P-please leave me in peace, cousin."

Now is the time for the root vegetable. "I thank you for what you have shared." Thessa bowed politely. "However, I must understand your Lady's plot. Laurus may have been in love with chaos for its own sake, but Lady Mnemosyne is not, or at least did not used to be."

"I... that is not a question I can answer." Derketo flinched as Thessa's narrowed her eyes. "Because I don't know! I merely follow my Lady's orders, as do my sisters."

Thessa sighed. "Where can I find Mnemosyne?" When Derketo hesitated, lowering her gaze to Thessa's tail, she added, "I have no wish to harm her. Only to talk."

Derketo bowed her head. "She is currently in residence in the Great Lake of Michigan."

Thessa assessed her response as truthful. "Farewell, cousin." She made a show of starting to swim away, then paused and looked back over her shoulder. "Oh, one more thing. Exactly how many swords have been created?"

"Twenty-four."

Yet only twenty-three Chosen have them. "And how many have been distributed?"

Derketo wrapped her arms tightly around herself. "What does it..."

Turning to face the lake mer fully, Thessa repeated, "How. *Many*?"

Derketo's shoulders slumped. "Twenty-three," she said. "Mine was the last." Her gaze shifted ever-so-slightly to the rock in which hers was lodged.

Thessa nodded to the rock and gazed meaningfully into Derketo's eyes.

"Fine." Derketo's voice held a whining undertone, but she dutifully swam over and slid the sword free of its rocky sheath in another shower of yellow-white sparks. She tossed it to Thessa.

She caught it easily by the hilt and immediately felt a powerful vibration surge from her hand up her arm and seemingly into her heart. Ancient mer runes had been carved along one side of the blade. It took Thessa a few minutes to recall her youthful education in early written mer language and decipher their meaning: *Power calls to Power.*

She shivered.

Thessa slid open a long compartment along the side of her tail and tucked the sword securely inside. When she turned to bid Derketo farewell and admonish her to behave, the lake mer was nowhere to be seen.

No matter. She'd gotten everything needed to move forward with her investigation.

The remaining answers would come from the Lady herself.

***

Thessa was already aggravated by the time she arrived on a remote shore of Lake Michigan, having had to fly there in a U.N.O.S.C. helicopter, which she despised as only an ocean-dweller forced to travel through an environment so alien to her natural habitat could. She issued a polite request for an audience, which the Lady either didn't hear or ignored. Increasingly less courteous requests also went unanswered. Finally, Thessa gave up on manners and dove in.

Even with her bionic tail propelling her at speeds unmatchable by any other sea creature, Lake Michigan presented an enormous challenge to explore, both in sheer size and depth. She might as well have been ordered to search the Atlantic Ocean for a particular shell. Adding to her aggravation she had Commander James's voice in her earpiece providing daily updates on the activities of the Chosen. As the election drew closer, their antics were increasing, with isolated skirmishes reported throughout the country. The current occupant of the White House, starting to become as concerned for his life as his re-election, had already begun engaging in his own saber-rattling.

After nearly a week Thessa let some of her frustration slip through during her report back. "Commander, I do not see how continuously reminding me that time is of the essence helps. I am searching this Great Lake as fast and thoroughly as possible!"

After a moment of silence that stretched just long enough for Thessa to worry she'd overstepped, James replied without a hint of rancor, "I'm hoping it reminds you that going fast isn't the only ability you possess. Instead of speeding up, agent, smarten up." She terminated transmission.

Her stinging words echoed in Thessa's mind as she surfaced. "Find another way," she murmured aloud. "A smarter way… of course!" She cursed herself for being so focused on the speed and strength afforded by her infernal tail that she'd forgotten the tool stored inside it.

Thessa triggered the long compartment to open and withdrew Derketo's sword. "Power calls to power," she recited as she held it aloft and concentrated on the subtle vibrations it released. She pivoted north, then east, then west - at which point she felt a tug.

Holding the sword in one hand before her, Thessa followed its pull toward the west. The sword's vibrations increased as she traveled through an isolated region of the lake until it began producing an audible hum. Looking just past its tip, Thessa spied golden caudal fins sliding below the water's surface about two clicks to the southwest. She accelerated, closed the distance in moments, and dove after her elusive prey.

"Mnemosyne," she called. "This cowardice belies your noble station! Turn and face me, Lady!"

The golden tail flashing through the dark water slowed as its owner whipped around to face Thessa, who pulled up short and suppressed a gasp.

Mnemosyne was a striking figure even to another mer. Her skin glowed with a pale golden hue. Her long hair was white-blonde threaded with dark red and gold strands that made it appear flames swirled around her face and shoulders. Her large, amber eyes, now focused on Thessa, seemed to spark with an inner fire barely contained by her mortal shell, threatening to burst forth at any moment to scorch the waters - and her uninvited guest - into steam.

Thessa wasn't one to be impressed by position or appearance. However, confronted by this formidable creature, she found herself drawing rapid, watery breaths through her gills as though she were a child about to be punished for swimming too close to a ship.

Mnemosyne assumed an upright position. She folded her arms,

golden tail swishing back and forth slowly beneath. Unlike other lake mer, she'd retained the gills shed by her descendants. She cocked her head to the left and said, "Why do you pursue me, daughter of Poseidon? You and yours hold no authority over my lakes."

Thessa brandished the sword in response. "This. Or should I say, these? By the authority of the U.N.O.S.C., I demand to know why caliburnium swords are being tossed out to surface-dwellers like bait fish to seals!"

"You *demand*?" Mnemosyne didn't raise her voice but Thessa felt the temperature of the water surrounding them rise.

She flinched. "I… I requested politely that you meet me and explain your reasoning. More than once." *By the Great Trident, I sound like a recalcitrant babe!* She hoped her discomfiture wasn't as obvious as it felt.

"I owe you no explanation. I certainly don't answer to your land-walker agency." Her gaze shifted from the sword to Thessa's tail, and she pressed her full lips into a straight line. "The mangled one. You are half land-walker yourself now, yes?"

That did it. Thessa's nervousness before the intimidating mer noble dissolved like a snail doused in salt. "I am Thessalonike, agent of the U.N.O.S.C., and in this matter, you *will* answer to me, Lady." She thrust the sword at Mnemosyne, who didn't flinch. "This is a caliburnium sword. One of many that have fallen into the hands of an assortment of surface-dwellers, or land-walkers, or whatever you like to call them. Each is now convinced they have been chosen to rule the United States. They are prepared to lead armies against the current government and one another for the privilege, yet none has demonstrated any qualifications to rule - if anything, they all seem equally deranged."

Mnemosyne raised one precisely arched eyebrow. "And this troubles you - why?"

"Their conflict threatens to destabilize the U.S., and with it the Treaty of Triton and related agreements that maintain peace between the surface-dwellers and merkind. I find that deeply troubling, as should you." Thessa closed the short distance between them in the space of a blink. "You may feel free to answer me here and now or, if you prefer, at the local U.N.O.S.C. base. But rest assured, my Lady, you *will* answer."

To her credit Mnemosyne didn't shrink back or otherwise display any outward signs of fear, which only increased Thessa's respect for her. Instead, she stroked her jaw while seeming to consider several options before responding, "Very well, daughter of Poseidon. Perhaps once my mission becomes clear, you will understand that I am not the villain you seem to think. You know the tales of the land-walker king known as Arthur - both their versions and ours?" Thessa nodded. "For thousands of swims, I have been presented as foolish for having bestowed one of the most powerful weapons in merdom to a walker who turned out to be a weak-minded, power-maddened disappointment.

Mnemosyne scowled. "I swear to you this was *not* the case. Arthur was every bit a hero when I offered him the sword to consolidate his kingdom and serve as a protector to that land and its waters. However, the fundamental property of caliburnium - to vibrate in tune with the sympathetic nervous system of land-walkers in such a way that they feel compelled to fight and die for the one who bears it - causes… side effects."

"Such as?" prompted Thessa.

"Over time its proximity makes the bearer paranoid, delusional. As you said, deranged." She smiled briefly, but her eyes were sad. "Arthur transformed from a brilliant natural tactician and noble man only interested in the welfare of others into a jealous lunatic who alienated those who loved him best. He eventually became so mad he dispatched his most loyal knights on a doomed quest for an object of fantasy. After he…" Mnemosyne shook her head sharply, as if to dispel an ugly memory. "Well, after, his one remaining devoted courtier returned the sword to my possession I knew I could never offer it to another. It seemed my greatest accomplishment - figuring out how to forge caliburnium into a powerful weapon - would only be remembered as my greatest failure."

Thessa frowned. "Then what you have done makes even less sense. Why would you not only repeat this error but compound it by distributing multiple, mind-distorting copies?"

Mnemosyne's expression hardened. "Because the surface governments have been chipping away at their vows to merkind, particularly when it comes to the interior waters. With each successive leader, they further infringe upon our protections. A few more chemicals are permitted to be poured into rivers and lakes. More boats permitted to travel closer to our homes. Garbage is dumped with less oversight and even fewer consequences. Our water temperatures rise, yet they refuse to even acknowledge that threat as reality!"

She raised her voice. "I heard the cries of my daughters, and realized that as this nation of yours leads, so do the others follow. Right now, under the current fool running it, our sovereignty continues to erode whilst the threats to our very existence increase." She sucked in water and released it slowly. In a calmer tone, she said, "At first, I intended to find a new champion, one who would value maintaining the health and safety of our waters for the good of all. I even went so far as to consult the Sea Witch for assistance on how to temper caliburnium in such a way that it would not drive its bearer insane."

Thessa groaned, imagining Laurus' delight at the request. This was the monster who'd sought to bioengineer an army of mer who could march on land and fight surface-dwellers on their own soil, after all. "She told you that was impossible, didn't she?"

"Indeed."

"And then she offered you an alternative."

Mnemosyne nodded once. "She analyzed the original sword and developed synthetic caliburnium to create more. She proposed I empower multiple land-walkers and use the negative side effects to foment war." She gazed into the distance, as though seeing through time. "Soon this land's walkers will resort to savagery. Once they have reduced their country to rubble and chaos, its waters will be saved."

Thessa glanced at the sword in her hand and wondered if exposure to its mind-warping properties affected mer over time. At least that might explain Mnemosyne's eagerness to go along with Laurus' scheme. "That does not make sense. If this country descends into civil war, *all* waters will be polluted by munitions and chemicals of warfare, not to mention the detritus of broken buildings, vehicles, and corpses."

"For a time, perhaps," said Mnemosyne with a shrug. "You have not lived as long as I, daughter of Poseidon. You do not understand the perspective near-immortality imparts. Eventually, there will be blessed little surface life remaining. This land will revert to the barren paradise it was when occupied by its earliest natives." She gave Thessa a knowing look. "And if the rest of the world does not improve its behavior, then I will forge more swords for my daughters to choose with until their lands fall as well."

Not without Laurus, you won't, thought Thessa. At least having gotten rid of the Sea Witch had ensured Mnemosyne could not expand her plot. Choosing her words cautiously, she said, "I understand your frustration, the nobility of your intent. But your plan is predicated on the belief that the damage will be mitigated by time. What about the many mer who will die because of this conflict between fanatics?"

At this, Mnemosyne's expression became so regretful that Thessa believed it was genuine - which made the Lady's next words even more chilling. "Again, you cannot see the water for the eddies. Loss of any mer life is regrettable. However, guaranteeing our continued existence as a species justifies their sacrifice."

Thessa closed her eyes. Instinct told her to attack, to eliminate Mnemosyne and leave her remains floating in the lake. As aged and formidable as she was, the bionic tail gave Thessa an advantage she was confident would allow her to prevail.

However, such action would not be free of consequences. To destroy a mer of such age and high station would bring reprisals, to the degree that no matter how James tried to shield her, she would ultimately have to be turned over to her people for prosecution. Otherwise, the very treaties U.N.O.S.C. was meant to protect would be violated, and possibly considered broken. Besides, killing Mnemosyne would do nothing to staunch the power of the twenty-three swords already in the hands of the Chosen.

Thessa chewed her lower lip thoughtfully. *Smarten up, agent. Use manipulation, not violence - at least not yet.* "You believe you can control the chaos you unleash." She studied Mnemosyne's expression, her slightest movements, for reactions to guide her strategy.

"I am the Lady," the regal mer said simply. "It was I who first identified the properties of caliburnium, who bathed in its power. It was I who forged the first sword. No one understands its properties as well or as thoroughly."

"The first sword. Excalibur, the surface-dwellers called it."

"It translates to *hard belly* in one of their languages." Mnemosyne smiled. "As in voracious. Even as it bestows power it makes the wielder endlessly crave more."

Thessa strove to maintain an even tone so as not to, as her colleague Martinez would say, tip her hand. "And which of the Chosen bears it now?"

"What?" Mnemosyne's eyes widened in what appeared to be genuine surprise. She chuckled. "None, of course. As though I would hand over Excalibur itself!"

"Why not? It is no longer unique. Just one of twenty-three identical to it." Thessa dangled her bait carefully. "Or would that be twenty-*four*?"

Mnemosyne's humor faded. She narrowed her eyes and stared into Thessa's so intensely, it felt as if the Lady was examining her very soul. It took all her fortitude not to look away. "Excalibur is merely a... prototype now. It lacks the... enhancements found in the new swords. There was no need to give up something that holds such sentimental value to me."

That is a lie, thought Thessa, her theory all but confirmed. The hook was set. It was time to reel. "Or," she said, "being the only true caliburnium sword, untainted by whatever experimentation the Sea Witch performed to duplicate it, its purity gives it power over the rest."

"That is a pretty theory," said Mnemosyne, feigning a casualness belied by her increasingly rigid posture.

"Here is another," said Thessa. "You would not give up Excalibur, just in case the destruction wrought by your Chosen did indeed get out of control. You have it here, ready to use to subjugate its inferiors and their bearers if necessary."

"Are you implying I would keep Excalibur where any other being could take possession of it without my express permission?" Mnemosyne's voice filled with quiet menace.

"Power calls to power." Thessa spun Derketo's sword by its hilt. "This helped me find you. But now I realize it wasn't *your* power that drew it." As if in response the sword halted in mid-spin and tugged against her grip as if seized by an enormous magnetic field. The sword's tip pointed down and to Thessa's right like a compass needle.

One instant Mnemosyne was in front of Thessa; the next she had vanished into the depths of Lake Michigan.

Thessa rolled her eyes and muttered, "Really?" Then she dove and followed in the Lady's wake.

Just as Mnemosyne's reached the bottom of the lake Thessa arrived at her side. She saw the Lady reaching for a golden hilt sticking out of a huge boulder and slapped her hand away.

Mnemosyne twisted around and grabbed Thessa by the shoulders. "Do you truly wish to challenge me, a queen of her kind, little mer*maiden*?" Her skin brightened, the golden glow forcing Thessa to avert her eyes. "I already told you why the power in Excalibur led to it being called hard belly by some land-walkers. You shall now learn why others called it *hard lightning!*"

A jolt of electricity surged through Thessa's body, nearly blinding her with agony. She convulsed, and Derketo's sword floated free of her twitching fingers.

When she could think again, Thessa feared that the Lady might have shorted out her tail. Without it, she would be trapped at the bottom of the lake, at Mnemosyne's mercy. It was unlikely she'd survive until James sent backup. She fought down panic by focusing on her training. *Remember, for all her power, the Lady is but flesh. You are more.* Still, she was handicapped by having to defeat Mnemosyne without executing her - a restriction the Lady didn't share.

As her nervous system slowly recovered from the shock, Thessa assessed the damage to her mortal and bionic halves, and felt a surge of relief. Her tail's systems were still online. *Good.* Now she could return her full attention to strategy.

Thus far, her encounter with Mnemosyne had revealed much. The Lady bore the arrogance of the powerful and entitled, accompanied by overconfidence in the outcome of her actions. *Which gives me the advantage.*

Feigning greater damage than had been inflicted, Thessa floated, motionless save for the occasional twitch she hoped looked convincingly involuntary. She kept her eyes open but unfocused.

Mnemosyne, her glow fading to normal, studied Thessa's face for another several moments before twisting her lips into a satisfied grin. Then she returned her full attention to the sword sheathed in the boulder.

Thessa slipped up behind her and split her tail into legs. She wrapped them around the Lady's torso, and squeezed.

Mnemosyne jackknifed forward and back, then thrashed from side to side. She started to glow again with building electrical current in preparation of inflicting another, likely higher-voltage shock.

Thessa increased the pressure carefully. She'd spent enough years with her bionic tail to thoroughly assess the extent of its force and how to apply it, including exactly how much could be exerted before bones shattered like shale. The glow from the electrical field surrounding Mnemosyne fluctuated, then stalled until she finally went limp.

Thessa immediately let go and left her opponent to float. She converted legs back into tail and turned her attention to the sword. *Why must they always wind up embedded in stones?* Despite the dire circumstances, she couldn't repress an amused grin at being about to enact a legend in real life.

The tales of Arthur were many and contradictory, among mer and surface-dwellers alike. Some said Excalibur was given to the future king by the Lady of the Lake directly. Others said she plunged it into a stone under the aegis that only a worthy champion could pull it free. *Am I meant to be the champion in this tale?* Thessa wondered. *Am I worthy?*

There was only one way to find out. She grasped the hilt of the sword and pulled.

It didn't so much as wobble.

Despite herself, Thessa experienced a rush of disappointment, but then she shook it off. *To Hades with destiny!* It was nothing but a matter of overcoming lake mer trickery.

Thessa swung her tail to one side, took aim, and smashed it against the side of the boulder. Half the great rock crumbled upon impact. She dealt it a second blow and the sword floated free.

She heard a moan from behind. "Thessalonike… no."

Thessa caught Excalibur by its golden hilt as it drifted upward. The sword lit up the dark water like a beacon, and sent vibrations surging through her that dwarfed what she'd felt from Derketo's copy. Its power enflamed her very soul.

Derketo's sword drifted back toward her from above, drawn by the magnetism of its superior once again. Thessa acted almost without thinking, slashing at the other sword with Excalibur. It sliced Derketo's sword in two with an ease that reminded Thessa of cutting through kelp with a scythe. The two halves floated off in different directions; its remaining, artificially infused power evaporating.

"One down," she said. "Twenty-three to go."

Mnemosyne shook her head weakly. "Foolish child. You are dooming us."

Thessa tucked Excalibur safely into her tail compartment. Part of her was afraid to continue wielding it, lest she find herself under the control of its intoxicating power. "No. I am saving us. From you."

She grasped Mnemosyne by the upper arm and ascended swiftly to the surface of Lake Michigan. Mnemosyne didn't resist. Whether that was due to the field of obeisance Excalibur exuded or simply that she was overwhelmed by the unfamiliar experience of defeat, Thessa couldn't be sure, nor did she care. She switched on her tail's retrieval beacon and let James know she had completed her mission.

As they awaited extraction, the subdued Lady said, "You have been warped in body and mind by the land-walkers. But, you could still become a champion to your own kind." She lowered her eyes briefly to indicate Thessa's tail. "Their unholy technology allows you to do what no other mer can, not even I." Gazing deeply into Thessa's eyes, she pleaded, "Use Excalibur. March across the land. Lead my Chosen under *your* banner."

Thessa hesitated, unable to keep from considering the offer - but only for a moment. "Do you know the problem with well-meaning megalomaniacs like you, my Lady? You never pause to consider alternatives to wholesale murder for achieving your goals."

***

U.N.O.S.C. confiscated all twenty-three remaining swords within weeks, and without an ounce of bloodshed. It became a simple task once their bearers found themselves inexplicably and irresistibly drawn to U.N.O.S.C. headquarters, where they knelt before Excalibur and offered their swords up at Thessa's command. They were then remanded to Raspmer Psychiatric Center for evaluation and treatment while their confused followers rapidly lost interest in their causes.

After some diplomatic wrangling, Mnemosyne was turned over to the Court of Triton, where she would likely receive a far too lenient sentence in deference to her stature. Thessa struggled to accept, not for the first time in her life, that some political compromises were unavoidable.

A week later Thessa and James found themselves regarding one another across the briefing room table again, only this time Excalibur lay between them. Its golden hilt rested mere inches from Thessa's fingertips. The sword's brilliance was only barely outshone by the fluorescent lighting.

Very quietly, Commander James said, "So. The pseudo-caliburnium swords have been melted down. Their bearers are in custody. Only this one, and you, remain."

Thessa caressed the cross guard. "Do you fear I intend to serve as Mnemosyne's final champion? Lead a mentally captive force of surface-dwellers through the streets of your capital against its contemptable administration?" Excalibur's power burned against her fingertips, urging her to take it up once more.

"The thought didn't even cross my mind," said James. Thessa looked up sharply, and was surprised to read the honesty in her commander's expression. "By now, I know my faith in you is not misplaced, agent."

Thessa felt a warmth from within headier than any exuded by Excalibur. That the person she had come to respect more than any other surface-dweller - no, more than anyone else, period - had such unwavering confidence in her only reinforced that she had come to the right decision.

She stood, lifted Excalibur flat by hilt and blade, and extended it across the table toward James with a deep bow. "Commander Summer James, you have already proven yourself to be a worthy champion of merkind. Please accept guardianship of Excalibur, and keep it safe."

As the silence following her offer stretched out, Thessa raised her eyes and took in the stunned look on James' face. For the first time since they'd met, it seemed her commanding officer was at a loss for words. But finally, James stood, reached across the table, and gingerly accepted Excalibur.

As Thessa straightened and saluted, James hefted the sword, testing its weight in one hand, then the other. For a moment she seemed taller, infused with an inner glow almost as bright as Mnemosyne's had been.

Suddenly nervous, Thessa added, "You understand you cannot wield it for long periods. The negative mental effects might take more time to corrupt your mind than one of the Sea Witch's warped copies, but still."

"Understood," said James. Her eyes were half-lidded, dreamy.

"However, should the instability gripping these United States increase..." Thessa paused meaningfully.

James turned and walked out of the room. "With me, agent."

Thessa followed, her heart thrumming. Had she made a mistake after all? Perhaps she should have turned Excalibur over to be melted into slag as well. But considering the current president and the potential threat he and his cronies posed, she'd concluded such action would be ill-advised.

James went into her quarters, leaving the door wide open for Thessa to follow. As the mer agent watched, her commander laid Excalibur gently on her bed. She went to her private locker, opened it using a key worn on a chain around her neck, and removed its few contents. Then she placed Excalibur gingerly within. After relocking the cabinet, she handed the key and chain to Thessa.

"This way, we can both be sure," James said. Then she did something so rare Thessa could only stare in response. James smiled. Widely, and with warmth. "Thank you, Thessa. I swear to do my utmost to prove myself worthy of this honor."

Thessa nodded approvingly. "Commander, you just did."

Heart of Frozen Tears

Diane Raetz

I gazed at the moon's reflection off of the Hudson River and wondered how painful burning to death under the sun's rays would be.

I was at my psychiatrist's office, in theory to talk about my "anxiety" problems. I had chosen Dr. Cerna because her eyes were both kind and sad. The sadness spoke to me. It told me that she, like me, had felt the kind of pain it wasn't easy to recover from. I hoped she would find her happiness. I knew I would never find mine.

She started the session as she always did by speaking about confidentiality. Instead of listening I thought more about dying.

The first time I died was seventy years ago in Ebensee Concentration Camp. I had been brought to the attention of Aribert Heim, the Butcher of Mauthausen. He was one of the heartless Nazi doctors who experimented mostly on the Jews in the concentration camps. During the months he tortured me he told me many times that I was a toy given to him to unleash his sadistic impulses on. He said that I was worse than a Jew. I was a woman who had tried to save Jews sentenced to die. And because of that, he had saved the worst of his experiments for me.

The night I died Heim had ripped my liver from my emaciated body without anesthesia. Before he killed me he shared that he was curious to see how much pain a human body could take. Dying at the Butcher's hands was an agony unlike any I'd ever experienced. Screams were torn out of me as I prayed to the Good God to take me.

And then came a peace that passed all my understanding. I was at the entrance to heaven. I would see my beautiful daughter again. All would be well. Joy filled my soul. Then I was ripped away and returned to Hell on Earth.

Heim had injected me with the blood of a prisoner who had survived all of his "experiments." I was brought back to that travesty of a medical laboratory to become the tortured undead. I was starved of blood, caged-the perfect victim to practice his ceaseless brand of sadistic medicine on.

As my psychiatrist droned on, I regretfully decided once again not to kill myself. I did not know if one such as I could achieve Heaven, but the Lord frowned on suicide. I would not risk angering Him more than my very unnatural state already had. If there was any chance that I would be able to see my precious baby again, I would not do anything to risk it. I had no chance of dying in a State of Grace-I could not step one foot into a church much less partake of the Body and Blood. Confession and Absolution were beyond me. For years I was almost beyond hope. And yet in this new and very non-religious city and time, many believed that the Lord would forgive without the blessings of the Church, that intent mattered. If they were right (and for me it was a dim but potent *if)*, then maybe I would see my child again. For surely the Lord didn't blame me for sheltering that poor Jewish family in my home from the vile Nazis. For that "crime" my two-year-old Elsie had been sent to the gas chamber and me to the Butcher's bloody experiments.

"I think you should go back to where it all began." I was jolted out of my memories by Dr. Cerna. My psychiatrist was almost as young as I'd been when I died. No more than thirty, her cap of black hair shone in the light. Her hazel eyes were older than the rest of her, full of a secret pain I instinctively responded to.

"*Wo ist das*?" I had been so lost in my memories that I'd reverted back to my native German. "I'm sorry. What were you saying?"

I wasn't supposed to see it, but she rolled her eyes in exasperation even though her voice stayed compassionate, caring. "Louise, it's pretty obvious that you haven't told me everything that's bothering you. You've been coming to me for years and I'm not sure I've been able to help you at all. I'm beginning to think we will never get to the root of your problems." She looked me up and down "You've got bags under your eyes, your skin is pale and drawn, your hands shake constantly, and your hair is so dry it's almost falling out. You're clearly not getting enough out of our sessions."

I couldn't tell her that my physical condition was a side effect of being a hundred and two year old vampire and that I'd never change. When I died I was a starved shell of myself. If I lived to be a thousand, I'd still look exactly the same.

"They help," I told her honestly. Without my meetings with Dr. Cerna, I could go weeks without talking to anyone except those I hunted. These therapy sessions were the dim highlight of my otherwise dark week.

"I'm glad to hear it. I'm not giving up on you. But I do have a couple of things I want you to do." She handed me a spiral bound notebook. "I want you to write down what has hurt you, what you're thinking about, and whatever you happen to feel. You don't ever have to let anyone see what you've written." She gave a little half smile, "Some of my patients even burn the pages so no one else can see them."

As I leaned over to take the book, I wasn't sure I would ever journal about my time in the concentration camp. Still, some part of me liked the idea of burning my story about living and dying in a concentration camp. Perhaps the flames would find its way to heaven and remind God and His Saints of the few of us left here on earth.

"Here's the other suggestion. Go back to the beginning, to whatever truly haunts you. Go back. Confront the ghosts that live inside you." Her voice was full of sorrow as she added, "It's hard. I know it's hard. But confronting your demons can be freeing." I took the notebook but didn't say a word as I held it. Finally she said, "Our time's up." As I walked out of the office she added, "Louise, think on what I said."

Later that evening, during my hunt, Dr. Cerna's words haunted me. Go back to the beginning? Impossible. After the Anschluss, my village of Kufstein had never been the same. Nazis occupied it, the English bombed it, the French reoccupied it, and now it was home to a tennis racket manufacturer. The hills of my youth survived, but my farm was long gone, devoured by the hands of time. As I thought about it, longing and fear tore twin daggers of pain into my heart. A red-eye flight might safely take me home so I could once again see where my darling Heinz wooed me and my precious daughter was born.

I shook helplessly. Kufstein was also where my darling Heinz had been forced into the army against his will. Not yet 25, he'd been killed on the Russian Front fighting a war he didn't believe in. My sweet baby Elsie was gassed in Ebensee, deemed too young and too useless to be the slave labor the Nazi monsters demanded. I wiped futilely at my eyes trying to clear the imaginary tears that my vampirism would not allow to flow. I slid to the ground silently keening. There would be no return to Kufstein for me. Even after seventy-six years, I wasn't strong enough for that.

The idea of returning to the home I once held dear made me wish I could cry. I rejected outright the thought of returning to Ebensee. Every violation the butcher had inflicted upon me was etched on my soul. I would not wander those halls, preserved now as a museum, with children one quarter my age who would gasp and shudder and take photos with their phones to post on social media with no ability to understand the horror that I had survived. I didn't hate those children. In fact, I envied their naiveté, but I would not share the horror of my life and death with them. It was more than vampiric flesh could bear.

"Fucking Muslim bitch." I was brutally torn out of my memories by two men who had dragged a scared woman wearing a hijab in an unlit alley. "Coming over here and trying to inflict Sharia Law on the rest of us."

"No, please. I wouldn't. I was born here…" The poor woman shook in fear as she tried to appease her tormentors.

One of the two men started groping at her through her heavy skirts "I bet you have a bomb hidden underneath there. Come on, Bobby. Let's take a look."

They pushed her against the wall in a way that was far too familiar. For a moment I flashed back to a shopping trip I'd taken with my best friend Rebecca. Brownshirts had thrown her against the wall chanting "Juden" and groped her while I stood frozen in fear. Like then, this woman's attackers used sex to cause terror. Unlike then, I wasn't a fragile woman helpless to stop them.

I surged forward, grabbing the two men and smashing their heads together, powerful in a way I hadn't been then. "Bloody bastards," I said, dropping them to the ground. The woman cowered, and I could only imagine what I looked like with my fangs out and bloodlust in my eyes. "Go." I pointed the way to safety, my voice guttural with rage and the need to feed.

With a whispered, "Thank you," she grabbed the edges of her long dress and ran.

"And now for you." I looked at the two men I'd dropped into the alley, my eyes glinting red.

"No, please. I won't… I didn't do anything." They babbled, speaking on top of each other. "I'll be good."

I deliberately licked one fang, wanting to increase their dread. Their minds were easy to read. This was not the first woman they'd assaulted in the name of "America." They used their so-called patriotism to attack Muslim, black, and Hispanic women. Their America was completely different than the one who had given me sanctuary all those years ago. My adopted country was better than this. I would not let these men continue their cruelty one more night in her name.

As I bent over to grab one of them, he pissed himself. Normally I would have been repulsed, but instead I relished the smell of his fear, knowing that he was suffering through the same terror he'd inflicted on so many others. With great delight, I clamped down on this neck and bit.

It was near dawn when I dropped the two would-be rapists on the doorsteps of the 22nd Precinct. They were down a few pints of blood and in the mood to confess to everything they'd ever done, up to and including stealing a dollar from the collection box of their local church when they were kids. I'd used my powers to ensure their full cooperation.

I was too far from my lair to get back before sunrise. I needed to go someplace where I wouldn't be bothered. Someplace without windows. Someplace that I could enter without an invitation. There was no movie theater nearby, which was my favorite place to hide when away from my den. Houses of worship were permanently denied to me. Hospitals were impossible-the smell of blood drove me crazy with hunger. I was afraid I would lose control and bite indiscriminately. I'd stayed in the subway system before, but I hated it. They reeked of people lost in despair and those too busy to notice. I was running out of time and had almost resigned myself to a day lurking in the subways when I noticed a small museum across the street. There were large windows near the front entrance in what I assumed was the lobby. The rest of the building appeared windowless. That would work, and it had to be better than a subway.

I ran across the street and climbed the fence. There was a slight chance it was electric, but I doubted it. Electric fences in NYC were rare. I didn't care if it was electric, in fact part of me almost hoped it was. Accidental death was not suicide and God probably would not keep me out of heaven for that. Instead, most places, including this museum, had security cameras and a half-asleep guard. Cameras aren't an issue for me. I don't show up on them. I forced the service entrance open and slid inside. Alarms went off, and I ran for the basement.

I mesmerized the security guard who found me to report the basement empty of all intruders. An hour later the security company wrapped up their investigation. They decided that since the footage showed no one entering the museum the open door and the alarm was likely caused by a short in the system.

Hours later the museum opened. I slipped out and began to roam the exhibits, easily avoiding the sunlit lobby. I marveled at the famous Tiffany stained glass, once only the province of churches, now available to all. It was backlit and appeared as though the sun was shining through it. I smiled wistfully at one resplendent with rolling hills of grapes. Heinz and I had traveled to the south of France when we were first married. The vines reminded me of that trip. We'd had such dreams. Dreams killed by a war waged by an evil monster.

The next exhibit I wandered into was a display of nineteenth and twentieth century dollhouses. I gazed on the well-loved small homes with a bittersweet smile. When Elsie was still an infant, Heinz had built her a dollhouse. One of the last things he'd said to us was that he'd be home in time to see Elsie play with it. But my Elsie hadn't lived long enough to play with her father's creation. The brutes had taken her first.

I turned and gasped with pain. Across the room, Theresa was displayed on a shelf of children's toys. She was a small stuffed doll I'd made for Elsie. She carried it with her when the Sturmschafuhrer took her. I remember standing tall and reassuring Elsie that Theresa would take care of her. Elsie hugged it tight and nodded, promising me she would be a brave girl and make me proud.

I hadn't cried when they'd taken my beautiful girl. I'd tried to make things as normal for her as possible. She would have been scared to see me sobbing uncontrollably. So I'd buried my tears and saw her off on a doomed railcar, hoping that she would be one of the few children of dissenters spared the gas chamber. That hope had been dashed. Heim had gleefully reported her death to me.

I reached out and grabbed the toy, ignoring the alarms that went off as soon as I touched the stuffed doll. I was faster than the security guards and could not show up on their cameras. I searched frantically for the "E" that I had embroidered on it. Longing for it to tell a different story than Airbert Heim told me. Hoping that Elsie had been adopted by a German couple. Praying that she'd lived. My heart was ripped out of me once again when I realized the "E" wasn't there. This doll was exactly the same pattern as the one I used, but the apron was free of any identifying marks.

Shaking, I put the doll back so it would look undisturbed when museum security responded to the alarm. I didn't cry. I hadn't cried since that horrible day when I held my tears to give Elsie hope but oh how I wanted to. They were locked inside my cold, unbeating heart. Sometimes I thought I'd tear apart from the force of them.

I wandered aimlessly through a couple of other exhibits, not seeing them. Thinking of Heinz, of Elsie, of the home that no longer existed.

Then I turned the corner and my heart stopped. Kufstein was in front of me, so real I thought I could touch it. Not the Kufstein of today, but *my* Kufstein. My home.

I greedily devoured the painting, wishing with all my soul that I was still in *my* Kufstein. I reached out, my fingers hovering just inches above the meticulously painted oil strokes. I wished that I could walk through the painting and be at the only home I had ever know true happiness, but of course, that was not to be.

My eyes were drawn first to the fortress on the hill. The round turret that had once signaled safety and prosperity and turned to fear as the hated Gestapo flew the Nazi flag from its tower. Then Saint Vitus's Church. I avoided looking at the cross, but smiled at the Gothic and baroque blend of architecture I'd known so long ago. I stared at the ancient wall designed to protect us from invading hoards armed with swords and bows, not tanks and guns. Not that it had mattered. Austria had fallen to Hitler without a single shot fired.

I went closer. Altstadt with its picturesque lanes and the Romerhofgasse with the tiny stores I'd shopped in during my mortal life. The Hofbrau where Heinz and I courted was there, painted white with tasteful brown trim. And Schaller's butchery was there. Mr. Schaller was my friend Gretel's father and always saved choice cuts of meat for me. Then the Neuhaus candy store where I used to buy Elsie's treats.

I fled the room, as close to tears as I'd been in seventy-six years. I'd bought Elsie a small chocolate cat the morning we'd been discovered. I never got a chance to give it to her. I'd put it away thinking it would be a special treat for my little girl on a day when she'd been very good.

I ran, looking up to see that I'd stumbled into in a room full of instruments of torture. Racks and Iron Maidens didn't deal half the blow to me that scalpels, syringes, shackles, and chains did. My undying vampiric body had survived being injected with petrol and phenol, my kidneys ripped from my body only to grow back the next day, my bones broken and feet amputated would regenerate in hours. Heim had been fascinated by my ability to regenerate. Daily, sometimes several times a day, he would remove my prison tattoo with a scalpel and watch as the skin on my breast grew back. He told me that he'd made a blanket to sleep under out of the skin he tore over and over from my chest.

I did not need to spend one minute in that room. My memories of the concentration camp were indelibly stamped on my soul.

I ran again, only looking up when I collided with a tall, strong body clad in a museum security guard's uniform. I estimated him to be about forty, shoulder-length white-blond hair shining in the light, smiling down on me. A silver nametag with "Percy" and a symbol of a winged sword that I assumed was the museum's logo was pinned to his left shoulder. "Are you alright, Miss?" he asked in an English accent.

On any other day I would have told him I was fine and brushed past without talking. But the exhibits in this museum seemed to be perfectly designed to flay open the scars on my heart. So I answered, "No." I told myself to keep running, but when he wrapped an arm around me I stayed.

I needed the comfort he silently offered me. Without a word he led me into a closed room with a sign on it indicating that it was closed pending a new exhibition.

"We can talk here," Percy told me. We sat down on a small bench placed in front of an exhibit of medieval related artwork that thankfully had nothing to do with me. "Tell me what's wrong," he said with a command in his voice I found myself instinctively responding to.

"Everything. Nothing." I shook my head knowing that my answer would make no sense to anyone. I searched for words while he waited patiently. "Painful thoughts," I finally came up with. "Memories."

Percy settled back against the bench, looking like a man who had all the time in the world. "Sharing can help," he said simply. He waited patiently.

I didn't know if I could do it. Not talking about my old life had become my normal.

When I was first freed from the concentration camp I'd shared stories with a few of the other women survivors, but it hadn't helped. We all had our wounds. We all had our losses, and at the time, none of us wanted to linger on them. We wanted to get on with our lives. Go forward, not back. To build anew. For a few years, I kept in touch with a couple of them, watching with envy when Helga and Ingrid met new men and built new families with them. My vampiric state had kept me from doing the same.

We sat there for longer than I can say. Finally, I turned to him and said, "My story is pretty unbelievable."

He smiled. "Why, sometimes I've believed six impossible things before breakfast."

I had read "Through the Looking Glass" and wondered if the guard was trying to warn me. "Are you the Red Queen?" The Red Queen was not to be trusted.

"Not at all, my dear. I'm far more trustworthy than she. But like Louis Carroll's immortal character, I too am able to believe in things that sound impossible."

I chewed my lip for a moment. I had nothing to lose. At the end of our conversation, I would simply mesmerize the security guard and ensure that he didn't remember our conversation. I couldn't do that with Doctor Cerna. She kept careful notes of our sessions and would notice holes in her memory after talking to me. But this nice man would simply be left with foggy memory of helping a patron in despair. Having made the decision, the words burst out almost without my control. "I'm a hundred-and-two-year-old concentration camp survivor and the exhibits made me remember my family. I miss them so much."

I held my breath, waiting for him to laugh at me. Or comment on the fact that I looked twenty-two, not one hundred and two. Instead he said, "Of course you do." His voice held all the sadness in the world. "It's hard outliving those you love." He stroked my hair back with hands that were infinitely tender. "Tell me about it."

It was the first time I'd been touched in kindness in a lifetime. I reached up and touched the hand he had against my hair. He didn't flinch away in fear of the vampire. Instead, he twisted his hand so it was holding mine and brought our combined hands down to his knee.

Somehow that gave me the courage I needed. "I was born in Austria to a farming family just outside of Kufstein in 1915. We worked hard and by most standards, my family did well. Because of that, my parents decided to send me to school and not just my brothers like many families chose to do.

"My first day in school I made two very close friends." I smiled, thinking back to that day. "Heinz was a blond boy who'd thrown a ball at me the moment we met and had been surprised when I caught it. Then I threw it back twice as fast. He always told me he fell in love with me that very second. It was a love that lasted until he died fighting in a war he didn't believe in, for a Fuehrer he hated, on the Russian front."

If I'd been human I would have been crying. My eyes burned with the need to cry tears that could never form. I clutched the security guard's hand tighter, needing him to be my anchor.

"Rebecca was the prettiest girl in school. She had the most gorgeous dark hair done all up in spiral curls that I envied the moment I saw them. She wore a dress trimmed with real lace and she had a doll with a porcelain face. I'd never seen anything like it. Everyone I knew had rag dolls.

"Rebecca knew more than the rest of us. Even on the first day of school she could read. Really read, not a couple of letters like I knew. I thought she was perfect. Way out of my league. I was too scared to talk to her at recess. I thought a rich banker's daughter wouldn't want to be friends with a farmer's daughter. Then a couple of kids started teasing her for being Jewish. Without thinking about it, Heinz and I jumped in between her and her bullies, fists up." I laughed a little at the memory. Two tow-haired kids that had already managed to get covered in dirt from playing in the yard, fists up, defending the princess from the older kids. Those boys had been shocked when Heinz and I had knocked them down and sent them running.

"That was all it took for the three of us to become the best of friends. Some of the older kids tried to tell us over the years that I shouldn't be friends with a Jew. That the '*Juden*' were taking all of the good jobs. That they were stealing money from everyone else. But for Heinz and me Rebecca was our friend and that was all that mattered." I smiled, lost in happier times.

Percy let me remember for a long moment. Finally he asked, "Then what happened?"

"Heinz and I were married in 1935. A few days before my wedding Rebecca and I went to Salzburg. We were shopping for a veil for me and a new dress for her to wear to my wedding. It was supposed to be a happy time for us. Our last girls' day before I wed." I shuddered, suddenly cold, thinking back to that fateful day. "Instead, on the way home, at the train station, some thugs assaulted us. They threw Rebecca up against a wall and called her *Juden*. They groped her and spat in her face. She was so scared."

Something trickled down my cheek. I caught the red-tinged tear on one finger and stared at it in disbelief. "How?"

"It's not important," Percy said. I started to argue. Crying when my tears had been frozen for over seventy years was very important to me. But he said with a gentle air of command I found impossible to resist, "I will tell you later. Right now I would very much like to hear the rest of your story."

Obedient to his will and my need to finally have someone know my history, I continued my story.

"I just stood there." I couldn't sit still. Instead I paced, running from the memories I couldn't forget. "I stood against a concrete wall only a couple of feet away from where my best friend was being assaulted and cowered. The news had been full of what happened to those who stood up against the Sturnabteil. I was afraid. But that was no excuse." My soul was full of self-loathing. I'd failed Rebecca. I'd failed myself. "She was my best friend and I did nothing. I should have pushed one of them on the tracks or run for help." Or realized how dangerous Salzburg had become and been content with a homemade veil.

"They got braver after no one stopped them. Other passengers just scurried by, their heads down, trying not to see. They tore her clothing. Exposed her breasts. Hit her across the face. One of them said that they would have raped her but they didn't want to lie with pigs. After she was huddled crying in the corner of the train station they kicked her in the stomach and moved on." I clenched my fists, wishing I could go back in time and beat the men who had hurt my beautiful friend.

Suddenly exhausted, I ignored the tears that were blinding me and sank back down next to the security guard. "I picked her up and covered her with my coat." And had apologized about a thousand times for not protecting her. "The train pulled up, and we got on and went home." On the ride home, we'd pretended that everything was the same. But it wasn't. Something in our friendship had broken forever. She was the persecuted and for the first time ever I hadn't defended her.

"You were afraid. Anyone would have been." His words offered me an absolution I refused to accept.

"I should have been there for her. I was a coward! I knew better, and I let them hurt Rebecca anyway. It didn't matter that anyone would have been scared. Evil wins if we don't fight back. Even when we're afraid. *Especially* when we're afraid. That day innocence was destroyed."

I clenched the bench I was sitting on so hard I heard the wood crack. I looked down, a little bemused. I hadn't made that kind of mistake with my strength in over seventy years.

"Three days later Rebecca stood next to me as I married Heinz. She smiled, gave me a hug and made me promise to live a happy life." She'd also hugged Heinz and threatened him with dire things if he didn't take good care of me. "The day after my wedding Rebecca and her family left for America. The Brown Shirts' attack on her had scared her family into running and ultimately saved her life.

"A year later my parents died of the flu. My brothers wanted no part of running the farm, so it was ours. They both were mechanics and moved down to the city." I shrugged, a movement that meant nothing and everything. "We didn't have a telephone yet and they weren't the type who wrote letters. It didn't take long for us to lose track of them. A year after that we had our beautiful daughter Elsie."

I took a deep breath. "Then came the *Anschluss.* Germany annexed us without a shot fired. Hitler's troops were welcomed with cheering crowds and mindless adulation." The theater in Kufstein had showed Hitler riding into Linz with the crowds celebrating madly. Applause filled our theater. I wanted to vomit. I still did.

"I argued with Heinz. I wanted to take Elsie and flee Austria for America. Rebecca had settled in Brooklyn and I knew we could go to her. We'd have to leave everything behind, but she would take us in. We would be safe. Heinz wanted to stay in Kufstein. He thought that we would be safe. That, no matter what, farming was a protected occupation. He loved his home and wanted to stay right where he was."

I shook, remembering the black day that Heinz was stolen

from me. I stared blindly at the priceless artwork hanging on the wall. I felt like I was a block of ice, frozen from the inside out. Percy put his hand on my shoulder and told me "Keep going." Somehow that warm human touch melted me just enough that I could continue.

"We were still arguing when Heinz was taken. What neither of us realized as we fought about our future was that we were known 'Jew lovers' and had been targeted by the Wehrmacht. Heinz was conscripted into the army less than two weeks after the annexation. I cried helplessly as they took him. He promised to come home to me. I prayed and prayed to Jesus and to the Virgin Mary that he would come home but he didn't."

I looked up at Percy, shocked that Jesus's holy name had passed through my mouth. As a vampire, His name was forbidden to me. I would have said something, but Percy put his finger to my lips. "Continue," he ordered me. I simply nodded, trusting that when I was done, he would explain the miraculous changes that were happening to me. "Heinz was taken," he said as though I had forgotten where I was in the story. He was wrong. Every moment was indelibly engraved in my heart.

I stared sightlessly at the picture of the castle in front of me remembering those hard days and bitterly cold winter nights after Heinz had been stolen away from me. I would have taken Elsie and run, but part of me couldn't bear to leave where Heinz and I had been so happy together. I needed to believe that he would come home to me, alive and in one piece. Leaving felt like a betrayal of our love. Of us.

I got up and slowly started walking around the room again, the pattern of the terrazzo floor blurred by tears. If I kept moving, the memories wouldn't overwhelm me. "One day I went into the barn to milk the cows before turning them out to pasture, when I found a Jewish family cowering in there. The Nazis had liquidated the Jewish ghetto the night before, but they'd managed to escape. Rebecca had introduced me to the Bauchman family several years before the war ever started, and they remembered me. They begged me to hide them. To let them stay in the hayloft. I looked at their four-year-old child, already old before his years, and I couldn't say no." The boy had the same clear gray eyes as my best friend.

"They swore that Aaron would stay quiet. That they would smother his cries in pillows if he cried." I hated saying the next bit, but it was a reality of being under Nazi occupation. Something I had demanded as the price of sanctuary. "They also promised that if the Nazis came and burned my barn down, they wouldn't run but would stay inside and die. That way Elsie and I wouldn't be murdered by the Nazis as well.

"I was very careful. I never brought food into the barn. Instead, I deliberately under-milked the cows and failed to collect a few eggs from the hens. They lived on the milk left in the cows, raw eggs, and on the oats I pretended to overfeed my livestock. We survived that way for six months. Then the Nazis came."

I collapsed to the floor, my legs boneless beneath me. Percy was next to me the next moment, his arm holding my head up off of the hard floor. "I'm here," he promised me. "You are not alone."

I held tight to the man and managed to finish my story. "The Sturmschafuhrer said he was there for a routine inspection. I stood there with Elsie at my side, watching as they stabbed pitchforks into bundles of hay. God wasn't with us. They hit Aaron. He cried out. He couldn't help it. He was just a boy." I wiped my eyes angrily with the back of my hand. "It had taken less than thirty minutes for them to find the rest of the family.

"I knew what was coming next. The Sturmschafuhrer ordered Elsie and me to be rounded up as well. He allowed me to get Elsie's coat and doll, dress her, and send her off with him. He left holding Elsie in one hand and Aaron in the other. And he sent them off on one of the rail cars to die."

I dissolved into tears, crying hysterically, and found myself being turned into Percy's shoulder. The wool of his uniform was scratchy against my skin until my tears turned it to a sodden mess.

"I don't understand it." I sobbed. "I never understood how he could smilingly condemn them to death. They were just children. Elsie was a baby. So helpless. So innocent. How could they do something like that? What kind of monster sees a baby and wants to kill her?"

I cried forever. Every tear I'd held back watching Elsie be carried away came out. Every tear I'd cried for Heinz. For me when I was in Ebensee. For Aaron and his parents and Rebecca and for the Muslim woman who had been tormented only the night before. Every tear of loneliness I'd held inside of me for the seventy-six years I'd lived without my loved ones came pouring out of me.

Finally, hours-or days-later, I was empty. I looked around the room and everything glistened, glittering diamond-bright through the remnants of my tears.

"How are you feeling now?" Percy asked.

"Light. Lost." I didn't know what I was going to do without the knot of grief that had held me captive for so long. "Tetherless."

"May I ask you a question?" There was something in his voice that said the question was very important to him.

The man had listened to me. Heard my story and helped free me from the past. I owed him more than he could possibly know. "Of course."

"If you had to do it all over again, would you still shelter the Bauchmans?"

Oh God in Heaven. That was a question I'd asked myself over and over again. My compassion had cost my daughter her life. For *nothing*. On the other hand, how could I have said no? Aaron, his mother Susan, his father Abel. None of them had done anything wrong except to be born into the "wrong" religion.

I didn't answer him directly. Instead, staring at the floor ashamed, I said, "It didn't make any difference. They all died anyway. And my daughter with them. She was mine to love. Mine to protect. I betrayed her by protecting them."

"Do you really believe that?" he asked. I turned to look at him. His face was stern, his eyes demanding. Forcing me to face my truth. "Do you really think that nothing would have been different?"

Staring into his eyes, I spoke what was in my heart. "No," I answered heavily. "If I'd turned them away, it would have been a stain on my soul. An act that would have put me beyond God's redemption." And with that I had the answer I'd hidden from for over seventy years. "I would have had sheltered them anyway. Anything else would have been wrong."

I cried again, this time in relief. I knew that for all that I had suffered, way back in my barn in Kufstein, my soul hadn't chosen wrong. I'd stayed true to myself and God's will.

When I wiped away my final tears, Percy asked, "What are you going to do now?"

I shook my head. "I don't know." I'd spent the last seventy years lost in despair, haunting the night, missing my loved ones. I still missed them, but my tears had freed me. I felt like I had a new lease on life. Living aimlessly wouldn't be enough.

"Do you still want to die?" His voice was infinitely kind.

That surprised me. I hadn't told him how close to suicide I'd come. Then again, he'd heard my story. Maybe my despair was obvious to anyone willing to listen. Although I didn't need to breathe, I drew a shaky cleansing breath. "No. I feel like I've wasted my life since I was freed. I need to do something with the rest of my immortal life. Something worthwhile." I wanted to make sure that there were no other Muslim women tormented by those who hid their sadism behind their alleged patriotism. No other Rebeccas tortured for their religions. No other Heinzes thrust into wars they didn't believe in. No other Elsies and Aarons killed because someone saw them as less than human. And no others like me, victims of wars fought to torture others. But I said none of that. It seemed too pretentious to believe I could make much of a difference, that I could stop the spread of evil. But I wanted to with all my heart. I wanted to transform all my pain into a shield that would protect the innocent.

He smiled as though he could hear my thoughts. "You are important. You can help change the world."

Staring into the eyes of a person who could apparently read my mind, my heart no longer burdened by my dead, I began to questions the changes in me. "How was I able to cry?" Vampires couldn't cry. I knew that from personal experience. I would have cried a thousand times if I'd been able to.

I looked at him, really looked at him. He bore a slight resemblance to my father. And I could see my Heinz in the shape of his shoulders. The tilt of his head was very like Mr. Bauchman, and his eyes were grey like Aaron's. He looked like every good man I'd ever known in my life.

"Who *are* you?"

"Does it matter?"

"God in Heaven!" I burst out. "Of course it does!" He'd freed me from invisible shackles and opened me up to living again.

My question changed. "What are you?" It seemed ridiculous to ask the next question, but, "Are you one of the Good Lord's saints?" A saint wouldn't want to have anything to do with a cursed vampire, but I couldn't think of anyone or anything else capable of making changes to my very nature.

He stood, and light haloed around him. I blinked against the brightness and when I reopened them he was clad in a blue surcoat emblazoned with white crosses over shining armor. "Not a saint, but one of God's warriors."

I fell to my knees in front of him. He lifted me back to my feet and said, "I am Father Perceval, leader of a small band of warrior who fight in God's name. And Louise, I am recruiting. Will you join us?"

With the heart of a woman no longer wounded and the bravery of the child I'd been I burst out, "Yes. Please."

From somewhere he produced a small wooden cup that shone with an unworldly light. "Take and drink," he said. Words spoken around the world as a promise of God's love and the openings that love gives us. "This is My Blood, given for you."

Trembling, I took the cup and drank, entering into my new life as a Warrior of the Grail.

The Titanic's House of Morgan

Russ Colchamiro

"It's murder, Arch. That's what it is. Friggin' murder."

Anthony Grenachi grumbled from the ladder as he beveled the corner of a jagged support beam. He pawed at his left knee. "Girlfriend's looking to bleed me dry, then kill me. I'm gonna die right here on this spot."

"Tony … Tone. Come on." Tony's assistant Archie Frye was touching up the chestnut brown paint on a strip of molding. An imported marble globe with Asia tilted forward sat upon an antique reading table. "That's yer problem. You like the crazies. Your wife … Marjorie … now *she* was a peach. So sad when she passed. But this one … Zanita? She's got three kids with three different baby daddies and none of 'em are yours! I know we all need the gentle touch now and then, but I'm not sure she knows *how* to be gentle. And she sure ain't good!"

"I know, I know," Tony said, eye level with leather-bound copies of medieval Welsh poetry, lined with precision. "But she's with me, she breaks up with me … she's back with me again. I can't control her. And it's not like we live together. It's just a Friday night thing. You know how it is."

Archie had lived with his 'roommate' Doug for the last nineteen years. He also never mentioned a girlfriend. Tony had wanted to ask - just so that Archie wouldn't feel the need to keep secrets, the inner pangs buried deep within - but didn't press the issue.

"You get yourself worked up over nothing, Tone. Just ditch this one. Relax. You gotta lie back, drink a cold one … and smile. You gotta live life while you still got it in you."

"Live? Aw for chrissakes. I'm fifty-one years old, Arch. I got a leaky roof, a truck with bald tires, a nephew on parole, and now I blew out my meniscus again. And the busy season's slowing down. We gotta take every job while we can. My health insurance nearly doubled last year and now the North Koreans are testing missiles. My stress is off the charts!"

They were doing touch-up work on the private, two-tiered library of 23 Wall Street in Lower Manhattan. The famed building - known as 'The Corner' - was originally owned by and built for industrialist and financier JP Morgan back in 1913. The property had changed hands a few times, and was under renovation.

Tony was about to knock off early and pack that bad knee in ice when Archie did what he always did just when Tony needed a distraction - went off on some wild tangent, usually a combination of tall tales, bizarre news, and conspiracy theories.

"Yo, Tony. Speaking of living life while you still got it ... you heard this story? Some Kangaroo Jack's building ... get this ... a new *Titanic*. As a *cruise ship!* Can you believe it! The *Titanic! Man*, that's some balls, huh?"

Despite himself, Tony felt the tension rod in his chest unscrew one turn. Archie was a half-decent contractor's assistant, but his rants were always amusing, if not bat crap crazy. Deep-based rock-n-roll howled through the paint-splattered radio hoisted on the toolbox.

"They're raising the what? The Titanic? Oh, come on."

"Not ... you know ... *raising* the Titanic," Archie said. "*Building* it. A new one."

"... wrapping up a Led Zeppelin two-for-Tuesday with 'Ramble On' and 'Misty Mountain Hop', we turn to the latest on traffic and the weather. But first ... in today's news, raised from the bottom of the North Atlantic Ocean, twelve thousand five hundred feet below the sea ... Australian billionaire and eccentric Clive Palmer has finalized his plans to recreate the Titanic. Down to the last detail, he's committed to delivering a world-class cruise ship that he claims will set the standards for quality, comfort, and safety, combining state-of-the art design and construction features with the texture and ambiance from the original ship."

"Tony! Tone! Check it out. This is it! Listen!"

"The original ill-fated voyage back in nineteen twelve was actually set to dock at our very own Chelsea Piers on the West Side of Manhattan. As we all know, it never made it. Palmer says the new ship - The Titanic II - will be the safest in the world, with some passengers willing to pay up to nine hundred thousand dollars for tickets on the maiden voyage. The new Titanic - under construction for Palmer by the CSC Jinling Shipyard in Jiangsu, China, will travel from that Far East city ... finally docking in Dubai. .... And now, today's forecast calls for ... "

"Hold on a second," Tony said. "Are you seriously telling me this maniac is going to build a cruise ship - a new Titanic, iceberg Titanic, *disaster* Titanic - and people think this is a good idea? Oh, for crap sakes.

What the -?"

Not a big guy - five foot nine, a hundred and sixty pounds - Tony doubled over, hand pressed against his temple. The diamond-splinter headaches - they had kicked in right after Tony started work on the library - were getting worse.

"Whoa. Tone. You okay?" Archie reached for the creaky ladder, held it steady. He was shorter and smaller than Tony, but deceptively strong. And most important, he was always there. "You seein' 'em again?"

Jaw clenched, Tony gritted his teeth, eyes squeezed shut. The pain was like a crowbar being plied to the crate in his head, popping the lid off its hinges. The combination of wood oil and old dust wafted up into his nasal cavity, scraping behind his eye.

"Ow, yeah. It's ..." He breathed in and out, slowly, forcing the air between his teeth in tight, controlled hisses. He kept at it until the pain subsided. "I'm not sleeping, Arch. My knee. The pain pills help, but not enough. I've been knocking back a couple of tall boys in front of the TV. Passing out in my chair. But when I wake up ... the movies I watch before bed ... my mind can't 'em let go. They come in flashes, just sloshing around in my brain."

"When's the surgery? For your knee?"

"End of next month. Forty-seven days. And then rehab. Not as bad as when I blew it out in high school, but I'm old, Arch. I just can't take the poundings like I used to. And my head is always killing me. Friggin' allergies."

Archie nodded in silence. Sometimes you just have to let a man say what he needs to say, feel what he needs to feel. And then, "Headaches could be from grinding your teeth, Tone. Get yourself one of them chompers. You know ... night guards. I wear one. Doug's got one, too. Ain't too sexy, but if it works ..."

"I don't know ... I just feel like ... it's something else. The pain, the stress. Like ... my wires are crossed. Like it's someone else's dream. I don't know, Arch. I just don't know."

The property they were working on - directly across from the New York Stock Exchange - was only four stories tall, on JP Morgan's orders. Boasting among his fellow millionaires, so wealthy was Morgan that he didn't require an enormous stone tower jutting into the heavens to show off his power and prestige. He showed off by not showing off. Less was more. He wouldn't even permit his name on the building. Everybody knew it was his. The "House of Morgan".

Tony had been commissioned - strictly as a favor by his pal, lead contractor Gerry Kuzmanoff - to help finish the library, a double-height, two-story room with dark, wooden arches, a vaulted ceiling, gold-plated lamps, and more than 15,000 immaculately kept volumes from around the world. It wasn't a large room, but like Morgan had laid out, it wasn't the size the mattered, but the location. Classic real estate.

Tony, whose throbbing head had settled down, eased off the aluminum ladder, nicked and scratched from years of abuse. He took a swig of water from a dented, plastic bottle. The radio was going:

"... the Yankees swept the Red Sox with last night's six to two victory. And in today's top story, Australian billionaire Clive Palmer says the Titanic II is set to be completed this year, updated for our modern times, but capturing the spirit of the original. The best of both worlds. 'The Titanic comes from a time when the world was different,' Palmer said. 'When there was a different culture, different ways of living. When people worked with each other more.' The experience on the new ship, the eccentric billionaire noted, will include Turkish baths, a smoking room, and a gymnasium as it would have appeared on the original ship. ..."

"See, that's what I mean, Tone." Archie wiped sweat from his forehead with the back of his arm. His overalls were covered in plaster and paint smears. "These millionaires, billionaires ... gazillionaires ... they knew that ship was in trouble. Not enough life boats in case there was trouble ... but they didn't care. Stroking the high-ticket passengers. Didn't want to block their view of the decks. Problem was ... that was just the tip of the iceberg. So to speak." Archie was proud of that one.

Brown, leather chairs and couches were covered in drop cloths. Same again with the coffee tables. The new owners were converting the property to a more modern facility, but the library - the Morgan Room - offset deep within the building, held its historical roots, and was being made accessible only to a select few tenants. The elite.

Tony sighed. "Oh, boy. Here we go. Okay. Lay it on me."

"Check it out, Tone. Check it out. So I'm watching the *History Channel* last week. All about the Titanic, right, because of this Palmer guy. So everybody - I'm talking *everybody* - still wants to know what really happened that night. It's like JFK. The great mystery nobody quite believes. But we all know the story. Titanic hits an iceberg. Ship sinks. Lots of people die. Tragedy. DiCaprio makes that movie. Then James Cameron goes back down there with his pods to see what else he can find. But why? To rescue old dinner plates? To find long-lost love letters? I mean ... maybe. But e*verybody* feels - like deep in their souls - that something else was going on."

Two weeks earlier they had redone an orthodontist's second floor bathroom in Bronxville. Today they were in the financial center of the world. Tony was used to knowing how much other guys had - and how much *he* didn't. But he was getting that feeling again, that loose, wobbly feeling, like his feet couldn't touch the floor even though he was standing up. Could have been the pain pills, but he took the last one three hours ago.

"And that's what so crazy, Tone. I mean … think about it. Here we are. You and me right now. We're banging around the House of Morgan. But did you know that Morgan himself - *same guy* - was an owner in White Star Line? That's who built the Titanic. True story! He had a private suite on the damn thing! Decked out and everything. He was over there. In England. He was supposed to be on the maiden voyage. But guess what …?"

Tony squinted. Diamond-splintered headaches. Piercing pain.

Flash. In his mind's eye he saw a stormy day. Docks. Huge ship. RMS Titanic on the side.

Flash. Well-groomed executive. Dark eyes. Squinting.

Flash. Interior cabin.

Flash. Fire.

Flash. Iceberg.

Tony squinted, shook it off. He squeezed the handle of the joint knife. Hard.

"So here's the thing, Tone. Turns out a fire may have damaged the Titanic - *before* it set sail. That's the rumor, anyway. Blaze went on for weeks, near the boiler room. It left these thirty-foot scorch marks. Weakened the steel. So that when the iceberg hit - wham! - it ripped a hole right through it. But here's the big question. Did the fire really break out before the launch, making the ship susceptible to iceberg damage … or did the damage from the iceberg cause the fire? Don't know."

Sharp pain shot through Tony's knee. He grimaced.

"But then there's this, and I gotta say, Tone, it's pretty wild. There's people out there who say JP Morgan himself … was behind the whole thing."

"What? Oh, come on, Arch. I know you love a good conspiracy, but how could JP Morgan sink the Titanic? Gimme a break."

"Good question, Tone. Good question. Take a look at the ship itself. There were no red flares on board to signal any boats for rescue, you know, just in case. Only white flares that signals everything is a-okay. Really? Not a single red flare? Like JP Morgan would ever put himself in danger. And Ed Smith? He was one of the most decorated captains of his time. He was the *man!* And he didn't make sure the ship was safe? Sound right to you?"

"Could've been an oversight," Tony grimaced, not totally believing it himself. "The pressure of debuting a new ship. Cut a few corners to get out on time? Wouldn't be the first time."

"I don't know, Tone. I don't know. But what we *do* know is that Morgan cancelled his own trip hours just before *The Titanic* was supposed to leave. And guess what else? A buddy of Morgan's, this guy Milton Hershey - he *also* cancelled at the last minute. And then he built an empire. You know. *Hershey* Hershey. Chocolate bar Hershey."

"Trips get cancelled all the time." Tony's pushback continued to weaken. "Doesn't mean anything. Maybe some business deal popped up. Whatever."

"Maybe yes, Tone. Maybe no. But here's where it starts to get real interesting. The Federal Reserve - you know, the Fed, controls the banking for the whole country - was formed the very next year. The Fed, man. The Fed!"

"So what?"

"The Astor Family, right? Astor Place, right near St. Marks off Fourth Avenue? We did that job across the street from it last year. Well, John Jacob Astor IV - the actual *richest man in the world* back then - he was *against* the Fed. He made a boatload off his real estate holdings right here in New York, and didn't want to be regulated. And other big wigs who were against the Fed, like this guy Benjamin Guggenheim and Isa Strauss …"

"Yeah …?"

Splinter headache. Something shifted inside him. Tony felt more on the way, tremors before a storm.

"All three guys were on the Titanic, mostly to meet with JP Morgan. But then Morgan cancels … and lives. *They* stay on the ship … and die. Fed gets created. JP Morgan's a banker. Was rich before that, got crazy rich after. And those three guys … the ones that died … not including anything else they might've invested in after that … you know what they would have been worth today?"

Flash. Interior cabin.

Flash. Compartment at the base of the wall.

"Give or take …eleven billion dollars, Tone. That's almost real money."

Designed in a classic architectural style by Trowbridge & Livingston built in 1913, the House of Morgan was designated a New York City landmark in 1965, later added to the National Register of Historic Places. The building was never getting torn down. Built to last.

"There was an even crazier conspiracy they talked about, Tone. It's unbelievable."

"Archie. Come on. You've already got JP Morgan sinking the Titanic so he can take over the country's banking system. That's not enough for you?"

"I know, I know, sounds crazy. But maybe crazy enough to be true. If you remember, the Titanic sank on April fourteenth, nineteen twelve. But do you know what happened about six months before?"

"JP Morgan bought stock in ice cube makers?"

"No, but that's actually not a bad idea. That day the Olympic - another cruise ship from White Star - collided with the HMS Hawke just off the coast of the Isle of Wight, in the English Channel. It was a huge problem for White Star. It meant taking the Olympic out of service for repairs. It also meant that the Titanic - which was originally scheduled to launch in March - got pushed back to April."

"… And? "

"White Star Line - JP Morgan's company - could not afford to delay the Titanic … at all. They had business and legal bills piling up, *plus* they had to dig into their own pockets to repair the Olympic. *And* they were losing revenue because the Olympic was out of service. Triple threat! Even rich guys lose money."

Splinter headache. Piercing.

"So … as the story goes … they came up with a plan…"

Flash. In his mind's eye Tony saw two ships.

Flash. Side by side.

Flash. Titanic.

Flash. Olympic.

Tony stared at Archie, but really, he was looking far beyond. He was starting to know things he didn't want to know. Like he was drawn to them. Like they wanted Tony to see.

"They switched the ships," Tony said. His hands fell to his side.

"Hey! You're catching on, Tone! The Titanic we know was never *really* the Titanic. It was the *Olympic*. They switched the nameplates to keep business going because nobody could tell the difference. And when the Titanic sank - which was really the damaged Olympic - they filed an insurance claim on that sunken ship, and cashed in. Only the top guys - including Morgan - knew that the Titanic was really the Olympic, and the Olympic was really the Titanic. There's even this photo of the two ships next two each other. They're identical. What a scam."

Electricity crackled in Tony's knee. It shot up to his head. Splinter headaches. Sharp. Piercing. Connected.

"Thing is, Tone … you look a little closer at those two ships, you check the photos … the Titanic had fourteen portholes. Evenly spaced. But when it left Southampton on that maiden voyage …"

Flash. "It had sixteen portholes," Tony said. "And they were uneven."

"Y-y-yeah …," Archie said, suspicious, curious. "How'd you know that?"

Flash. In his mind's eye Tony saw a shipyard. Belfast. Harland and Wolff. The image was clear, yet distant, grainy, yet vibrant. Men in wool coats. Rain pounded the coastline. The wind howled. But he could hear them, without realizing, repeating what they said, like he was right there with them:

"They swapped out the bloody ships," a dockworker said.

"Shut yer trap," a man in a top hat said, pointing, ferocity behind his eyes, "or you'll never work again. Not you, not yer family. No one! Ya hear?"

"Whoa," Archie said. "I didn't even know about that one. How'd you …?"

Flash. Tony was back on the docks, JP Morgan standing in the doorway of his private suite, on the Titanic. The day it was scheduled to leave Southampton:

"Careful with those!" he commanded several dockworkers, who removed bronze statues from Morgan's private suite. "They're worth more than your bloodline will earn in a century."

Tony nearly doubled over.

"And Tone … back in the day … any time there was an advertisement for the Titanic or White Star Line, the pictures the company used for them …? They were always - and I'm talking every time - the Olympic and its interior. If the Titanic was the jewel of the fleet, why would they use photos of the Olympic?"

Though the House of Morgan was only four stories tall, the foundations were constructed deep and strong enough to support a forty-story tower if ever there was a desire to build up, like a fortified castle lording over the mainland. But while the exterior had aged well, the interior elements splintered through neglect.

"Hey Arch," Tony said, pushing through to do actual work. "This look right to you?" He pointed to the base of a short staircase, leading to the library's second tier of books. "The moulding. It's loose." He fiddled with the wood strip, pressing it flush against the baseboard. It didn't hold. Muted light caught the golden tassel dangling from Kahlil Gibran's "The Prophet" - 1923 first edition hardcover. "I'm not sure -"

"The inner slat. It's not the right size," Archie said. "It's off by at least an inch. We'll have to shave it down." Archie dug through the tool box for a metal hand file with a serrated surface. Tony hoped it would keep them busy, but he knew better. Much like the piercing headaches drilling into his mind, the conspiracies continued. And escalated.

"*History Channel* played the Titanic special for like two weeks straight. I think I saw it about ten times. There's another theory, Tone, one more I just can't shake."

"Archie. Stop." Tony closed his eyes, the pain behind his temple so intense he now heard a high-pitched whistle, like a microchip about to short circuit. "You're killing me. I get it. JP Morgan and pals lied, stole, and cheated their way to the top. Call Ripley's. But what you do want from me?" He reached for his head again, pressed against his temple in hopes of muting the pain. It didn't work. "Ow. Damn. How's it any different than the jackass we got in the White House?"

Archie was a talker. Tony knew that. It was one of the reasons Tony liked having him around. It helped pass the time. But every now and then - not often, but sometimes - Archie would grab onto a thread, and pull on it, until it finally unspooled.

That's why Tony knew the look Archie had - not the regular fanboy look, like his bar buddies Doug and Eric whining about the Knicks.

Or his neighbor's kid Lucas exploding into hysterics because one of the nerd web sites listed *Guardians of the Galaxy Vol. 2* ahead of *Black Panther* in its recent rankings of the best Marvel superhero movies.

Most people have hobbies. Some are passionate about them. Maybe even crazy. When it came to conspiracy nuts, sometimes, dangerously so.

"It's spookier than that, Tone. So there's this book, right, from eighteen ninety-eight - about fifteen years *before* the Titanic - called *The Wreck of the Titan*. In the book, there's this famous cruise ship, the *Titan*. Rich owner has his own suite, he's booked on the voyage. But at the very last minute … he cancels. Then the ship hits an iceberg and sinks. Sound familiar? That's some clairvoyant stuff, Tone! Or spirits. Or black magic. Or something!"

Tony's heart sped up. He clenched.

"And then, Tone. The author? Morgan Robertson? When people started asking him questions about how similar his book was to the actual Titanic … before he could talk about how he wrote that book … and why? He died. He didn't have a heart attack, didn't stroke out, didn't choke on a steak or a chicken wing. He was *poisoned*."

But there was another look with Archie, like coming home at night and immediately sensing something's amiss - a dust bunny out of place, a lamp tilted in the wrong direction - only to discover your home has in fact been robbed. The otherwise imperceptible shifts of energy in our little worlds become known to us. The disruption. The jeopardy.

This was one of those times.

Tony's hands trembled. Something was wrong. Something was coming.

"Maybe they're connected, maybe they're not," Archie said, "but rumor has it … JP Morgan had treasure on the Titanic worth more than all the riches in the world combined." Archie's eyes held steady, unblinking. The air around him seemed to constrict, as if the most infinitesimal movement - a quarter blink, a sigh - would trigger an earthquake from which there would be no recovery.

Trying to focus on the repairs, to ward off whatever wanted to reveal itself to him, Tony knelt down, pulled the moulding off the wall.

Treasures. He didn't want to hear about treasures, didn't want to know.

He reached inside the wall, when his hand came up against a wood surface. It moved. "What the…?" Both hands in now, he took hold, and removed a box. A wood box. He stood up. Held it out.

Carved into the center of the hand-crafted box was a narrow-eyed dragon, within a circle, curled around a crackling fire pit. A metal latch secured the box closed.

Deafening, high-pitched whir. Piercing headache. Throbbing knee.

Terrified, yet compelled to draw closer, Tony placed his hand on the metal latch. He opened the lid. Within, the box was lined with red felt. Within the felt lining was a narrow ravine. Within that ravine, was a pouch. A green pouch, with a gold draw string.

Tony's hand - as if moving under its own will, as if the hand belonged to another man from another realm from another time - slid toward the pouch. He removed it, loosened the draw string.

Crossing the threshold in the air delineating outside the pouch, and within, unrelenting power surged through him. Feeding on that incredible energy, Tony withdrew the object within. It was shaped like half a pool cue.

The object was simultaneously heavy as an anvil and yet light as the wind.

Before his metamorphosis, he found himself in the middle of the library, occupying a glowing green sphere, set apart from the world. He looked upon the object in his hand. He looked to Archie. He looked straight ahead.

And in a mighty explosion Tony levitated, his body surging with electricity. Like the sphere, it was green. His head, arms, and back pulled back like a diver from a rock cliff, hovering above the earth before his descent into the sea.

Flash. In his mind's eye Tony saw JP Morgan kneeling over a hand-crafted box - identical to the one Tony had just opened.

Flash. JP Morgan opened the box.

Flash. A box lined with felt.

"Some people say Morgan was lucky," said Archie, whose voice changed, croaking as Tony had never heard it before. "Others say he was smart. And others … they say he had powers. Magic power. Second sight."

Flash. JP Morgan reached into the box. The felt lining. The ravine. The satchel.

"They say he had come to learn of an ancient power, buried for a thousand years," Archie croaked. "In the days of old, the Knights of the Round table were ruled by a great and mighty warrior. We know of him as Arthur. King Arthur. And his greatest advisor, his friend … his mentor … was the greatest sorcerer the world had ever known."

Flash. In his mind's eye Tony saw a wizard.

"And his name," Archie said, "was Merlin. With him he carried his robe, his hat, his walking staff … and his wand."

Flash. A magic wand.

Flash. The mighty wizard seemed ten feet tall. White beard. Immense power.

"Before the mighty wizard was defeated," Archie said, "he hid his wand, to keep it from the clutches of evil men, who would seek to harness its power. The stories say that JP Morgan discovered that wand in England, and planned to transport it with him back to New York, on the Titanic. Whether he ultimately used the wand to sink the Titanic or the wand warned him of its demise … no one but Morgan truly knows. But as history surely proved, after the Titanic found its watery grave, Morgan rose to power - if only for a short time - that few could have imagined."

Flash. The wizard stood.

Flash. The wizard fell.

Tony dropped to the ground. And then he rose. In his hands, he now realized, wasn't a pool cue, but a wand.

A magic wand.

Merlin's wand.

"It is said that only Merlin himself can harness the wand's power. That anyone but he who dares to manipulate its force will meet an early and horrible demise. JP Morgan's life force expired just a year after finding that wand. He died in Rome. In his bed. His fortunes a fraction of what he thought they would have been. But before his soul shrivelled to dust … before the wand rejected his body, mind, and soul … he realized what he had done. That the power was not meant for him, nor could it be. So he hid the wand, where it laid in wait for its rightful master."

Tony held the wand in his hand, surging with power.

"Merlin's body may have left this Earth," Archie said, green magic swirling within the library, "but his spirit remained, passed on, waiting for rebirth. Connecting mage … with magic."

In a blast of green lightning the man Anthony Grenachi had known himself to be - the man his consciousness looked upon in the mirror, existentially alone - was obliterated. The flesh and blood vessel for the ancient power had served its purpose.

In Tony's place - revealing his true nature - was a great and mighty sorcerer.

Merlin lived again.

"I've been awaiting your return, master Merlin. It has been so long. You are needed more than ever."

"Yes," the great wizard said, his robes flowing over him. "Archibald the Sly, my loyal squire. We have much to accomplish. You have looked over me well these long and troubled centuries. I was trapped within the realm. The Sorceress Zonata shot into my knee an arrow of yellow magic. Poisoned magic. Crippled my power. Hobbled me. Kept me numbed and in pain, lost within a labyrinth of demons and lies. The path to my healing - and waking - was a labor of trials and tribulations, and those who sought to bring darkness over the light. I feared I would never find my way. The warrior princess Illilan found me near death, hiding below the trees, perched within their roots. She killed Zonata's foot soldiers, and nursed me back to health. Her cunning and bravery are beyond reproach. I am in her debt."

"I never lost faith in you," said Archibald the Sly. "Your many hosts struggled with their path, driven to the brink of madness. They were unprepared … ignorant … of the power within them. Within you. They felt the calling, but those wounded warriors understood not their true purpose, protecting your magic soul. I strove to keep their focus, guiding their journeys through the mortal realm, through one life after the next, always near the source, but never, until now, holding it within their hands. You were finally ready."

"Yes, squire. I felt their conflict. But I could not assist. Once again your patience - and loyalty - have proved a wealth not even magic can supplicate. Your loneliness must have been profound."

"Mine is only to serve. Command me, great Mage. What is our quest?"

Merlin the great levitated, engulfed by the glow of green magic. "We must find our lord. We seek Arthur."

"But where, my master, where is the mighty king?"

"Bonded to our fates, as ours is bonded his to his, here among us, in this city of York. This New York. And like us - like me - the warrior within is unknown to him. We must find our hero … lest his mortal enemies find him first."

"Then we must go at once," said Archibald the Sly. "Lead me, and I will follow."

The limestone holding the House of Morgan together nearly cracked to its foundation, as if Tintagel Castle itself were about to emerge from underneath. "To off we will," Merlin said, his voice reclaiming its ancient heft.

"Where do we begin?"

"As I am most powerful with my wand - a conduit and source for magic most pure, green magic - our king is most mighty with his sword. I sense the power of the blade. It has reforged. Once again, it calls out, beckoning to its master. This city is built upon ancient bedrock. We will find that stone. With the stone … we will find the sword."

Merlin surged with power. The mage reborn. Magic flowed from his wand, flowed through him.

"And with the sword," the great sorcerer said, "we will find our one true King."

Sir Gawain and the Errant Son

Austin Camacho

It is said that the road to Camelot is paved with gold, but often the road away from it is paved with blood. That was the case this day when I came upon a young, tow-headed man lying still with an arrow growing from the center of his chest.

I quickly leapt from my steed but as I knelt beside him I could see I was too late. He worked to push words past his death pain and so I bent my head to his lips to try to capture them.

"Lord Montagu" was all I heard before his life's breath slipped away. This was clearly not his own name. The man wore the silk garments a lord would give to his vassal. It seemed this man may be from this Lord Montagu's keep. And as I was on a mission from King Arthur to extend the offer of his peace and protection to all the fiefdoms in this area, Lord Montagu could well have been one of the men I needed to call upon. Sadly it seemed I would be bearing bad news.

I stood as a hay-laden wagon approached. A young woman, perhaps in her late teens, pulled the reins as I stepped in front of her horse. She was comely with flaxen hair and a wary expression on her face.

"Good sir," she began, "If you are a brigand I must tell you that I have nothing worth your effort to steal, nor will I say anything about the man you have slain. Please allow me to go my way."

"Be calm," I said, raising a gauntlet-covered palm. "I mean you no ill. I am Sir Gawain, a knight of King Arthur's Round Table. I have only just come upon this man who spoke the name Lord Montagu just before passing on. Do you know of such a lord?"

The serf girl lowered her gaze. "Indeed I do, sir. In fact there are two men who answer thus. Lord Montagu the senior holds the keep three or four leagues distant. His son, the Lord Edward Montagu, holds the lands we stand upon now. His castle stands just over this next ridge."

"Then I shall start there," I said. I hefted the dead man from the road and placed him on the hay at the back of the wagon. The maiden recoiled at his sight, as if this were the first dead man she had seen. I mounted up, and rode at her side toward the castle. I learned then that her name was Margery and that she was happy to share what she knew of this land.

"So did the senior Lord Montagu give these lands to his son?" I asked. "A generous lord, then."

The girl blanched. "Sir, really not my place to say, but it was more like a banishment. I know not the details, but the senior lord was ill pleased with his son and exiled him to this bleak corner of his realm, where the rocky land yields little. The two have feuded of late."

Indeed, Edward Montagu's castle was modest and ill maintained to my eye. As we neared the drawbridge lowered and I was ushered to the lord's reception chamber. Two serfs loaded the dead man onto a small wheeled cart and accompanied me. I bid Margery follow to bear witness to events.

Edward sat on a velvet throne with a man cloaked in chain mail on either side. As we entered Edward leapt to his feet and his guards laid hands on their sword handles. The lord was short but portly, his jowls straining to the side as his face drew into a pained grimace.

"What evil is this?" he shouted. "Loyal Merek dead! This is my fourth loss. And you," He pointed a finger at me, "are you the villain sent by my father to slay my men?"

"Why, I have harmed no man," I protested.

"Well, you look able." Edward said. Then he pointed to one of his guards. "Carac!"

Hearing his name, the man drew his sword and moved toward me. I drew as well, and assumed a ready stance. His attack was fierce but clumsy. I parried his blade and easily disarmed him. I rested the tip of my sword against his throat. He backed against a wall and was still.

"Would you see your man slain for naught?"

Edward settled back into his throne. "I would bid you spare him. I see your skill is impressive. Why kill a commoner, even a man at arms, for anger when you can gain 100 gold coins for killing a lord. My father."

"You would see the senior Lord Montagu dead?" I asked, sheathing my blade.

Edward stepped toward me. "He and his men have slain now five of my finest followers. I would see him in his grave, and have the coin to back up that request."

I considered his words in silence for a moment. I am no stranger to family conflicts, as my mother, Arthur's sister, still stood as the greatest threat to him. Yet in order to establish Arthur's peace in this realm I felt the need to confirm the truth. I decided to keep my name and my mission to myself.

"Your offer is interesting. How shall I find Lord Montagu?"

In response Edward flipped a coin toward the flaxen haired lass. "Guide this stalwart to my father's castle. He will surely welcome a travelling knight into his presence without suspicion. "

Seeing Edward did not prepare me for the senior Lord Montagu. The true lord was tall, trim, and well-muscled, as much a warrior as his son was not. It was easy to see why Edward may have been a disappointment. And he greeted us with only one armed guard present. However his wizened vizier stood by, cloaked in a wizard's gown such as Merlin often wore.

"And what brings you to my castle, good Sir Knight?" Montagu's voice boomed out, courteous yet demanding. I offered a respectful bow as is due a lord in his home.

"My Lord, I am late of Edward Montagu's castle and I must say yours is certainly five times as grand. Sadly I must admit to bringing grim tidings. Your son, it seems, wishes you grave ill, and even asked me to come here and dispatch you."

"Arrogant pup," Montagu bellowed, pulling his broadsword from its scabbard. "I could kill you now…"

I saw Montagu blink as the speed with which I unlimbered my own weapon and aimed its tip at his chest. Behind me Margery gasped.

"I *could* kill you," Montagu said in a calmer tone, lowering his weapon, "but it appears that would be a total waste of talent. Now, was it truly your intent to slay me, here in my own castle?"

At that moment a different plan came to my mind, as I needed to know if the thoughts of the father mirrored those of the son. Sheathing my blade I said, "In truth I had determined to take the better offer."

Montagu roared with laughter. "Indeed a wise mercenary. Well you have chosen the wise choice. I will give you 500 gold coins to send the young pup to Hell. In fact, I know him to have a small band of fighters and would offer a thousand coins to see them all dispatched."

I shook my head. "Sir, I have no desire to go to war with an entire keep. Besides, I would have to gather other fighters for such a mission."

At that the vizier stepped forward. "But surely Edward himself would be no challenge to one as skilled as you," he said in an accent I did not recognize. If Edward believes you work for him it should be no challenge to get close enough to slip the knife in."

"The boy is no warrior," Montagu added.

"Surely true," I said, "but even if I did such a deed I would still have to escape his castle."

The vizier turned to his Lord. "Sir, I may have the solution to that issue, if I may be permitted a moment with our stalwart."

Montagu waved us off dismissively and the vizier took my arm and led me off into a dark hallway. I believe this man was more comfortable in the dark.

"You are a stranger here," the vizier began in hushed tones, "so you need to know what is really going on between my lord and his son. A neighboring fiefdom has a very effective tax collector, but to deliver the gathered wealth to their petty king they must ride through the Montagu forest. For safe passage that king, Bayonne by name, pays Lord Montagu a percentage of the tax money. This has been a profitable arrangement for all concerned, at least until recently."

"What has all this to do with Edward?" I asked.

"Lord Montagu's son, jealous of this wealth, has sneaked a small band of warriors onto Lord Montagu's land and attacked these shipments. Twice he has raided and stolen the tax wagons, leaving my lord with the responsibility of replacing those funds."

I raised a hand to stop him. "Have there been casualties?'

"Indeed. Two of my Lord's best fighters have been slain in cowardly sneak attacks, and three of King Bayonne's drivers were killed. But our men fought back hard, taking at least four of Edward's men into the afterworld with them."

I wondered if this was the four men Edward alluded to, killed by his father. Arthur would be horrified to know of this kind of infighting in an area under Camelot's peace. But before I called in an army to suppress such wasteful killing I hoped to resolve the situation myself. And it seemed the vizier may have read my thoughts.

"There is a quick and easy way for you to bring this to an end."

"And what might that be?" I asked.

The vizier stepped closer, lowering his voice still more. "A narrow river flows through Lord Montagu's forest. The heavily laden tax chest cannot ford this river safely so must cross at the narrow bridge not far from here. This is where Edward has struck on his previous raids."

"Edward goes on these raids himself?" I appeared to study the tapestry hung along the hall when in fact I was looking closely into the vizier's eyes.

"Oh yes. Edward is quite brave when accompanied by armed

soldiers. I can direct you to a good vantage point. When his men go forward to attack the cart he will be alone and an easy mark for one such as you."

Returning to the King's chamber I found Margery where I left her, standing quietly as befit her station. When I explained my mission to her she surprised me.

"Sir, I know it is not my place to ask, but I would very much like to accompany you on your journey."

She may have been in doubt about her safety in Lord Montagu's castle, and I could hardly blame her. As she had helped me, and accompanied me thus far her safety was now my responsibility.

"Can you ride? I cannot wait for a wagon."

"Sir," she said, a mischievous glint in her eye, "I am no palace-born lady. I sit a horse as well as any man, and believe your stallion would have no trouble if I were to straddle him behind you."

Once in the saddle I pulled her up behind me, and will admit that the ride was made more pleasant by her arms wrapped across my chest.

The wizened vizier's directions were clear and plain, but I only followed them for a short distance. His story had not run quite true to me, and I was far more interested in the vizier's plans than the site of a planned robbery. I doubled back, but kept a good distance from my quarry. The vizier climbed into a stately carriage which was surely comfortable and also easy for me to follow without being seen, thanks to the ruts its wheels left on the trail.

Within an hour's ride we came upon a modest cottage. The vizier's carriage drew up quite near another equally majestic carriage. Both drivers sat in place.

"With both carriages on the same side of the cottage I should be able to work around to the other side to see what the vizier is up to," I told Margery as I dismounted. "Stay here and be quiet. I will return shortly."

Tall grass surrounding the cottage made it easy for me to move with stealth despite my chain mail coverlet. Moving closer I noted a window at the back of the thatch roofed structure, out of view of the carriage sitting near the front door. I crouched and crept up to within two horses' lengths of the opening. I watched the vizier pace back and forth, waving a finger as he spoke. I dared not get close enough to hear his words, but I didn't need to know the conversation. Once I saw Edward Montagu stride past, responding to the vizier, much became clear.

While they continued to talk I returned to Margery, still undetected. To her credit she asked no questions, but stood by for direction.

"Lass, I need you to mount up and return to Lord Montagu's castle."

"But, Sir, how will you get back?"

"Worry not about me," I told her. "I shall be along shortly. Wait for me at the main gate."

With the slightest courtesy she climbed aboard my steed and rode off toward the castle. Once she was out of sight I moved back toward the house. The two drivers were nodding, making it easy for me to slip into one of the carriages undetected. Once inside I crouched low, drew my dirk and waited for the passenger with whom I was eager to renew acquaintances.

My wait was not long. I heard Edward's heavy tread on the grass well before he opened the carriage door. With a loud huff he heaved himself inside and had plopped onto the seat before he even noticed me. I quieted him with a finger to my lips and the edge of my dirk against his throat. Curiosity must have overwhelmed his common sense because he still spoke, albeit in a low whisper.

"I expected to see you again when you had finished your mission, but what is this?"

"This," I said, "is a change in plans. Now direct your man to head for home, as the vizier surely will. When we are well beyond the vizier's sight or hearing, we will turn around."

Fear shone from Edward's cowardly eyes. "Where are you taking me?"

"You and I need to have a meeting with your father."

Lord Montagu sat bolt upright when I led Edward into his chamber with my small blade still pressed against his throat. The vizier had arrived ahead of me, and still only one guard stood by Montagu. I slammed Edward down into a chair, watching the other faces. The guard was impassive, Lord Montagu broke into a broad grin, and even the vizier allowed himself a small smile.

"So you chose to bring him here for his end," Montagu said.

"Lord, you and I have business to conclude. But I think your man need not be privy to it." I nodded toward the guard, who turned to his Lord for guidance. Montagu scratched at his chin for a second.

"Indeed, no one else need witness what comes next." Montagu waved a hand, and the guard stalked out of the room. Once he was gone Montagu rose and strode across the room toward a chest I assumed held his ready coins.

"Shall I presume you want to see your pay before you finish your work?" he asked.

"That is one logical ending," I said, "if I was who and what you presume. Or I could just as easily get paid and then kill you both." Montagu spun toward me, and Edward raised his chin a bit from my dirk's blade. I had their attention now. "Or," I continued, "I might be wiser to take money from you both and make a deal for your vizier, who has made fools of the two of you."

At this the vizier leaped to his feet. "How dare you? Who are you to make such an accusation?"

It was time for the truth. "You would know now if you were not so vile that you assume the worst in everyone you meet. Know that I am no low mercenary or free-lance. I am Sir Gawain, a knight of King Arthur's Round Table. Arthur has dispatched me and others to secure the peace in all his wide realm and I come here to find a blood feud within a family, and a lord taking counsel from a pernicious snake sowing seeds of hatred for his own gain."

"Listen not to this liar," the vizier said, as I watched his right hand slip into the billowing left sleeve of his wizard's gown. Montagu's eyes were on me, as he raised a hand toward his vizier.

"Quiet. I have heard of this Arthur. He and his are known far and wide for their honor. But tell me, Gawain, why do you speak thus about my vizier?"

"Lord Montagu, I saw him conspiring with Edward in secret. Have you never wondered how your son knew the day and path of the tax shipment moving across your land? It can only be your vizier who told him, in return for a share of the stolen wealth. And unknown to Edward I'm sure, the vizier told me where to meet Edward, at a certain bridge, where the next robbery would take place. He said I could kill Edward there."

"What?" At this Edward bounded to his feet. "Today he told me the money wagon would be diverted to the bridge, not the usual path. Were you arranging for my death?" Edward pointed at the vizier.

"I would also guess that it was the vizier who told you that Edward killed the two wagon drivers, to sow more dissent between you two."

"Lies!" This time Edward's eyes went to his father. "It is true that I sent my men to kill yours to steal the money as revenge for your treatment of me. But it was your vizier himself whose arrows cut down the wagon drivers. I did not think them worthy of death but he did."

"Indeed," I said. "He would not want any witnesses to his presence at the crime."

The vizier's face glowed with hatred. "You'll not bring me down," he shouted. His right hand drew clear of his sleeve and with it came a dagger which he flung toward me. But I anticipated his attack and dodged to the side. I drew my sword as the dagger point drove into the back of the chair Edward had used. The vizier rushed to Lord Montagu and drew his sword. He slashed at me but I turned the blade aside with my own. Our swords clanged together once, twice, a third time. His next parry was too slow and I drove my blade deep into his left side. When I withdrew it the vizier dropped to his knees, then fell forward, dead before his face hit the ground.

I spun quickly, expecting threats from two other possible sources. But I saw that Edward, no warrior himself, had fled the room. That left only Lord Montagu who, to my surprise, lowered his bulk to one knee before me.

"Sir Knight, you have shamed me by showing me my own ignorance and gullibility. I can offer little in my own defense, but I *can* and *do* swear fealty to Arthur, and commit to maintaining his peace throughout my realm, to include the end of this feud between myself and my son Edward."

"Lord Montagu, that is all I or my liege would ever ask," I said, wiping the blood from my sword onto the vizier's gown then sheathing my weapon. "If I can secure the same commitment from Edward I will consider this mission a success."

Lord Montagu bid me stay for a feast that even, but I longed to return to Arthur with a good report. I barely stepped beyond the castle gate when Margery trotted up to me on my own steed.

"Are you ready to return to your own keep, Sir Knight?" she asked, dismounting.

"Indeed, fair maiden, my work here is done. If you recover your wagon I will escort you home, and then be on my way."

We rode easily side by side again. I began to tell tales of life in Camelot, and Margery expressed her desire to one day see that shining structure. She was comely, and smart, and would surely be a good companion. I will admit I was on the verge of inviting her to travel on with me when I spotted the body, barely a quarter mile from Lord Montagu's castle, just off the side of the road.

I leaped from my horse and ran to the dead man but I was far too late. Edward Montagu would not be pledging his fealty to anyone. The punctures to his neck, small by any standard, were still more than enough to bring a quick death. A blade needn't be large to be deadly, it just needs to be pushed into the right place.

My stride was slow and heavy as I returned to the road. I walked to the wagon and grasped the reins with one hand. To her credit, Margery did not turn her gaze away.

"You were swift to get here and back to the castle before I departed," I said. "And your blood must be cold to show no agitation when you met me at the gate. Now, must I ask you for your knife to compare with the wounds?"

"No, Lord," she said with no hint of shame. "I'll not deny this deed. I was the death of Edward, the younger Lord Montagu."

"Surely you know I must return you to Lord Montagu senior for judgement. But first, tell me the reason. Can it be that when you saw the dead man who began this adventure you did not turn away because of unfamiliarity with death, but instead because of familiarity with the man?"

"Sir, I believe you to be a wizard to divine such," Margery said. "Dear Merek was my betrothed. We were to be married next full moon. I was crushed to see him lying dead in your arms, although I feared telling you, not knowing what side of the conflict you would land on. And when I learned that it was Lord Edward Montagu who sent him to his death - not as a warrior but as a thief - I swore vengeance if ever it presented itself. Thus, I am guilty and will accept whatever consequences you deem necessary."

My heart lifted when finally the golden spires of Camelot came into view, aglow in the twilight. I had a fine adventure to recount to my brothers of the round table. Arthur's peace was spreading throughout the land and in one corner of the land there was one less petty lord to deal with. I thought at that moment that Margery, settling into her cottage for the night, must be thinking similar thoughts. After sending her home without a word to Edward's father I reflected that justice was a slippery thing, sometimes dark, but always final. Should it not also be fair?

Knight Moves

Quintin Peterson

Last Night
2105 Hours

SIN Task Force HQ
601 Indiana Avenue, NW
Washington, DC

The HQ of the special criminal investigations unit known as SIN, the location of which was known only to Arthur King and his team, was located on the top floor of a commercial and residential use high-rise in the 600 block of Indiana Avenue, N.W., overlooking the D.C. Superior Court, the Henry J. Daley Municipal Building, One Judiciary Square, the Navy Memorial, Smithsonian Institution buildings, the National Archives, and beyond. With all eyes on him, Metropolitan Police Department Commander Arthur King stood at one of the picture windows, looking out over the city. In the distance, a storm was brewing.

As the work of the Special Investigations Network task force involved clandestine operations, King had arranged for his HQ, code named: Camelot, to be offsite from all involved law enforcement agencies, specifically, the U.S. Marshals Service, U.S. Park Police, U.S. Capitol Police, Secret Service Uniformed Division, FBI, DEA, ATF, ICE, and the District of Columbia Metropolitan Police Department. Proceeds from civil asset forfeitures seized from the villains the unit took down paid for the fancy digs and funded all operations.

With the resources of the involved law enforcement agencies at its disposal, along with the invaluable assistance of a confidential informant codenamed Merlin, the special unit had been highly successful. Over the past eighteen months, the task force had taken down the drug suppliers for the Carver Court Crew, and the Simple City Crew. The Sizov Syndicate had cornered the market on the new synthetic narcotic known as Coffin, which like crack or crank could be smoked or snorted, or injected like heroin.

Finally, King turned and walked away from the window and over to the round table he'd special ordered. He sat down and joined the dozen peace officers seated around the table and assessed the team he'd assembled for his special investigations task force, who by coincidence or providence, were, like him, members of the law enforcement biker club, the Blue Knights:

Three fellow MPDC officers, Captain Ryan Norman, Lt. Patrick Liu, and Sgt. Florian Bellevue; two from the U.S. Marshals Service, Marshal Cary Taylor and Marshal Nathan Garland; two from U.S. Capitol Police, Lt. Dana Pannell and Sgt. Mark Lane; one from the Secret Service, Agent Cameron Lyon; one from the FBI, Agent Karl Ritter; one from the DEA, Agent James Percival; one from ATF, Agent Hank Morgan; and one from ICE, Agent Dakota Kaye.

Commander King said, "This unit's mission has been successful thus far. We've brought several villains to justice and made the city safer. But tonight, we face our greatest challenge. In order to collar an extremely dangerous individual who is key to our investigation into the Sizov Syndicate, we must risk it all. If we fail, it could mean the end of the Special Investigations Network.

"Through our ongoing surveillance of scumbags of interest, a man going by the name of David Franklin has been identified as a major player in the Sizov Syndicate. I won't go into it now, but I happen to know that Franklin is not this key player's real name. He is someone I know from back in the day."

"Really," said Agent Ritter. "Who is he?"

King said, "I don't care to share that information at the moment, Keiser."

"Wish you wouldn't call me that, sir."

The team laughed.

King smiled and said, "Well, that's the nickname I gave you and it's yours for as long as I live, Keiser. Deal with it."

King continued, "Anyway, I contacted 'Franklin' to solicit his cooperation in our investigation in exchange for a deal. He has agreed to meet with me tonight in a public place, because he knows that I wouldn't endanger the lives of innocent bystanders to bring him in should the meet be a ruse to arrest him, which it is. And contrary to what 'Franklin' thinks he knows about me, I *am* willing to risk the safety of innocent bystanders to lock his ass up.

"The meet is set to take place at midnight in the Ragin' Cajun Supper

Club, up on Mount Olivet Road. Captain Norman, I want you, Keiser, and Lane inside the joint at least an hour before the meet. Eyeball the patrons, look for people who could possibly be there as Franklin's back-up. They'll be there for our meeting for sure. We'll be using Tac Channel 2, so make sure you set your radios to that frequency.

"Hang back while I talk with Franklin. We'll take him outside the club. The last thing we want is a shootout in there or we can kiss this unit goodbye. But if a shootout *does* jump off, shoot straight and only hit the bad guys. Please.

"I want the rest of you to be set up outside the club around 2300, front and back of the joint, teamed up however you like, in whatever vehicles you like. When 'Franklin' exits the club, we'll make our move.

"Any questions?"

The team members shook their heads.

Arthur King stood and said, "Let's roll."

2342 Hours

Ragin' Cajun Supper Club
Mount Olivet Road, NE
Washington, DC

Commander King parked his police department-issued black Toyota Avalon on Mount Olivet Road in front of the Ragin' Cajun Supper Club, an eternally dark and smoky Ptomaine Domain specializing in so-so pseudo Cajun cuisine and outstanding, authentic pole dancing.

He climbed out of the police cruiser, locked it down, and in the pouring rain proceeded briskly to the strip joint and through its front door.

A pole dancer was on stage gyrating to *Slave to the Rhythm* by Grace Jones when King stepped inside. The place was dark and malodorous, the stagnant air thick with cigarette smoke and the perpetual funk of greasy-spoon cooking and sweaty pole dancers dowsed in cheap perfume. King weaved through the seated crowd and sat in the shadows at an empty table in back. A half-naked waitress with bad acne caked over with makeup took his order, a Jack and Coke, and returned with his drink just as the man King had come to meet stepped to the table.

"Get me one of those, baby," the man told the waitress.

The waitress nodded and stepped away. The man sat down opposite

King, the light of the candle in the little red jar set in the center of the rickety wooden table flickering on their shadowy faces. They leaned in close so they could hear each other above the music.

"Art," he said with a nod.

King returned the nod and replied, "Jack Dulac. You look great for a dead man, Duke."

Dulac said, "Now, let me get this straight: We worked undercover together two years to interrupt the street-level distribution of narcotics in the city. You discovered that the operation was a scam Senator Gaul put together to identify and eliminate the competition for his East Coast drug distribution operation. So, now you want to do what you *thought* you were doing for two years; you want to *really* do the job. You used the blackmail material I gave you when I stood down…"

"Faked your death," King corrected him.

Dulac nodded. "You used the blackmail material I gave you so that you could leverage whatever you wanted from the powers-that-be, just to start your own multi-law-enforcement-agency task force. Now you're a man on a mission; a crusader. Got your own Untouchables. And I particularly like your Knights of the Round Table theme. Very theatrical." Dulac snorted a laugh. "All this drama because you want to make a difference or is it simply because we hurt your feelings?"

"You betrayed me," King retorted. "You shot me twice in the chest and then ran off with my girl. *That* hurt my feelings, yes."

They stopped talking when the half-naked waitress returned with Duke's glass of Jack and Coke and set it on the rickety table. To her delight, Duke handed her a twenty dollar bill and told her to keep the change. After she walked away, he leaned back in.

"You're better off without Gwendolyn," Dulac snapped. "Believe that."

"Where is she?" King asked.

Dulac shrugged and said, "Hell if I know. She took her cut and split."

King said, "Was it worth it?"

Dulac asked, "Was what worth it?"

King said, "Betraying me?"

"C'mon," Dulac snorted. "It wasn't personal. It was business. Hell, I like you, Art. That's why you're still alive. I shot you in the vest. I could have shot you in the head just as easily. And I gave you your cut, plus that blackmail material on government officials. I'm your friend, dummy."

"Stealing my girl wasn't very friendly, Duke."

"Gwen wasn't your girl, Art, you just made the mistake of falling in love with her. She was just a gold-digger, and that's putting it mildly. She jumped at the chance to betray you just so she could get paid. She wanted me to kill you to get you out of the way after we ripped off the Tudor Cartel. Cold bitch. Forget her. I have."

"I haven't," said King. "I *can't*. I can't forget about you either, Duke."

Dulac said, "Did you really want to talk a deal or is this a trap?"

"You tell me, Duke. Would I endanger innocent bystanders to clip you?"

Dulac said, "Not in the old days, Art. Never." He shrugged and added, "But nowadays I'm not sure. So, what are you offering me?"

"Immunity," King said. "Give us what we need to take down Sizov and you walk."

"How far could I walk when the rest of that crazy Russian crew found out what I did, Art? You think I'm going to let you paint a bullseye on me? What for? Just so you can be the hero? No thanks."

"Then you're going down, Duke."

Dulac smirked and then said, "Art, I don't have a problem with you and your crew. Honestly. I'm all for live and let live, you know? Let me be and I'll let you be. But, if you want a fight, I'll fight you like the third monkey on the ramp to Noah's Ark."

"So be it," said King. "It's already raining."

Just then Special Agent Karl "Keiser" Ritter, who had been sitting at a table nearby, stood, put his S&W 9mm service handgun in Dulac's right ear, and proclaimed, "You are under arrest, Duke!"

Dulac snorted, "Be serious, Keiser."

Just as King had figured, Dulac had brought backup. Special Agent Ritter caught the first round. The 9mm slug caught him in the back and twirled him like a ballerina. More gunfire exploded throughout the club before his body hit the floor.

In the exchange of gunfire, a couple of patrons and a pole dancer caught stray rounds. No fatal wounds, thank God. Screaming people fled the club as good guys and bad guys took cover and fired, over and over. The good guys won by a score of 3 to 1.

In the pandemonium, Dulac escaped.

Arthur King knelt and checked the kid for a pulse. There was none. He slowly shook his head and then stood.

Looking down at the body of Special Agent Karl "Keiser" Ritter, he remembered the first raid he'd taken him on:

As they had been gearing up, King had noticed Ritter putting bullet-proof vest shock plates into the pouch in front of the wearer's heart. Ritter had installed the Teflon plate first and then the slightly curved metal plate on top of the Teflon plate, facing outward. King schooled him, "That's wrong, Keiser. And I thought the master race knew *everything*." He took the body armor from Ritter and as he rearranged the shock plates, explained, "The metal one goes under the Teflon one. If the metal one is on the outside, a bullet can ricochet off it, up into your chin, or down into your junk. The Teflon plate on the outside will catch the bullet and the metal one behind it will prevent penetration. There."

A lot of good that advice had done Agent Ritter; he'd been shot in the back and the slug apparently hit him in the heart, on the opposite side of the extra protection of the double-shock plates. Damn. Then again, if he'd stuck to the plan, he'd still be alive.

King drew his hand-held radio from his belt and switched the frequency from the tactical channel his unit had been operating on for this bust to the Citywide channel. He advised the dispatcher, "This is Camelot 1. 10-33! Have multiple gunshot victims inside the Ragin' Cajun Supper Club on Mount Olivet Road. Send back up and emergency medical services ASAP. Officer down!"

***

This Morning
0905 Hours

Federal Bureau of Investigation
Washington, DC Field Office
Fourth Street, NW

FBI Special Agent Kevin Balin watched Commander Arthur King on the CCTV monitor in the room adjacent to the interrogation room where the commander sat in a gray lacquered metal chair at a white lacquered metal desk, both of which were bolted to the floor of the white room, which was bathed in bright, fluorescent light.

"What's this guy's story?" Agent Balin asked.

"He's the best," answered Chief Turman.

Agent Balin turned to him and said, "Then why is Agent Ritter dead?"

Chief Turman shrugged and said, "This is a dangerous job."

"That is true," said Agent Balin. "But I think Commander King is personally responsible for Agent Ritter's death, and not just because he blew the operation last night. I'm going to see that he burns for it."

Chief Turman smirked and said, "Good luck with that."

Agent Balin said, "King's unit has seized a lot of money and property. The fancy digs the unit operates out of on Indiana Avenue, N.W., costs a pretty penny. Yeah, King and his team are living high on the hog."

Chief Turman asked, "You've been to the unit's HQ?"

"Indeed I have," said Balin.

Chief Turman said, "I see." He paused for a moment and then continued, "What I want to know is why you're coming after Commander King? The people of this city owe him their gratitude…"

"I think he's dirty," Balin snapped. He inhaled deeply and then calmly said, "You are welcome to watch while I interrogate Commander King."

"I'll leave when King leaves."

Agent Balin nodded and opened the door. "Start recording," he told the tech seated at the controls of the AV equipment. He then exited the room.

Agent Balin entered the interrogation room and closed the door behind him. He strode to the table where King sat, took the seat opposite the commander, and placed his file on the table.

"Commander King, I am Special Agent Balin. I have been assigned to investigate the homicide of Special Agent Ritter.

"Our conversation is being recorded, commander. Now, for the record, you were in charge of the operation last night that resulted in the death of Agent Ritter?"

"That is correct," said Commander King.

Agent Balin nodded and said, "Before we get into the incident at that strip club last night, let's discuss this special investigations unit of yours, for the record." He looked inside of the folder he was holding and said, "Special Investigations Network. SIN for short." He looked up from the folder and complimented King, "Catchy."

King did not reply.

Balin looked at the file again and continued, "Your unit is comprised of thirteen people from multiple law enforcement agencies, with DC police officers sworn in as special deputy U.S. Marshals, essentially making them federal officers." Balin turned his gaze back to King and said, "So you and your folks can go after criminals anywhere in these United States."

"Villains," King corrected Agent Balin.

"Beg pardon?" said Balin.

"We can go after *villains* anywhere in the U.S.," said Commander King. "And beyond, if necessary."

Agent Balin smirked and said, "Villains, criminals. You say tomato and I say tomato. What's the difference?"

Commander King said, "SIN wasn't created to snare ordinary criminals, it was created to take down *extraordinary* criminals, masterminds and kingpins, the fat cats who profit from turning neighborhoods into hellholes by flooding them with narcotics and guns. *Any* actively evil individuals who've ruthlessly acquired wealth and power at the expense of others on a large scale, we're taking them off the board. *Those* are the scumbags we target. You know the kind, I'm sure.

"Anyway, there's a big difference between a common criminal and a villain is what I'm saying."

Agent Balin nodded and said, "Okay. I hear you." He sighed and continued, "Tell me; what is the source of your unit's funding, commander?"

King said, "My people's salaries are paid by their agencies, but asset forfeiture is the life's blood of the unit."

"So," said Agent Balin, "whatever assets you seize go directly into the unit's operating budget. One could argue that that is a conflict of interest."

"How so?" asked King.

"C'mon, Commander King. Don't be obtuse. Every criminal the Special Investigations Network takes down is a payday for the unit. That money pays for the unit's fancy digs in a high-rent area. SIN's headquarters is located on the top floor of that high-rise located on the 600 block of Indiana Avenue, N.W., for Christ's sake. That's a high rent area."

King remained silent.

Finally Balin continued, "That business with the round table you conduct your meetings at, commander, whose idea was that? Yours?"

"Yes," said King.

"So, it was also your idea to dub SIN HQ 'Camelot,' wasn't it? And the call signs for your team, Camelot 1 through Camelot 13, all yours, am I right?"

Commander King said, "By coincidence, we're all members of the Blue Knights. It seemed fitting that we codename our HQ 'Camelot.'"

Agent Balin pressed, "The codename for your HQ, the call signs, the unit insignia on your black baseball caps and on the backs of your black windbreakers raid gear, your ideas too? All of it?"

Commander King nodded and then said, "How did you know?"

Agent Balin chortled and said, "You're just easy to read, I guess. By the way, commander, just out of curiosity, what was Agent Ritter's call sign?"

Commander King said, "Camelot 13."

Agent Balin nodded and then said, "It would seem that 13 is a bad luck number after all. Tell me what happened last night at the…" he referred his file…"the Ragin' Cajun Supper Club."

"We developed information that led us to the identity of a key figure in the Sizov Syndicate, a man going by the name of David Franklin. During the course of our investigation, I learned Franklin's true identity was that of a man who faked his own death a couple of years ago: my old partner, Jack Dulac.

"Jack and I worked a deep cover assignment for two years with the Janus Project, a multi-law-enforcement-agency task force designed to disrupt street-level distribution of narcotics, supposedly using the combined resources of the special investigations network. It was the brainchild of Senator Robert Gaul from the great state of Texas. But you know that, Agent Balin."

Agent Balin opened his mouth to speak, but King cut him off.

"Anyway, Jack shot me twice in the chest, faked his own death, and left town with my girl and a shitload of drug money. Well, he reinvented himself and resurfaced as David Franklin. But you know that, too."

Balin opened his mouth to speak, but King cut him off again.

"As I was saying, I got word to him that I knew his true identity and set up a meet…"

Agent Balin interrupted, "Inside a busy business establishment, where the situation could not be controlled?"

"Jack picked the spot. He knew I wouldn't risk the lives of innocent bystanders to try to take him in. That is why I had to meet him there. He thought he had the upper hand on me, which gave me the upper hand on him…"

"Or so you thought."

"I had the place staked out, my people both inside the club and out.

The plan was to take him outside the club. Agent Ritter knew the plan, but he jumped the gun. He pulled a gun on Dulac and Jack's men opened fire. Ritter got it first."

Agent Balin said, "So you're saying Agent Ritter was responsible for his own death?"

Commander King said, "No. I am simply stating that he knew the plan, but deviated from it."

Agent Balin said, "Yeah, well I think you're responsible for Agent Ritter's death, not because you're incompetent, but because you're still partners with Duke Dulac. I think you set up the SIN Unit so you and your buddy could continue the criminal enterprise you started back when you were working the Janus Project. Ritter was on to you, so you orchestrated the meet to have him taken out in that shootout in the strip joint."

"How did you come to that conclusion?" King asked.

Agent Balin smirked and said, "Ritter told me."

King smirked and said, "Which do you play, Poker or Chess?"

Agent Balin said, "Chess."

"Yeah," said King. "I figured you were a Chess man. You can't bluff worth shit."

"Is that right?" said Agent Balin. "Thing is, I'm not bluffing. Right now I have a team executing search warrants at your HQ and your residence. I am confident they will find drugs and drug money at your home, as well as intel on your criminal enterprise at your HQ."

"The stuff you tried to plant you mean?" said King.

"What?" said Agent Balin. "I did no such thing..."

King interrupted, "I play Poker *and* chess, but I prefer chess. I don't like relying on luck, I prefer strategy.

"When I learned that the Janus Project was bogus, I knew Senator Gaul had to have had partners inside one or more of the involved federal law enforcement agencies in order to pull off the scam: taking out his drug trafficking competitors under the guise of the war on drugs. I knew that when I started my on special investigations task force, the person or persons unknown would make sure to have one of their own put on the task force when I had Chief Turman contact the involved agencies and request applicants for the SIN Unit. And so I put all of the task force members under surveillance from day one.

"Ritter was your man...and Dulac, too. That's how Dulac knew about the round table in 'Camelot.' That's how you knew Dulac's nickname is Duke; that's how Dulac knew Ritter's nickname was Keiser. Dulac called

Ritter that last night when he pulled his gun on him; just like you slipped up here today and called Dulac 'Duke' when there's no way you could have known his nickname unless you knew him. And I suspect you told Agent Ritter to take out Dulac in a line-of-duty shooting inside the Ragin' Cajun, knowing that a shootout would ensue when he drew his gun."

"That's outrageous," Balin protested.

King continued, "You didn't want Jack Dulac taken in; you're partners. Ritter *thought* he was your partner, but he was expendable. Putting a black mark on SIN for a senseless shootout in a public place and getting the unit shut down was well worth it to you and your boss, Senator Robert Gaul. He couldn't stand the heat from my unit targeting his drug operations in D.C.

"So, I'm afraid no one is serving search warrants on my business, my home, or my offices. Search warrants are being served on *your* home and *your* office, with the cooperation of the Office of the Attorney General and the Department of Justice. And an arrest warrant will be served shortly.

"The man you paid to kill Ritter in the shootout, just so you could set me up for a charge of conspiracy to commit murder, on top of multiple RICO charges, has already rolled over on you, just like the men you paid to plant drugs and money in my business offices and my home this morning. Thanks to our ongoing surveillance operations, they were caught in the act and also have all rolled over on you. And Dulac turned himself in this morning. He's cut a deal and has rolled over on you and your partners in crime, too. Just like you will. Hell, your own agency has been watching you since I identified Ritter as your inside man in the early days of SIN."

Two FBI agents entered the interrogation room, disarmed Balin, and took him into custody. When he was in handcuffs, one of the agents read him his rights.

Special Agent Balin smirked and said, "I guess you weren't bluffing about being a chess player, too. And a master at that."

King replied, "My favorite chess piece is the knight. It moves sideways and, if your opponent sleeps on it, he never sees it coming."

Balin scowled at King for a time and then turned and walked through the door, flanked by his two colleagues.

Chief Turman was waiting in the hallway when they walked Agent Balin out.

Turman motioned to the escorting agents, indicating he wanted just a moment with Balin, and then told him, "I have never been to Commander King's HQ. It is a secret location known only to members of the task force.

And I am prepared to testify in open court that you admitted to me here today that you have been there."

Arthur King interjected, "That won't be necessary." Kevin Balin's eyes locked with his and he continued, "Your man Ritter told you the location of Camelot, and then took you there after hours. We have you both on audio and video, not only there, but at several other meetings at various locations we documented during the course of our investigation.

"What bothers me is, I liked Keiser. I was going to cut him a deal. He might have been a great man if he hadn't lost his way and let you get your claws into him...and unwittingly set himself up to be your pawn sacrifice.

"Karl Ritter was a criminal, but he wasn't a villain, like you."

Tears welling in his eyes, the disgraced agent looked away and then down at the floor as his colleagues escorted him away, down the long hallway.

Patrick Thomas

They say time heals all wounds but I don't buy that, although the idea that it wounds all heels is a nice one. Not necessarily true however. I've been around upwards of a thousand years and there are some grudges I still carry. To this day I blame Lancelot as much as Mordred for the fall of Camelot, but there's someone I blame more than either of them. No, it's not Morgan LeFay. She ended up reforming and these days actually helps guard Arthur's resting place until he comes again at England's hour of greatest need. Personally, I was convinced it would happen during the blitzes of World War II but apparently, there is something much worse in store for England at some point in the future.

The knight whose actions insured the fall of Camelot disappeared centuries ago after his dastardly act. A number of us knights spent years trying to track him down with no luck. Sir Accolon betrayed the Round Table and I had hoped he died a horrible and painful death, but always knew he could still be around – I am. So are a handful of other knights. Sure it's only a small fraction of the hundred and fifty members of the Round Table at its height but after so many centuries I still think it's impressive that any of us are still alive to fight the good fight.

Forever is a mighty long time and immortals are subject to the frailties of any other person. We get lonely, we get sad. We reminisce about the good old days, although for most of us that can cover more than one era.

That's why it's lucky that there's a place like the Eternity Club for us to visit and meet with old friends and even make new ones. That wasn't the case tonight.

"I'll kill you!" I screamed.

And I meant it. I know it may seem uncharacteristic for me, especially as a Knight of the Round Table, to shout a death threat then tackle someone. The behavior was even worse coming from the former Jester of Camelot, but I had reason.

I ran across the room in my powder blue tuxedo and leapt at the man. Considering I don't reach five foot with boots on, I was impressed that I hit him around the chest and knocked the traitor into the mahogany walls and then onto the marble floor of the Eternity Club.

We rolled around a bit and I ended up on top, hitting him in the face with my fists. Not that the damage did any good in the long run, but at least it made me feel better. Or at least it did until Jack Wisp, the owner of the Eternity Club, dragged me off my intended victim.

"Dagonet, what in blazes are you doing?" Wisp said with an anger I'd never seen directed my way before.

Jack was scary, even in my circles. The man beat the Devil and now controls soulfire. One touch of those flames and you'll be reliving every good and bad thing you've ever done. Those the fire claims experience how their actions affected not just the people they hurt, but those around them that were hurt as well. It's driven many a strong man or woman to the other side of insanity. Among his more notable accomplishments, Wisp took out Hitler. Typically, soulfire burns the spirit, not the body, but it incinerated Hitler.

"This is a recruitment gala. Everyone is welcome and there is no fighting."

Wisp held two recruitment galas a year. They were big old school parties and usually a lot of fun. Black-tie was the minimum for the dress code, although you could wear clothes from any era as long as they were fancy.

"And normally I'm more than happy to follow those rules, but I've been looking for this bastard for over a thousand years and I'm not about to let him go now," I said.

The betraying whoreson smirked as he got to his feet. I tried to rush him again, but Wisp was so strong I couldn't break his grip without hurting him. I wasn't about to do that to a friend.

Lendor – at least what that's what the butler called himself these days – rushed over and took hold of one of my arms and then the other so Wisp could let go. The proprietor of the Eternity Club reached down and offered a hand up to the man I hated more than Mordred.

As Wisp was apologizing for my behavior, Lendor whispered in my ear, "Dagonet, what's wrong? I've known you more than a thousand years you almost never lose your temper."

Lendor's attention to be focused on me so much he hadn't looked at Wisp's guest.

"It's Sir Accolon!" I said.

The color drained from Lendor's face and he got a look of anger that I hadn't seen since we fought Mordred's armies and he had to throw

Excalibur into a lake.

Lendor let go of me and rushed Accolon, landing an uppercut on his chin that knocked Accolon back five feet and onto the floor.

"Bedivere Lendor, what in blazes?" Wisp looked like somebody had shot his puppy. When I first knew Sir Bedivere he was a Knight and the butler of the Round Table. He has loyally served as a butler for the Eternity Club since it opened in the 1700s, more than fifty years before the Revolutionary War. I severely doubt in all that time he's ever struck a guest who wasn't breaking the rules. I would say Wisp counted him among his closest friends and this act was viewed as a betrayal.

"I'm sorry, sir, but that man is Sir Accolon and he is responsible for the fall of Camelot," Bedivere Lender said. By this point, the rest of the gala, including the orchestra that had been playing a hip-hop waltz, had stopped. All eyes were upon us.

"I thought Mordred was responsible for Camelot's demise," Wisp said.

"Only because he was able to wound Arthur and kill him. If not for the actions of this man, Arthur would not have died," Bedivere said.

"Was he Mordred's chief general?" Wisp said.

"No, he stole Excalibur's scabbard and ran off," I said.

"What difference would that make?" Wisp said.

From out of nowhere, a bolt of lightning struck Accolon, making him convulse and twitch but otherwise leaving him unharmed.

"The sheath was made by my brother Merlin," said the on again-off again love of much of my long life, the white-haired Ganeda. Poor Gani was shaking in anger. "The scabbard was more impressive than Excalibur itself. It protected its wearer from all harm and disease, ensuring that Arthur would never die. But our King was overconfident and would only wear the sheath in battle. This scumbag stole it then disappeared from Camelot. Because Arthur did not have the sheath, he was weakened and eventually Mordred killed him. If Accolon had not stolen the sheath, Camelot would still exist today and this world would be a far better place."

"Be that as it may, he is over a thousand years old…"

"Only because he's wearing the sheath under his clothes," I said. "It shouldn't count if he stole his immortality."

"Many of those here stole their immortality. I acknowledge you have a significant grievance, but that does not change the fact that I do not allow violence in the Eternity Club."

"Very well, sir. Never let it be said that I shirked my duties," Bedivere said and left the room.

"This man will be granted safe passage away from here," Wisp said.

Two rather large men pushed their way through the crowd, their faces just as angry as the rest of ours.

"Like hell he will." That came from Sir Marrok and as he said it the werewolf knight transferred into his hybrid human-wolf form

The man next to Marrok was dressed in a tuxedo that would've done James Bond proud. He wasn't the tallest or the biggest man in the room, but I'd lay on odds that he was the strongest. Even a custom-tailored tuxedo couldn't hide Hercules's muscles. The Greco-Roman demigod had also been a Knight of the Round Table. As Sir Bors, he had ended up on the wrong side of the battle between Lancelot and Arthur but he always acted with honor.

"Arthur's death shall finally be avenged," whispered Hercules, a sound that coming from him was more terrifying than any other man's shout.

Hercules and the Wolf Knight moved towards Accolon who had stopped twitching and was now crawling backward on the floor in well-deserved terror. Before the two knights could lay hands on the sniveling coward, Wisp turned and yelled, "Stop!"

That alone wasn't enough to stop those two, but the flames that burst from Wisp's head and hands were. When you've lived as long as we have, the prospect of whether all the bad you've done would be balanced out by the good was terrifying. The two men stopped in their tracks.

"I respectfully request that the former Sir Accolon be turned over to the surviving members of Camelot for trial and execution," Sir Marrok said.

Wisp simply shook his head.

Even the combined forces of the five of us would be hard-pressed to beat Wisp in a fair fight and as he was a friend and we were Knights of the Round Table that was the only way it could go down.

The Wolf Knight growled. "Don't make me invoke the..."

Flames shot out Wisp's right hand towards Marrok's fur-covered face. The soulfire was so close it could have licked his nose.

"Don't you dare even consider invoking the Pantheon Accords or I will ban you from the Eternity Club. I did not know this man's history, but anyone who comes to here invited is under my protection while they are here. All of you stand down and allow him to leave."

Accolon stood and laughed at us.

"All these centuries and you only found me by chance. After tonight you won't ever find me again. I'll admit I'm surprised to see so many of you still around but you got lucky here. If I see any of you again I'll kill you."

Wisp retracted the flames from Marrok and turned to face Accolon. "Your invitation to join the Eternity Club is hereby rescinded. Don't darken my door again. These people are among the noblest I have ever known, so if they want you dead it's with good reason. Now that they know you're still alive, I doubt any of them will rest until they find you again. So if you find that amusing, continue to laugh. I'll grant you a thirty-minute head start before I allow them to leave. I suggest you make the most of that time."

"Now wait a moment. I was promised your protection…"

"Which you've gotten and my offer is only good while you're here. In your application, you were asked to list all your past identities and possible conflicts with other members of the club. You made no mention of any of this, which means you are in violation of our agreement which was based on that application and the reason for your being invited here. That means you're lucky I'm giving you thirty minutes, of which you only have twenty-eight left. If you'd like to keep talking, I'm sure they won't mind."

That got Accolon's back up. He was hardly the best of us, but he wasn't the worst knight. And even the worst knight of the Round Table was a superb fighter.

"You don't scare me. You can't kill me."

Now it was Wisp's turn to laugh. "What makes you think I need to kill you to hurt you?" The fire extended from his hands to just before Accolon's throat. "Your scabbard won't do anything to stop this."

Accolon tried to act tough but turned to leave which is when Bedivere reappeared with a wool trench coat that he held out for Accolon.

"Your coat," Bedivere said holding it so that Accolon could slip into it. The betrayer of Camelot chuckled and turned his back and slipped into his coat then pulled it on and brushed off the shoulders with a dismissive wave of his hands and left.

"Wisp, are you really going to make us wait the whole thirty minutes?" Hercules said.

Wisp took a deep breath and the flames surrounding him disappeared, then he nodded. "Might as well use the time to gather the rest of your number."

It wasn't an unreasonable suggestion. With one exception, not counting Accolon, the rest of the surviving Knights of the Round Table were in the Eternity Club. The exception had become a watchman for a sacred task and wouldn't be able to join us even if he wanted to.

"I will meet you there," Bedivere said and left.

The gala was not limited to the ballroom. There were many immortals who didn't look normal anymore. There are two types of immortals – regular and eternal. Us regular types will live a very long time as long as we're not killed. Eternals can't be killed. However, they can fall ill or worse. Wisp had care facilities for those immortals who couldn't care for themselves. There were several who had wished for immortality but not youth and survived as bags of flesh that couldn't die. There was a couple that Zeus turned into trees that graced an indoor courtyard. There were animals and statues and worse.

And of course, there was the Hall of Heads filled with eternals who had their heads separated from their bodies. There was well over a dozen, probably the most famous of which was Orpheus. Hot on his heels in terms of notoriety was the head of the Green Knight. He never really got bored with his beheading game although he claimed to only choose those worthy of death for their crimes – drug lords and such. A while back when someone realized that the Green Knight would be separating their head from their body at the neck, they got the bright idea of immobilizing and stealing his body. It was a good plan too because if he couldn't reattach his head, then he couldn't finish the bet.

If anything, losing his body had only made him more annoying as all he could do is talk. Still, he was one of us so we needed to let him know what was happening even though we'd have to leave him behind.

The other knight we were going to bring with us to hunt Accolon was the young corpse. At least that's what Sir Kay nicknamed him.

Mordred was not Arthur's only son. I helped raise the other one. When Anir died, Arthur and I were both beside ourselves with grief so we set off into Faerie and managed to get the cauldron of life from King Oberon and bring it back to Camelot where we planned to use it to revive Anir.

Unfortunately, Arthur was foolish enough to let Mordred stand guard over the cauldron. Mordred tainted its magic so that whatever came out was what we'd today call a zombie.

Camelot was about to be overrun by the dead and the only way to destroy the cauldron by having a live human climb inside. It was a suicide mission. I volunteered for the task and stopped for a moment to say my goodbyes. Sagramore used that opportunity to get into the cauldron himself. It worked and returned the twisted dead to their final rests. However, Sagramore became a living corpse, one who would always heal from any wound, although he looked dead.

I've carried a lot of guilt about what happened to him. Although he's sworn he forgave me long ago it does little to assuage my guilt. These days he's the Shadow's Sword in the Undercity of New York City, working for the living shadow and protecting those outcasts who would otherwise be preyed on by the stronger.

I knew he'd want to be in on this. I went to the largest parlor where those immortals who no longer looked human spent much of the time. The braver among them would join the main ball. No one would stop them but even among the long-lived, there can be looks of scorn and pity. In the indoor courtyards and parlors, there are a host of animals and other creatures who had once been human as well as many from the Hall of Heads who were brought out and laid upon pedestals so they could look others in the eyes.

Thanks to the way magic works, many of them were still able to talk and draw breath despite no longer having lungs.

As we entered the enclosed courtyard I had to duck to avoid being hit by the head of the Green Knight as it shot at my head like a soccer ball. The reason for that was a simple one – a minotaur named Nilos had kicked it across the courtyard with his hoof.

As I ducked Marrok reached out and caught him by his hair.

"Are you okay?" I said.

"Never better," the Green Knight replied.

"And you're being kicked why?" Marrok said.

"I bet Nilos that he couldn't kick me through the doorway and I've won," he said.

"No, you haven't. My aim was good and if my kick not been interfered with by the werewolf you would've went through the door," the minotaur said.

"Oh well. Would of, could of, should of. I didn't go through which means I win."

"I demand another try without any outside interference," Nilos said.

Marrok held the living severed head up so he could look it in the eyes. "And you're okay with being kicked?"

"Most assuredly, as there is little else that I can do these days."

The Wolf Knight shrugged and held the head out in front of him as if was a football then drop kicked it so it flew back across the courtyard to Nilos. "Have fun then."

Sir Sagramore had been over in the corner talking with a woman who had all of her skin burned off in a fire. She couldn't die and so lived her immortal life in great pain.

Not all eternals can regenerate.

The Dead Knight excused himself and came over to join us.

"Is it time for the toast already?"

"Something more important has come up," I said.

Sagramore raised a single eyebrow. Whenever we all meet we always raise a toast to Camelot. "Accolon showed up for the membership drive."

I wouldn't have guessed that the dead man could look any paler but he somehow managed it. In one swift motion, he reached beneath his black trench coat and pulled out his blade, a short sword made from his own leg bone. Once while captured and imprisoned he ripped off his own leg, tore off the flesh and used his tibia to grind down his femur into a blade that proved much more durable than mere steel. He has carried it ever since. Fortunately, his leg grew back.

The minotaur kicked again and the head flew between the lot of us.

"What? Accolon alive?" the Green Knight said as he sped past us and did indeed make it out the door.

"Wisp gave him the right of protection and a half-hour head start," I said.

Sagramore sheathed his blade beneath his coat. "How much longer do we have to wait?"

Without looking at her watch, Gani said, "Six minutes."

"Let's go find Bedivere so we can get out of here," Hercules said.

As we left the courtyard we walked past the Green Knight's head.

"Wait! You can't leave without me," he said.

"We can't very well bring you. You're a severed head. People would ask questions," Gani said.

"My current physical condition doesn't matter. I was just as much a Knight of the Round Table as all of you, begging the Lady Ganieda's pardon. By right I should be included in this," he said.

Hercules rolled his eyes as did Gani.

"You've got to be kidding me," Marrok said.

"He's annoying but he was irritating when he served Camelot as well. What's more, he's right," I said. As I bent down to pick him up by the hair. "He's coming."

"Fine, but you're carrying him and dealing with any attention he brings," Gani said.

I grinned. "I could just strap him onto my shoulder and use my coat to hide the strap and tell people we're conjoined twins." Or Zaphod Beeblebrox but not everyone is well read enough to get that joke.

Hercules laughed.

"You're really going to do it, aren't you?" Marrok said.

"Do you have to ask?" Gani said.

"It's something that I would actually find quite amusing," Sagramore said quite deadpan.

"Don't I get a say in this?" the head said.

"Not if you want to come with us," Marrok said.

"There is another option. Take me to Bedivere and I'll show you," the Green Knight's head said.

"You're not going anywhere until you fulfill the terms of our bet. There's no way you can argue this time. I kicked you through the door. Now tell me the secret of how you can survive the beheading game," Nilos demanded.

"Fair enough. Back in the days before I became a Knight of Camelot I wooed a woman passionately but not wisely. I was not careful and her husband found me out and challenged me to a rite of combat. I won by beheading him. My lover was quite happy with the situation as she had grown weary of her husband and had likely arranged for him to find us so that we would be forced to fight. I had no problem with that as it was a common enough occurrence. Unfortunately, she labored under the unfortunate delusion that I would now step up and marry her. When I told her that was not going to happen, she cast a spell on me.

"While she apparently knew the details of the spell, she'd never cast it before so while I was still weak and dizzy from the magic, she picked up her husband's sword and decapitated me with every intention of mounting my head on the wall like some game trophy, knowing full well that I would be alive and aware of everything that happened. What she didn't count on was that I would still have control of my body and I crawled forward, grabbed hold of my head and put it back atop my body where it healed as good as new. I would've left matters there but she was so upset she summoned a demon to kill me instead. The demon and I fought. I managed to send it back to Hell but to close the portal I had to throw her after the demon.

"Ever since I've had the ability to be beheaded and return my head to its proper place. That is until the last time my opponent got the bright idea of immobilizing then kidnapping my body. My control of my body is limited by distance so I have no idea where it is or how to find it which explains my current predicament."

"But that means there's no way for me to duplicate it," Nilos said.

"I never said you would be. I agreed to tell you how I was able to do it, not how you would be able to."

"Two minutes people," Gani said and we went back to the main ballroom where we met Bedivere driving a power wheelchair that had a manikin sitting where the body should be.

"I knew Dagonet would not leave you behind so I got the chair."

"See, I told you so," said the Green Knight's head.

Bedivere Lendor held out his hands and I handed him the head which he gently placed on the manikin's neck and fashioned a turtleneck-style strap to keep it there. The Green Knight opened his mouth and put it around what looked like a straw and took off across the ballroom in the power chair.

"How's he driving?" Hercules said.

"There's a tiny joystick on the mouthpiece which he can use his tongue to work. Excuse me for a moment," Bedivere said and walked up to wisp.

"Sir, I'm afraid I'm going need the rest of the night off and perhaps some more time after that."

"Lendor, it does not look good for someone in my employ to be in a hunting party against a prospective member. It will tarnish the reputation of the Eternity Club," Wisp said.

"In my very long life, I have had the privilege of serving three great men. You are the third. The first was Alexander the Great. The second was Arthur, King of the Britons. I cannot let his death go unavenged any more than I could yours. Because of Morgan LeFay's spell, most of the world believes Camelot to be a myth or fairytale when the truth is that it was the most glorious civilization that ever existed on this Earth. Had Arthur lived, Camelot would've existed to this day. At least that's what Merlin's prophecy saw. This man did not just take Arthur. He took an age of peace and prosperity from this world that people shall likely never see again. If what I'm going to do is a problem, I will tender my resignation to protect your reputation and that of the Eternity Club."

Wisp nodded. "I accept your resignation but when this is done I would like you to return."

"Thank you," Bedivere said.

"Did he put an address on his application?" I doubted he'd be foolish enough to go back there, but it would give us a place to start.

"No," Bedivere said then made an exaggerated expression as he looked down at his tuxedo jacket. "Oh my, what is this?" The eternal butler reached down above his breast pocket and pulled up a single hair. "It appears as if a hair from Accolon's jacket has transferred itself to me. How fortunate that I was no longer in the Eternity Club's employ when I found it."

Wisp tried to hide his expression so I wasn't sure if it was a scowl or a smile. "Very fortunate. Now the lot of you get out of here. The time is up."

Bedivere handed the hair to Gani who literally jumped up and down with excitement.

While her magi brother had far more power than Gani ever did, while he is trapped Merlin allows her to tap into his mystic abilities.

She's always been smarter than him and she's never stopped studying new ways to do magic. Any mage worth their salt would be able to use something with genetic material to track down the person it came from.

Gani had what looked what looked like a designer clutch but thanks to some spell weaving was a *lot* bigger on the inside than it was on the outside. She reached into it and pulled out a glass globe. It was pretty ingenious. She unscrewed the top then placed the hair inside. The hair wrapped itself around an arrow floating inside the globe.

Gani waved her hand, said a few words and the globe started to glow. Now the arrow would point towards the person the hair came from. It could point not only forward, backward, right, and left but also up and down and diagonally. The arrow got get thicker the closer you got to the target. It was pointed south and up.

"He's airborne," Gani said.

"He probably caught a helicopter down on Penn's Landing," said the head of the Green Knight. Sagramore gave him a questioning look. "We don't just stay in the Hall of Heads. We do go on field trips. I've done the Liberty Bell tour twenty-seven times."

"I could call Paddy and see if he'll loan us Baby," Hercules said. These days Herc works as a bouncer at Bulfinche's Pub. And his boss was a leprechaun named Paddy Moran. Baby was his flying 1930 Cadillac.

Gani laughed and reached inside her clutch. She pulled out a rolled-up carpet and unfolded it. "I think I've got this covered."

Marrok looked at the flying carpet warily. The Wolf Knight had never gotten over his fear of flying. "Is there going be enough room for all of us on that?"

Gani had made a larger flying carpet in service to Camelot that could carry several men on horses but it was destroyed a long time ago. Her personal carpet was sleek, swift, and had significantly less surface area.

"We've known each other for over a millennia. I think we can squeeze together," Gani said.

And squeeze together we did. The carpet was only about four by six feet and the Green Knight's motorized wheelchair took up a lot of that room so the lot of us ended up standing around it and holding on. Although most of us used only one hand, Marrok held on with two.

The carpet lifted off the floor and Gani pointed her fingers at and used magic to open the front double doors of the Eternity Club and we flew out.

Belvedere looked behind us and frowned at the still open doors.

"Lady Ganieda, if you wouldn't mind…"

Gani smiled and pointed her fingers in the door shut behind us, satisfying the butler.

"Should we pick up Father Sundry?" Sagramore said.

Sundry was the man who raised me when my parents put me out to die, although man might've been stretching the term a bit. He had been one of the demons known as Legion that Jesus had exorcised by putting them in a herd of pigs that then drowned. Although it's not related in the Bible, one of those pigs turned around and bowed down before Jesus, begging his forgiveness. The Nazarene was moved and not only forgave him but transformed the body of the pig into that of a human. Sundry became the 13th apostle and he's still around and trying to do good on the Earth. He was a surviving member of the King's Council of Camelot along with Bedivere, Gani, and myself.

I shook my head. "Although he would understand what we're going to do when we catch the traitor, he would not want to be a party to murder, no matter how justified by past crimes it might be."

"Do we know anything about what Accolon's been doing for the last few years?" Hercules said, looking at Bedivere.

The butler nodded. "I had reviewed his application before I knew who he really was. He claims to be living in Columbia and working as a mercenary."

"Makes sense since the scabbard would keep him from being killed," Marrok said.

"So we should assume he'll have a have a lot of ordinance when we catch up to him," Hercules said.

We passed a confused hawk that Gani shifted the carpet's path to fly around. The sudden movement made Marrok grab on tighter to the wheelchair until his knuckles were white.

Gani was messing with him and added a forty-five-degree tilt to the maneuvers. It wasn't necessary but made everyone else a little nervous with the exception of the Green Knight and me. I'd spent enough time back in the days of Camelot riding with Gani to know that she had an adhesion spell on her carpet. Anyone Gani wanted to stay on would stay fixed to the carpet even if she flew upside down. I think the Green Knight wasn't nervous just because he was happy to be outside.

We flew the better part of an hour. The bad part about flying on a carpet is you can get pretty cold even at relatively low altitudes and I was freezing. My powder blue tux with the ruffles was wasn't enough to keep me warm, but nobody else seemed to notice. Sagramore was a living corpse and zombies don't get bothered by the cold. Hercules was, well, Hercules. Marrok had transformed into his wolf-human hybrid form so he had a fur coat. The Green Knight just didn't seem to care. Gani had simply pulled a white fur coat out of her bag and put it on.

As much as I tried to tough it out, eventually I started to shiver and Gani noticed. She reached into her clutch and pulled out a waist-length white fur coat and handed it to me. The other Knights snickered but I said thanks and put it on. The sleeves were too long and the waste actually went down below my buttocks, but it was a lot better than freezing.

There had been a time that instead of handing me a coat, Gani would've had me snuggle up with her inside of her coat.

I miss those days.

"So when we do catch him, who gets to do it?" Sagramore said.

The Green Knight's head bobbed up and down and on top of his manikin body and yelled, "Me! Me!"

"And what exactly are you going to do to him?" Hercules said.

"I'll nip him in the ankle."

"And you can yell it's only a flesh wound," I said.

"Exactly!" the Green Knight shouted.

"I think we need someone who has a chance of winning," Gani said.

"Spoilsport," the Green Knight said.

"Unfortunately by the sexist laws of Camelot, I can't participate in trial by combat even though I would win easily," Gani said.

And with her mystic skills, she undoubtedly would at that. "It was a different time and only Arthur can change the laws of Camelot and he's not available right now," I said.

"And as sexist as those laws may seem by today's standards, your abilities and skills *were* recognized by Arthur. As the only woman on the King's Council you were the second-highest ranked woman in the kingdom," Belvedere said. The first of course being Guinevere.

There was no question of us ganging up on Accolon as that would be against the rules of Camelot. The time-honored tradition that one could be exonerated by winning a trial by combat was done strictly one on one. Since this was a crime against the king, any combat would need to be against the King's champion. As Knights of the Round Table, all of us – other than Gani – qualified.

"I say so long as we take the Green Knight out of the mix, we let him choose which one of us he wants to face," Hercules said.

"That'll take all the fun out of it. He'll obviously choose Dagonet," Marrok said.

"I guess even an evil traitor can have good taste," I joked, but I didn't disagree with the Wolf Knight's assessment. Hercules was one of the strongest men who ever lived and had thousands of years of fighting experience. Marrok was an insanely powerful werewolf. Sagramore and Belvedere couldn't be killed by normal means. He stood the best chance of winning against me.

"I guess we'll assume it's a safe bet that he'll be facing Dagonet. Obviously, you'll need to get the scabbard away from him during the battle," Hercules said.

"Thank you for pointing out the obvious to me. Although I may not be on the same power level as the rest of you, I don't do too badly. I seem to remember besting you in trial by combat, Hercules." Hercules had been bullying me. The only way little old jester me could defend myself was to be made a Knight and Arthur made it happen.

Hercules smiled. "You got lucky one time and you just won't let it go."

"We have to hold onto the little things," I said.

"That's why we keep you around," Marrok said, winking at me.

The arrow and the globe had been getting steadily bigger and now we could see a small dot in the sky. Gani had been right. It was a helicopter, which was a good thing for us. If he'd gone by private jet we never would've caught him.

"I can take out the chopper from here," Gani said.

Belvedere shook his head. "Accolon would be fine but you might hurt his pilot. We'll need to get closer before we take him out of the sky."

The flying carpet closed the distance on the chopper in short order. We tried to stay in the pilot's blind spot as long as we could, but eventually they noticed us. Accolon was leaning out of the side of the helicopter courtesy of a strap and he was pointing a weapon at us.

"RPG!" Herc said.

Gani started fishing in her bag.

"Don't worry, I got this," I said and pulled Hayden off of my wrist sheath. Hayden is an amazing sword that Gani made for me so I'd survive my trial by combat with Hercules. Not only is it invisible, but the blade can elongate, allowing me to hit the rocket-powered grenade and trigger the explosion well before it reached us. Gani zoomed the carpet in closer and Accolon fired at us with a machine gun. Belvedere and Sagramore moved to the front edge of the carpet and stood to shoulder to shield the rest of us. Although the bullets were making holes in their backs, the pair healed almost as fast as they were shot. Other than a lot of pain, they were fine.

While taking cover behind my two comrades I telescoped Hayden's blade again and hit the engine several times by telescoping my blade in and out. My attack had the desired effect. The helicopter blades slowed down, forcing the pilot to make an emergency landing. We were over farmland so there were no worries about people being hurt when they put down.

Hercules leapt off the carpet into the field and started running beneath the floundering helicopter like an outfielder trying to catch a pop-fly.

I've seen Hercules do a lot of amazing things over the years, but he still continues to impress me. He caught the helicopter and broke its momentum before putting it gently down in the field.

Hercules has a bulletproof lion-skin trench coat, but he didn't have it on. It wasn't exactly black-tie wear. I was a little nervous when Accolon pointed the machine gun at Herc's face but Hercules leapt quicker than the traitor could pull the trigger. Herc crushed the barrel of the gun in one hand and grabbed the front of Accolon's tuxedo with the other, yanking him out of the plane

The pilot reached for his sidearm but Marrok had already pulled his own magic sword out. Shiftan was a broadsword that could transform from the size of a toothpick to something larger than a man. The Wolf Knight liked it big in battle and was strong enough to hold it. He pointed the tip of his blade at the pilot's throat.

"Do you really want to pull that?"

The pilot rapidly shook his head as he stared at the werewolf. Marrok held his free hand out and the pilot gingerly gave him the gun.

The Wolf Knight tossed the gun across the field. Hercules dragged Accolon away from the helicopter like he was a rag doll then threw him almost as far as Marrok had thrown the gun. Gani landed the carpet and stood in front of and above Accolon.

"Sir Accolon, you are charged with high treason by the King's Council." As Gani, Belvedere, and I made up three-fourths of the surviving Council, we were able to bring the charges. "We offer you either a swift trial and execution or trial by combat with any of the King's champions present that have limbs. Which do you choose?"

"I choose trial by combat."

And like Marrok surmised, he chose to fight me.

"So to be clear, by the rules set forth in Camelot, if I win this fight, I will be free and not persecuted anymore by any of you?" Accolon said.

Gani smiled but it was a look of a predator sizing up her prey. "Of course."

"I don't suppose you'll allow me the use of firearms?"

Belvedere shook his head. "Trial by combat is not a duel. Only that which is on the list of approved weapons may be used. What is your choice?"

Accolon looked at me and smirked. "Against the Jester? Might be fun to joust. I doubt he could even climb on the horse himself, but I'll be merciful and quick. I choose swords." Accolon looked at Marrok. "May I use your broadsword?"

"Only if you don't mind me sticking it inside your chest."

"Pass."

Gani reached into her purse and pulled out a broadsword and flung it so it landed point first in the dirt between Accolon's feet. The traitor picked it up and tested the balance in his hands and seemed pleased with it.

"The trial by combat begins now," Gani said.

Accolon creased his brow. "What, no one's going to give the Jester a blade?"

I smiled. The thing about the Round Table was not all the knights stayed in Camelot all the time. Accolon hadn't witnessed my match with Hercules. We never fought in battle together and he knew me primarily from my time as a jester, not a knight. He had no idea that I had Hayden.

"Don't worry, I'm covered."

With that, I telescoped Hayden's blade so that the point went through his right shoulder and out the other side.

Accolon screamed in pain, but the wound healed itself back together in seconds.

He looked at his shoulder, then at me. "That took longer than normal. This is why I detest magic weapons. I don't know how any of you besides the wolf and the witch are still alive, but you can stab me as many times as you want and I won't die. I only have to kill you once to win."

I shot Hayden out again and shredded Accolon's tuxedo pants so they fell to his ankles, revealing silk boxer shorts and Arthur's stolen scabbard. The belt was strapped around his waist and down the outside of his left leg.

Accolon kicked off the tattered pants and removed his tuxedo jacket. While he stripped I planted the tip of Hayden on the ground and telescoped the blade so it thrust me forward. My feet slammed into his chest, knocking him to the dirt. The impact covered what I was actually doing.

I rolled away as Accolon took a swing at me, barely getting Hayden up in time to parry a blow that would've tore through my neck. We both regained our feet at roughly the same time. Accolon was faster than me and charged, swinging the broadsword. This time instead of parrying I used Hayden to telescope me up into the air and then retracted the blade so I landed on his head, knocking him to the ground face first. I needed him to roll him over so I could get to his front. Accolon obliged by spinning onto his back and I went in. Unfortunately, he swung the blade as he rolled and it cut into my chest between a pair of ribs. It hurt like hell so I used Hayden to propel me back out of the reach of his blade, but not before I did what I set out to do.

"First blood is mine. I think I'll finish you with my next blow."

"Why bother? I just won."

Accolon looked confused, so I held up the belt and scabbard that it had taken me two tries to undo and pull off him. The traitor did a very satisfying double take at what I held and then looked down to his bare waist and side.

"No! Give it back!" Accolon rushed forward but he was no longer a young man. With each step he aged and I only had to take three steps backward before he collapsed.

"Sagramore, he looks even worse than you," the Green Knight said before using his mouth control to run over Accolon with his power wheelchair. Twice. It took all of two minutes for Accolon's body to turn to dust.

Gani whipped up a small dust devil and blew his remains far away.

We are stood looking at each other and exchanged nods.

"Let's go back to the Eternity Club for that toast," Sagramore said.

Gani motioned and the carpet flew over towards us.

It is difficult to tell with all his fur but it looked like Marrok's face had gotten much paler. "Since there is no need for us to follow anymore isn't there a quicker way we can get back?"

Gani grinned. "There could be, but I think I'm out of chalk."

Marrok crossed his arms in front of his chest and stared. Gani stuck out her tongue and rolled up the carpet and put it back in her purse. Then she took out a piece of chalk and drew a door on a large oak tree. She also drew a button on the side of the door and pushed it. Several seconds later, elevator doors appeared on the tree then opened.

The Green Knight rolled in first and the rest of us followed leaving a very confused pilot behind.

There were hundreds of buttons inside and one was labeled Eternity Club. Gani pushed it and the doors closed. About ten seconds later they opened again in a side hallway of the Eternity Club.

We walked in silence to the bar. Wisp saw us and Bedivere nodded to him. Wisp nodded back.

Wisp brought us our drinks himself.

"Lendor, I'm a like to offer you your job back," Wisp said.

"Thank you, Jack. In the morning I'll accept but I think I'm going to take the rest of the night off with my friends."

"Of course. You'll excuse me as I have other guests to attend to," Wisp said.

We each took our glasses. Well except for the Green Knight. His glass of whiskey was placed strategically in front of him with a straw sticking out. Then we bowed our heads, although again in the case of the Green Knight that's all he could really do.

After a respectful moment of silence, Sagramore raised his glass. "To the memory of Camelot, her king Arthur, and our fallen brothers of the Round Table," the Dead Knight said.

"To Merlin," Gani said.

"And for Arthur finally getting justice for the crime that ultimately caused his death," Belvedere added.

"And for those of us still fortunate enough to live on and continue the good fight," the Green Knight said. We drank and remembered.

"Now what are we going to do with this?" I said holding up the shealth.

"What do you mean we, kemosabe? You won the fight so by right it's yours. It's up to you what to do with it," Marrok said.

I nodded.

"I don't want it. I've survived this long without it. It is not mine to wear or to give away. It belonged only to one man who one day return to us in Britain's hour of greatest need. Until then, I will save it for Arthur so the next time Camelot will not fall."

THE OSPREY'S QUEST

D. C. Brod

The osprey glided over the docks and warehouses of Caernarfon, Wales, riding on the thermals to maintain her height. It was early - barely dawn - and aside from fishermen, few people cluttered the streets. The man she followed rode a bicycle, jacket buttoned to his chin and shoulders hunched against the sharp wind off the Menai Strait. She could make out his features, tense with concentration.

He stopped at the door to one of the warehouses. The faded, weather-beaten sign on the building read "Super Storage."

Turning to face the wind, the osprey hovered as she watched the man unlock the door and enter, rolling the bicycle in with him. With a flap of her wings, the raptor soared across the street and came to land on a discarded saw horse, hopped off and made her way toward the dark between two buildings, cursing each awkward step.

Several minutes later, a young woman stepped from the shadows and crossed the street, plucking a brown feather from her black jacket. She was slight with chestnut hair highlighted by a streak of moss green that fell over her left eye. She stopped at Super Storage, looked around and, finding the street empty, tried the door. Locked. She removed a small pick from her back pocket and began working at the lock. This ought to be easy by now, she thought, but her fingers still felt clumsy. She never imagined she'd need an enchantment for breaking and entering.

The lock finally gave and she inched the door open to peer in, preparing to cast an enchantment that would render her invisible to all but the most adept of her kind. But all she saw was a dark concrete floor. She stuck her head in. Dim light seeped through filthy windows, electrifying dust particles and revealing a large, empty room. She stepped in, looked around and saw the bicycle leaning against a wall behind the door. At the back were three offices, and she inspected each of these. All were empty except for a sad, broken swivel chair in one. The back door was in the corner. It opened onto an alley, empty except for three dumpsters. She walked up and down the alley's length, checking inside and around each bin to see if the man was hiding. He didn't seem the hiding type, although she wasn't sure why she thought this. Perhaps he'd fled when he heard her fumbling with the lock. Or while she was shedding her feathers, he had picked up something and walked out the same way he'd come in. But why would he leave his bicycle?

Annoyed, she kicked at a piece of gravel. Neve never lost her quarry. Colin Archer had been easy until now. In the three days she'd been tailing him, he'd done nothing worth reporting to her client. He worked at a tech company in the industrial estate west of the city, where he arrived at eight every morning and didn't leave until after five. Neve hoped he packed a sandwich in the canvas messenger bag he carried at all times. One day he had gone to a pub with a few friends after work. It was someone's birthday, and he had one beer and stayed for less than an hour. While he was there, he'd stopped a fight between two drunks just by talking them down. Neve wasn't close enough to hear what he said, but the men backed off each other. The barman offered Colin a drink, which he declined. He lived in a flat near the Town Centre. Aside from the evening he'd gone to the pub and once when he stopped at the grocer's, he went straight home and stayed there until he left for work the next morning. No one, not even his fiancé, Sara Cooke, visited him.

Four days ago Neve had received a call from Sara who was looking for a private detective. Since Neve had no office, they'd agreed to meet at a pub in Caernarfon. When Neve arrived at The Four Alls, Sara Cooke was waiting for her at one of the round, wooden tables in the beer garden drinking a glass of white wine. She had a round face and blond hair. Her lips were bright red and her eye shadow an equally vibrant shade of blue. She looked like a doll.

Neve approached the table. "Sara Cooke?"

"That's right." She smiled. "And you're Neve."

Sara pronounced it Neev rather than Nev, but Neve didn't correct her.

"I am."

"No last name?" She cocked her chin.

Neve sat across from her and didn't answer. Not only did she find small talk tedious, she hadn't slept well last night, having wakened several times, always from a dream set in the cave near Y Lliwedd's peak. It had been a long time since she'd thought about that cave, much less dreamed about it.

Sara fiddled with the stem of her wine glass as she chewed her lip. Then she looked up as though startled. "Oh. Can I get you a drink? Some wine? Beer?"

Neve folded her arms on the table. "What did you want to hire me for?"

"You do confidential investigations."

"That's right."

"I hear you're quite good at it."

"Who'd you hear that from?"

"My mum's solicitor, Ewan Banes."

Neve just nodded. Banes had given her a lot of work over the last seven years.

Sara continued to stare into the depths of the pale golden wine.

Neve said, "There's someone you'd like to know a bit more about?"

She nodded, a little sad. "My fiancé." Looking up from her glass, she said, "I just want to be sure, you know? Because these days you never know. Why, I've got a friend who married a bloke who turned out to have a wife and three kids in Spain. The rotter. I don't want that for me. You know what I mean?"

Sara wasn't wearing an engagement ring, but that didn't necessarily mean anything.

"Is there some reason you don't trust him?"

"No. Not really." Sara paused. "It's just ..."

Neve waited.

"It's just that I haven't had a lot of luck with men, you know." She gave Neve a small, hopeful smile.

Neve knew exactly what she meant and waited to see if there was anything else Sara wanted to tell her.

With a shrug, Sara said, "I'd do this myself, but I'm afraid he'd see me." She emitted a nervous giggle. "I don't want him to think I'm a stalker, you know."

Neve couldn't tell if she was serious. Not that it mattered. "Tell me more about your fiancé."

Colin Archer was a "computer technician of some sort" at Digital Perceptions in Caernarfon, and he was "quite good at what he does." Whatever it was he did. The photo Sara texted Neve was of a slender man who appeared to be in his twenties - possibly a bit younger than Sara - with dark hair and eyes that were as intense as a storm. It was as though he was looking right at her. And for a moment, Neve felt a connection. A common memory. But then it was gone.

"He won't know, will he?"

"He'll not suspect a thing," Neve said.

"Do you know how long it will take?"

"Probably a few days. It depends."

Now three days had passed, and until Colin Archer had disappeared into a warehouse at dawn, Neve thought there was nothing to him. Although it was strange that he had begun appearing in her Y Lliwedd dream, now occurring nightly. But her dreams often included odds and ends from her current life so she didn't think much of it.

Neve was meeting Sara at noon to give her an update, and she wanted to be able to tell her something more than "your fiancé disappeared into a building." She glanced at her watch. Just past nine. Three hours should be enough time to see if she could dig up a connection between Colin Archer and Super Storage.

She walked until she found a cab and had the driver take her to the library on Pavillion Hill and its bank of computers where she began her search. Neve quickly learned that Colin had a degree in software modeling and design from Cambridge University and had worked at Digital Perceptions for six years. He had a limited presence on social media - just a Facebook account, but he seldom posted. He had a lot of photos, but they were mostly scenic - the ocean, sunsets, Snowdonia - and mostly quite good. There were only a handful of photos featuring people. In only one - a group picture - did she see Sara Cooke. Neve checked out Sara's Facebook page. Quite the opposite of her fiancé, Sara posted every nuance of her life, usually with an accompanying photo. There she was with a garish pink cocktail, with her friends at a party, and posing in the new dress she'd purchased. Given all her photos, there were only a few with Colin in them, and none were of just the two of them. Well, Neve thought, it wouldn't be the first time a woman hired her to check up on a man she wanted to pursue. Although Neve couldn't help but think Colin could do better.

Now, Neve, don't be judgy.

She looked up Super Storage and learned nothing other than the fact that it had been built prior to World War II and was not currently in use. It was owned by a company with several holdings in Caernarfon. Not much more to it.

She moved on to Digital Perceptions, where Colin plied his trade. She hadn't given much thought to where he worked – it seemed boring. Sara had mentioned that they'd met there. She was an administrative assistant. As it turned out, Digital Perceptions was a privately owned internet marketing company with offices in Europe and the States. While this was more interesting than an empty warehouse, Neve didn't see where it helped her figure out Colin's disappearing act.

Neve arrived at The Four Alls twenty minutes early. She'd overstayed her time on the library's computer and had tired of the dirty looks from the guy who was waiting for her to finish. The pub was crowded, and it was a few moments before she spotted Sara at an inside table. She began to approach, then saw that Sara wasn't alone. She sat with an older man - early fifties - and their heads were almost touching as though they were sharing either secrets or an intimate moment. Perhaps both. Neve found an empty spot at the bar and ordered a lager and lime. She had a taste for coffee but didn't think the pub's version of a soy latte would satisfy her fussy habit.

She paid for her drink and took a sip as she walked toward Sara and her companion. They were no longer head to head, and Sara was gazing worriedly into her wine glass. Neve stopped at their table.

"Sara?"

They both looked up. Sara's eyes widened and the man looked annoyed.

"Neve! You're…"

"Early. I know."

The man stood, pulling on a brown leather bomber jacket. "I've got a meeting."

"Ah, yes," Sara said. "Thanks for, em, filling me in."

He downed the rest of his pint and gave Neve a not-so-subtle once-over as he walked past her. She stifled her urge to turn him into a newt.

"I do some … freelance writing for him." Sara said as Neve set her drink on the table and sat across from her client.

"You're still not going to let me buy you a drink," Sara continued with forced cheeriness.

"Thanks, but I charge enough already."

A flicker of confusion crossed Sara's face, but then she returned to the hopeful, scared, and anxious Sara who Neve was used to. "I hope you don't think I'm being pushy, setting up this meet. I mean, I know you'll let me know if you find out anything. It's just…"

Fearing a long-winded sentence, Neve interrupted. "Actually, I did." She hesitated, wondering if Sara had not been entirely forthcoming with her. But then, she told herself, she was only being paid to follow the fiancé - or whatever he was to Sara - and not to question her motives. So Neve told her what Colin had been up to - not much - until that morning. "He went into a warehouse, an empty warehouse, and someone must have picked him up behind it. He left his bike there."

Neve watched her client sort this out, anticipating her response. And when Sara finally said, "Where was it? Did it have a name?" Neve had to admit this wasn't what she'd expected.

Neve told her.

"Well." Sara canted her chin. "That's a bit odd, but it doesn't prove he's cheating. Does it?"

"No, it doesn't." It raised a thousand other questions, but, again, this wasn't Neve's business. *So why did she care?*

"Well," Sara said, neatly folding the corners of her paper napkin over the wine glass's base. "I'm afraid I can't afford to keep you on anymore."

Neve shrugged. "It's up to you."

"Em, sure. Can you send me a bill?"

"I'm afraid not. Cash only. Remember?"

"Oh, that's right." She seemed none too happy about it but pulled a wad of crumpled bills out of her bag and paid Neve.

Neve left her sipping her white wine and made straightaway to the nearest empty alley where she slipped into her feathers.

By the time Sara left the pub, a large white and sable osprey was perched on the roof across the street and the raptor saw Sara's older man follow her out. He called Sara's name; she kept walking. Sprinting, he caught up with her, grabbed her arm, and spun her around toward him. He said something unintelligible and released her. Rigid, Sara watched as he turned his back and walked away.

Flying back to her lake, which someone had named Llyn Dinas, Neve realized that her urge for coffee had not abated. Attempting to ignore it, she tried to make sense of what she'd observed. What was going on between Sara Cooke, supposedly the devoted fiancé of Colin Archer, and that older man? Neve didn't think they were lovers. Not after the way he'd grabbed her. At least she hoped they weren't. Whoever he was, Neve wanted to know more about him. Perhaps she needed to take a closer look at Sara's Facebook page. She had over a thousand friends; maybe bomber-jacket man was one of them. That meant Neve would have to go to Beddgelert, less than five kilometers from her home, where she could use the internet café. She could also assuage her coffee craving. But first she'd have to pick up her laptop.

Her nook in the vast and timeless cavern she called home had changed little over the millennia, even when Merlin had shared it with her. It was still protected and illuminated by enchantments, was home to whatever duck or otter that happened to wander in, and it was - and would always be – Neve's lifeline. Over the years, each time she had emerged to join Merlin in one of their quests, she had discovered something - some contemporary item - that she found so clever or charming that she wanted to have it. Which was why she had a gramophone and a selection of classical LPs, had purchased watercolor paints on every venture since the seventeenth century, and had a solar-powered lava lamp hanging from a low branch of her oak tree. And as meaningless as time was to her, she adored her Mickey Mouse watch.

She collected her computer and slid it, along with a notebook and pen into her tote. As she set out on the Glaslyn River in her canoe, she anticipated the creamy, nutty latte Caffi Colwyn served.

In less than a half hour, she was pulling the canoe out of the water beneath Beddgelert's foot bridge and noted, not for the first time, that rowing a canoe was almost as good for her shoulders as flying.

As she walked toward the café, she scanned the outdoor seating for an empty spot. That was when she saw him.

Sitting at a table pushed against the stone wall, reading a newspaper with coffee and a half-eaten scone in front of him was her mentor, one-time and probably future lover, as well as a number of other things. She immediately understood her persistent coffee craving. How did he always do that?

He had looked up and was watching her, newspaper lowered, and so she moved toward him, not wanting him to think she'd been caught off guard, even though they both knew she had. But she moved slowly. She liked giving him plenty of time to appreciate what he'd walked away from so many years ago.

When she reached the table, she dropped her bag on a green chair and walked past him and into the café where she ordered her latte, which would probably disappoint her now. She returned with the lidded cup and stood beside him. He looked her up and down, appraising her as he always did.

"How many calves were orphaned in order to wrap you in leather?"

"None." She sat across from him and positioned her cup on the white metal table. "Unless there's such a thing as a Pleatherpuss."

Removing the lid, she took a small sip. Tasty.

As he smiled, she remembered how she loved his smiles. Partly because she was one of the few people who knew how to wrest one from him. After all these years, she still knew his features by heart - the narrow face and nose, the eyes so sad they seemed to have suffered a thousand lifetimes.

He'd trimmed his salt and pepper beard so it was more contemporary. All things considered, he looked rather good.

"Merlin," she said.

"It's good to see you too, Nimue."

"Neve. It's Neve now."

"Neve," he said as though trying out the sound of it.

How long it had been? Decades, certainly. But time, when offered in such large pieces, had a way of folding into itself.

"More than seventy years," he said as though she'd spoken aloud.

"That's right."

She wondered who the object of this quest would be. Who had appeared in Merlin's visions? Who would Arthur be this time? Over the years, she'd had many moments of skepticism, asking herself what could any one person do these days. It was different when England was ruled by disparate tribes of warriors. One man who was thoughtful, fair, and reasonably bright could make a difference. But now? Yet Merlin had always found someone who *had* made a difference.

Ever since she'd emerged from her cave and into this new century seven years ago, she'd known he would come. He always did. She'd had a feeling that this time would be different. What troubled her about this feeling was that it was both foreboding and hopeful, and she had trouble reconciling the two. Sometimes it manifested as a subtle vibration beneath her skin, gentle as a purring cat but persistent and consuming.

He was watching her, his expression curious. Merlin liked to lead the conversation, and she wondered what he was waiting for.

"All right," she said, setting down her coffee. "What lucky soul stumbled into your vision this time?"

His brows drew together, creating that deep vertical crease she'd come to know so well. "Nimue…"

"Neve."

"It wasn't me."

She cocked her chin. "What do you mean?"

"I didn't summon you here." He paused. "You summoned me."

"I did no such thing." But even as the words left her mouth, she saw that he was right.

And this was, of course, unprecedented.

"And you came?"

"What else could I do?" he said, sounding testy. With a sigh, he added, "Lately my visions have been filled with despair rather than hope."

It was difficult not to become jaded. Painful to give the world someone who could change it, and then watch it try to destroy that person. More often than not, it did destroy him, and then the place where that goodness had been often disappeared, like a minor depression covered by drifting sand. Gone.

She felt as though she'd just been assigned a responsibility she didn't know the half of yet.

In the past, whenever Merlin summoned her, she felt him in her head.

"Was *I* in *your* head?" she asked, taking a drink to hide her smile.

"Yes, you were. In fact, the last few days you were like a fly I couldn't swat."

"You say the sweetest things." She licked a bit of foam from her upper lip.

He studied her without responding.

"Why me?" she asked.

"Why, indeed."

"You can't stand this, can you?"

"Well, you must admit I am the more … seasoned … in this area."

"Perhaps all that mentoring of yours paid off."

"A teacher, no matter how altruistic, never gives everything away."

"And don't I know that." She thought for a moment. "Why now?"

He shrugged and looked away. This must be hard for him. He didn't know how to be anything other than a mentor. Or so he believed. Over the years, their student/mentor roles had undergone many shifts. Some subtle, some not so much.

When Merlin turned to her, he must have seen her smile; she saw a flash of amusement in his eyes as they held onto hers for a moment.

Then he said, "What has been occupying your mind while you've been … what is it you do these days?"

He had a way of knowing what she was up to, but she'd play along. "I'm a private investigator."

"Ah, yes. A noble calling."

"You know, it rather is." She refused to rise to his taunt. "I protect people. And I'm well suited to following wayward spouses. No one expects to be tailed by an osprey. I don't require binoculars, and if I'm worried I'll lose him in a crowd, I can always mark him on the head."

Merlin smiled. "You always manage to find a place for yourself in whatever time you occupy, don't you?"

"I'm curious. That's all."

He nodded, and with a sigh he sat back. "So, tell me why I'm here."

Just as she was about to panic - how could she tell him he'd come to her for no reason at all? - she remembered how she'd spent the last few days. And then there were those dreams.

"Actually, I am working on a curious case. Thought it was nothing at first. Just a paranoid woman wanting to know what her fiancé was up to. But then it got interesting this morning." She told him about Colin Archer.

As she spoke, she watched him, remembering how he often stared past her as she told him something, and how, at first, she'd thought she bored him. But this was how he consumed information - by imagining it. Occasionally, he would stop her with a question, nod as she explained, and then she would continue.

Seeing him for the first time after a long separation always sent her back to those years they had together. Where the days had disappeared into the flow of time. And now, the promise of being together again, at least for a while, filled her with pleasant anticipation. They were always good together. At least for a century or two.

When she finished, he said, "And you believe this Colin fellow is the one we're looking for."

"I do." She recalled how Colin's photo had triggered some memory in her. A common memory. She pulled her phone out of her tote and tapped on the photo file. She set Colin's image in front of Merlin. He picked up the phone by its edges, as though unwilling to embrace it in his hand. "I can barely see this." Neve snatched the phone, and with her thumb and forefinger zoomed in on the image, focusing on the eyes. She set it in front of Merlin. It was several moments before he responded. "Perhaps." He drew the word out.

"'Perhaps,'" she snorted. "This is him."

He raised his eyes to her.

"And, you know what." She crossed her arms on the table and leaned toward him. "I know why it was me this time."

"Enlighten me."

"Because I'll wager you don't know an iPad from an iPhone."

"I'm not ashamed."

"Of course not."

"Besides, why would I want to? The discourse those devices engender is such that I have to keep reminding myself that humanity is worth saving."

"I know what you mean. I do." She paused. "But, you know, it's not all bad."

"Really? Name one thing that isn't."

Instead of giving him an example, she said, "Social media is in its infancy. Beginnings are messy."

Merlin sighed.

She leaned toward him. "We need to check him out. You know it."

He didn't argue; but he didn't appear convinced either.

"I've had dreams about this man."

"Well," he said. "I suppose he's not bad looking."

"You know what I mean. You have visions; I have dreams." She'd never thought they were the same, but perhaps they were. "I've been dreaming about Y Lliwedd." The cave where Arthur's knights awaited summoning was a myth. But that didn't mean it wasn't a sign. "Since I've been following Colin, he has appeared in this dream. Last night he was astride a piebald stallion. Bedwyr was beside him on Aliwn."

Merlin rested his chin on his palm, tapping a forefinger against his cheek. It was a gesture she knew well. He was going to go along with her, but didn't want to seem too eager.

"Tell you what," she said. "If I'm wrong, you can come back to the lake with me. We've got some catching up to do."

His eyes crinkled before his smile appeared.

The next morning, an osprey and a peregrine falcon perched on the roof of a building adjacent to Super Storage. An ornithologist would have found their behavior curious. Ospreys and falcons didn't normally associate with each other, and they never bonded. While Neve conceded that there was no bonding going on, there was definitely a relationship.

Neve wasn't used to having Merlin with her on her stakeouts; she liked being alone. After two hours, his constant presence was starting to rattle her. He seemed impatient, pacing and flapping his wings as if that would speed things up. She'd finally started flapping her own wings and that stopped him for a while. (There was no comparing the paltry wingspan of a peregrine falcon to an osprey's.)

They had agreed that if Colin showed up, she would fly to the other side of the warehouse and see if he exited. If he didn't, she would go in and find him. He couldn't disappear. She and Merlin might be able to pull that off but she was fairly certain Colin hadn't studied enchantments at Cambridge.

It was shortly past eight when Colin arrived on his bicycle, unlocked the door and entered the building. Neve flew to the back alley where she hovered for a few minutes, waiting to see if he was leaving. When he didn't appear, she lit on the edge of one of the dumpsters, hopped down, changed back to her flightless self, and walked around the building, motioning to the falcon across the way that she was going in.

After checking to see if the warehouse was empty, she slipped in and immediately made herself invisible. It wasn't so much an invisibility spell as a way of blending in with her surroundings so seamlessly that no one would be able to see her.

All right, Neve. If he's not here and not in the back, you missed something the last time. She walked the length of the warehouse, peering into offices again, and found what she was looking for in the rear corner opposite the back door - a trap door flush with the cement floor. It opened to a flight of stairs leading into the dark. An old bomb shelter? Neve switched on a pen light and descended. The steps ended in a solid metal door. She tried the handle. It wasn't locked. She switched off the light and cracked the door an inch. It opened into a lighted room that appeared to be small. All she could see was an office chair and a table filled with electronic equipment. The steady clack of computer keys was the only sound. She pushed the door open a few more inches and stuck her head in. When she saw Colin at a long desk facing the opposite wall, she slipped in and closed the door behind her. He looked over his shoulder at the faint sound, hesitated, then went back to work. Three large computer displays took up most of the desk's surface and Colin was engrossed with the center screen. Neve looked around. The room was no more than four or five meters square, and it was good that Merlin had not come in with her. As it was, she'd have to be careful to avoid Colin. He might not be able to see her, but he was bound to think something was afoot if he started running into invisible objects. She moved so she was a few feet behind him and could see what he was doing but was careful not to disturb the air around him.

He was entering some kind of code. She might know bounds more about computers than Merlin, but this was a foreign language to her. Colin began to hum softly - it sounded like a Beatles song. "Eight Days a Week"? He tapped the return key, sat back, and crossed his arms over his chest. "Okay, Harold. Let's hear it."

Then he pushed back his chair so abruptly, Neve had to jump out of the way. When she did, she jammed her hip into the corner of the electronics table. She tried to stifle her cry of pain and surprise, but Colin was looking around the room as though he expected to find someone.

Two things happened at exactly the same time: the computer's email chime went off, and the door to the stairs opened. *Please be invisible.* She turned toward the door. But the person entering was not invisible and was, in fact, Sara Cooke followed by her friend from the pub.

"Sara?" Colin said. "What…" Then he focused on the man behind her and his jaw sagged.

Neve retreated to the corner beside the electronics table.

"Mr. Whitacre?" Colin spoke as though he didn't trust his eyes. He turned toward Sara. "What's going on?"

Whitacre pushed past Sara to stand in front the computer. "I've come to see this software Sara has told me about."

"I…" Colin looked at Sara. "You told him?"

She shrugged. "I told you he'd want to buy it, but no, you wouldn't think of selling it."

"Why would I? And why would you think I would?"

"For the money," she said, as though it were obvious. "This whole thing was my idea, remember? I think it's mine to sell too."

Colin shook his head, staring wide-eyed at Sara. "Your idea? You read something nasty one of your so-called friends said about you on Facebook and imagine that it'd be wicked if there were a program that would call out a liar."

"I did." She gave Whitacre a proud smile.

"And then you spent ten minutes on what a backstabber your friend was and another ten responding to her in kind."

She shrugged modestly.

"And I develop a program that can automatically fact check every piece of data posted."

"Still, it was *my* idea."

Whitacre had moved closer to the computer and was reading the screen. "Whoever Harold is, he's quite happy with the results." He looked up at Colin. "So the beta testing is going well."

Colin didn't answer. Whitacre smiled at him. "I had no idea you were so talented. Why didn't you tell me about this? I'm Chief Technology Officer. Surely you knew I'd be interested." He turned toward the screen. "Digital Perceptions is going to find this most useful."

"It's not yours," Colin said.

"I think our solicitors will have something to say about that."

Whitacre began looking around the room as though sizing it up, and Neve pressed into the wall. "You did all your work here?" Whitacre asked. "None of it at DP?"

"None of it."

Whitacre continued as though Colin hadn't spoken. "We're prepared to compensate you, of course. A nice bonus."

"I don't want your money."

Out of the corner of her eye, Neve saw the door open a few inches, then close. Not enough room for anyone - even a wiry wizard - to slip in. But Merlin was out there.

"Of course not, Colin. You're above all that." He walked closer to Colin. "But surely you see the potential for this? We'd have the power to post any fact we want to use."

"That's not what it's for. It's to disseminate truth, not more lies."

Whitacre glanced at Sara and nodded toward Colin. "This is why he'll never get ahead, you know," he told her. "Very short-sighted."

"Actually, I'm not," Colin said. "I'm quite able to see the implications of this. For good or ill. And I'm not willing to take it your way."

"All right. If you insist. I'll leave you here. With your computers and your ideals. You just give me the code."

"Why would I do that?"

Whitacre removed a small gun from his jacket and pointed it at Colin.

Sara was starting to look concerned. "David," she said. "You told me..."

"Shut up, Sara."

She did.

Colin said to her, "I always thought you had an ass for a boss. A pity I wasn't as perceptive about my friends."

Sara looked down at the floor.

"Enough of this," Whitacre said to Colin. "The code."

Colin shook his head. "No."

Nodding as though he'd expected this response, Whitacre said, "That's why I brought her along." Without turning away from Colin, Whitacre reached back and grabbed Sara by the forearm. She let out a little yelp. Pulling her up alongside him, he pressed the gun to her head. "I know she's a little snake, but you, Colin, are one of the good guys ... You don't want to be responsible for her death. The code."

Colin swallowed but didn't move.

"You think I won't kill her? She means less than nothing to me. She's not even worth much a secretary." He released Sara long enough to reach into his jeans pocket and produce a flash drive, which he tossed to Colin.

It hit the floor with a clink.

"I don't have time for this." Whitacre grabbed Sara's arm again, pressed the gun to her head and began counting, "One … two …"

Sara had turned white, and her voice sounded like a squeak when she said, "I'm sorry, Colin. I'm so…"

Whitacre jerked her arm. "Don't worry, dear. You won't know what hit you."

Just as Neve wondered whether Whitacre intended to count to three or ten, Colin bent down and retrieved the drive.

"There's a good boy," Whitacre said as though he were talking to an obedient dog.

The process didn't take long and Whitacre, who apparently knew a few things about computers, stood behind Colin the whole time. When the code had been downloaded, he slipped the flash drive into his pocket. "Thank you, Colin."

Colin spun around in his chair and gave Whitacre a look of disgust and maybe a little inevitability. He had to know his chances of surviving the next few minutes were bad. "This won't work for you."

"It will."

"No." He shook his head. "Evil always loses."

Whitacre said, "Colin, it's all about perspective."

"No. It's not. What you're going to do *is* wrong."

"I know what this has the potential to do. Don't worry. I'm not going to take down a government or assassinate a leader."

"But you are going to…"

"Please, spare me the lecture." With that he pointed the gun at Colin.

Sara gasped and Neve launched herself from the corner, smacking into Colin's wheeled chair and sending them both flying. She heard the shot and the explosion as a bullet hit the computer's screen. Sara was screaming and Whitacre stood frozen, mouth agape. Neve scrambled, looking for something to throw. Her hand brushed the keyboard on the floor, which she grabbed and hurled at Whitacre. It smacked his arm and he dropped the gun.

Sara, still screaming, eyes wide as she took in a sight she couldn't explain, turned and fumbled for the door, lurching it open. As she tried to flee, she bashed into an invisible wall, fell backwards, staggering, then managed to pick herself up and make her escape, whimpering as she stumbled up the steps.

Whitacre dove for the gun at the same time Neve did. She got to it first, scuttled backwards and stood, pointing the gun at Whitacre who gaped at the floating gun aimed at his head. Behind him, a disembodied voice said, "You have no idea what else Colin is capable of."

Neve said, "Colin, get the flash drive."

Colin, eyes wide, turned in the direction of each voice. Then he took a deep breath, nodded to himself once as though prioritizing, thrust his hand into Whitacre's pocket, and pulled out the flash drive.

Neve wagged the gun at Whitacre. "Leave. While you're still able."

Whitacre jerked himself up, emitted a strangled cry, and bolted out the door, which swung shut behind him.

Colin looked from the gun now hanging at Neve's side, to the door. He seemed reluctant to move. "All right," he said, hesitant. "I suppose thanks are in order, but I make a point of never thanking someone I can't see."

Neve dropped her spell first. As Colin stared at the slight woman, Merlin appeared behind him. "I've heard a lot about you, Colin."

Colin glanced at Merlin, then turned back to Neve. He tucked the drive into his jeans pocket. "I don't know who you - or what - you are, but you're not getting this either."

"We don't want that," Merlin said. "We just want to talk. And when we're through talking, if you'd like, we'll leave you be."

Colin was still staring at Neve. "Talk?"

Merlin stepped between the two of them. "You owe us that, don't you?"

He shook his head as though clearing it and made a point of looking at Merlin. "Yes. I… I suppose."

"Tell me one thing first," Neve said. "Sara wasn't your fiancé, was she?" Because if she was, then they needed to work on his judgment issues.

Colin's eyes widened in disbelief. "What? No!"

"Good."

Neve tried not to smile as she waited for Merlin to explain to Colin, in the masterful way that had served him so well over these many years, that Colin wasn't seeing things; that his vision was good and noble and could grow exponentially; and that he and Neve would be there to help him.

But when she looked at Merlin, he was watching her, that amused expression tweaking the corners of his mouth.

He gave her a gracious nod and said, "You're on."

The Reluctant Lady

Susanne Wolf and John L. French

I love not to be constrained to love; for love must arise of the heart, and not by no constraint.

-Thomas Malory, Le Morte d'Arthur

It was a bright summer afternoon, when she could have read in the gardens, or gone swimming in the sea, or taken a walk in the forest. Instead, the Lady Dandrane was imprisoned in a carriage with Sir Claudin, travelling through the woods to Camelot.

Dandrane had last seen Claudin towards the end of King Arthur's Yule festivities. It was there that her brother Percival had announced her engagement to the knight. And now, having crossed the sea to her mother's keep at springtime, he was escorting her to Camelot, where Arthur himself, in order to honor her brother, one his best and bravest knights, was to preside over her wedding come Pentecost. Dandrane had dreaded that day for the last half year, and now that it was but a fortnight away it was as if she was riding to her execution.

Fortunately Sine, Dandrane's servant, companion, and only close friend, was also in the coach, seated across from Dandrane and Claudin. She was perusing a manuscript of the ballad *The Court Painter*. It was a song about a princess who refused to obey her lord, choosing instead as a lover a handsome rogue, a scoundrel of less than noble blood. It was supposed to be somewhat bawdy and not fit for the delicate eyes and ears of young ladies. It was said to have been written by a minstrel called Elric, who claimed to be a natural son of a prominent knight.

For her own reasons, ones she did not dare share with Claudin or even Sine, Dandrane smiled when she thought of Elric the minstrel.

Sine had obtained a copy from a squire. When Dandrane asked how she had done so, Sine smiled and blushed, and said only that she had made a promise or two she did not intend to keep.

Dandrane yearned to read the ballad, to dive into the forbidden fantasy it contained. All of Elric's tales spoke of the exploits of ladies and princesses who had affairs with those they should not. Some, like his ballad of *Tristan and Iseult,* were banned in Arthur's kingdom, as being not proper for even knights to hear. As might be expected, these were the most popular and most often sung in taverns.

Dandrane feared what would happen if Claudin caught her or Sine reading what he would call "complete rubbish." He would be sure to tell Dandrane's brother. And when they discovered Sine had been supplying the princess with the banned material her servant would be dismissed or worse, and Dandrane would be given a companion chosen by her brother, one who would no doubt act as a spy.

Dandrane tried to lose herself in the landscape racing by. Her blue eyes eagerly took in the various wood and stone buildings lining the side of the roads - homes, farms, taverns as well as the various people milling around them. She thought back to ports she had seen - the ships at the docks, the sailors in their billowing white shirts and leather pants, the merchants and dock workers going and coming as they pleased.

Dandrane tried to imagine herself amid that scene, going where she wanted and doing what she wanted, rather than at the side of this knight she barely knew and didn't care for.

But it was hard to ignore Claudin when he was right there, looking over her shoulder.

"It feels so good to be back on land again."

Dandrane rolled her eyes. "You got seasick, didn't you?"

"Yes, although it pains me to admit it. Both travelling to and returning with you. That storm we ran into in the middle of the trip didn't help."

Dandrane didn't know what her brother was thinking when he promised her to Claudin. No, that was not correct, she did know. Claudin was the son of Claudas, a Frankish king who had initially opposed Arthur's taking the throne. This marriage was meant to forge a bond between the two kingdoms - Arthur's Britain and Claudas's *Terre Deserte* - making Dandrane just a pawn in the game of nations.

The more she got to know Claudin the more Dandrane realized how little they had in common. Dandrane liked the arts - sculpture, painting, poetry, and reading. She had never seen Claudin with a book. Dandrane liked animals; Claudin liked hunting them. At least he had refrained from speaking of the hunt once Dandrane expressed her disapproval of killing animals for sport. Dandrane loved the sea; Claudin hated it - or, as he put it, the sea hated him.

"It wasn't all bad," Claudin continued, as if Dandrane wasn't completely ignoring him. "On my journey to you I did see some dolphins.

A school of them came right up to the boat. They made me think of you. I forgot all about being seasick then."

Dandrane didn't know how to respond. Dolphins were her favorite animals - they were part of her maternal grandfather's crest - but she didn't want to show any interest in what Claudin had to say. However, as hard as she tried to ignore him, she could not suppress her enthusiasm.

"Really?" Dandrane turned away from the window to face him, wide-eyed with excitement. "That's wonderful! Did you see them do any tricks?"

She could have kicked herself for acting too eager. Claudin was many things, but he wasn't stupid. He knew how to get Dandrane's attention even when she was determined to have nothing to do with him.

"Oh, yes! They were doing all kinds of jumps and flips. It was quite amazing to watch."

"I'm sure it was," Dandrane muttered through clenched teeth.

"You know what else made the trip worth it?"

"What?" She was almost afraid to ask. She knew what the answer would be.

"You, my lady."

She tried not to flinch as Claudin put an arm around her shoulder. Or breathe too deeply. It had been a long trip with no chance to bathe. Perfume could only overcome so much.

"On my journey to your mother's keep, I kept reminding myself that the ship was taking me to my future bride, a beautiful and charming noble woman. And on our return to the shores of Britain I told myself that soon I would be married to this same wonderful lady. That was more than enough to sustain me."

This wedding will be a dream come true for you, thought Dandrane. *But for me, it's a living nightmare.*

"Remember last Yule at the banquet, when your brother made the announcement?"

Dandrane nodded. It was a memory she wished she could forget. She could picture herself seated in the Grand Hall at Tintagel. She had finished her meal and was awaiting the minstrel when Percival made his announcement. She remembered being angry when earlier he had told her of the arranged marriage, when he reminded her of the duty they owed Arthur and his kingdom. She replied that his duty consisted of fighting errant knights, keeping the king's peace, and rescuing maidens trapped in towers. Hers was to be one of those maidens, trapped in the tower of a loveless union.

"Claudin is a good man and a brave knight. I'm sure in time you will come to love him, as our mother came to love our father."

"Then why, dear Brother, do they live in separate keeps? No, in separate lands?"

To this Percival had no answer. Instead he said only, "Think of Britain and do your duty, Sister." He then went down to the Great Hall.

When Percival made the announcement, Dandrane could have burst into tears, or thrown up her meal right then and there. So she could not help but think that it was one of the worst days of her entire life.

"That was probably one of the best days of my life." Claudin sighed, still seemingly not noticing that she was paying more attention to the countryside than to him. "Too bad I ruined it when I dropped my goblet and spilled wine all over your dress."

Dandrane recalled that part as well. Claudin had apologized profusely and promised her a new gown. Dandrane said that would not be necessary; she would have her dress cleaned. But the next day at breakfast Claudin handed her a box, which contained a shimmery gold gown with a red sash. And of course after everyone saw the dress and gushed over it, Dandrane had no choice but to wear it at the betrothal party that evening.

"I did make up for it with the gold gown. You looked beautiful in that dress. Then again, you always look beautiful."

Claudin's kiss felt cold against Dandrane's cheek. For the past year she had existed as an empty shell, completely heartless and soulless. She was nothing but a pretty doll to play with, a marionette pulled by invisible strings.

The betrothal party was overall a disaster. Dandrane had found Prince Claudin's presence suffocating. Dandrane longed to escape from his painfully loving gaze, his bright crescent moon smile. But the prince had insisted she dance with him all night; and even though he only stepped on her toes once, he hadn't shed his habit of using perfume in place of bathing.

Dandrane tried to maintain eye contact and smile every once in a while. She didn't want Claudin to ask her what was wrong. She might be able to lie to everyone else, she couldn't lie to herself. She couldn't stop think about how miserable she would be for the rest of her days .

Dandrane feared she would go mad.

"Claudin." She pulled away from the prince. "Could you get me a drink?"

The prince nodded. "Of course. Anything for you, my lady."

The second he turned his back, Dandrane scurried off. She meandered her way around the dancing couples, the people mingling on the fringes, and the servers holding trays laden with food. Dandrane sauntered out of the ballroom, slipping out the double doors that lead to the garden.

And that was when she met Elric the minstrel.

He was sprawled out on the lawn, but quickly rose to his feet. He had dark hair, gray eyes, and tanned skin. What struck Dandrane the most were his eyes. She felt like she could drown in those gray pools, get sucked to the bottom, and never surface again.

But when she looked closer, Dandrane gasped at his roughed up appearance. His face was bruised, with a black eye and a busted lip. His clothes were wrinkled, torn and streaked with dirt. Dandrane was outraged.

"Good Sir, what has happened?" Dandrane asked in concern.

"Forgive my appearance, my Lady," the young man replied as did he best to execute a courtly bow despite his injuries. "I am but a lowly minstrel. I fear that I ran into those who do not appreciate my tales and ballads."

"Remain here and I will fetch a physician, and my brother. He will see justice done. It is not right that a minstrel and one of Arthur's guests be treated so."

"I could not agree more, my lady, but it was one of the King's guests, or rather his men-at arms, who did treat me so."

"But why? What did you ever do to them?"

"As I said, I am a minstrel. And offtimes the songs we minstrels write do not please everyone, particularly those of whom we sing. My latest endeavor tells of how the enchanter Eliavres took the form of Sir Caradoc in order to woo and seduce the knight's bride Ysave. It is said that the Caradoc the younger is not his father's true heir but rather the natural son of the enchanter."

"Sir Caradoc, is he not one of Arthur's guests?"

"Yes he is, unless it is again Eliavres in disguise. Whoever it is, he objected to my presence and so sent his servants to express that displeasure."

"Whoever it is, the King must be told of this breach of courtesy and chivalry."

"I appreciate this thought, my lady, but given that Arthur was engendered by a similar deception on the part of his father, I doubt if my plight would receive much sympathy."

Dandrane suddenly remembered something. "Wait, the ballad of which you speak. Is it *The Deceived Bride*?"

"For my sins, it is, my Lady."

"Then you are the minstrel Elric."

Another painful bow. "That is my name, my Lady, my only name, as my father refuses to give me his. Like the younger Caradoc, I am a natural son."

Elric paused, then smiled and continued, "I am pleased that you have heard of me and my works. But I thought high born ladies were not supposed to listen to such ballads."

Like a fellow conspirator, Dandrane grinned back. "We're not."

Suddenly the young man squeezed his eyes shut, his hands clutching the sides of his head. "I'm starting to feel a bit dizzy. I need to sit down."

He wandered a little ways away and collapsed in the shadow of a griffin-shaped topiary. Dandrane rushed to his side. "Ar-are you well?" she asked in a shaky voice.

"I'll be fine," he managed. "Once my head stops spinning and my ears stop ringing."

That was hardly reassuring. Dandrane was astounded at how he could be so calm and casual about the whole thing. She wouldn't have handled a thrashing like that nearly as well.

After a minute or two of silence the young man said, "I feel a lot better now."

"Are you sure?" Dandrane pressed.

"Yes. I think I might have tried to stand up too quickly before."

The young man turned to Dandrane. His eyes shone like silver, like two moons gazing at her. Dandrane trembled. She felt a little uneasy. She had not spent much time with any man to whom she was not related.

"You want to hear a secret?" Elric whispered.

"Yes." Dandrane tried to convince herself it was okay for her to be in the company of the young man if all they were doing was talking. No doubt Claudin and her brother would say otherwise.

"My father is a knight, one who sits at the Round Table. He may even be in the Great Hall tonight."

"May be. Your mother did not tell you his name?"

"I asked her more than once. She always said to wait until I grew older. Well, my lady, I did grow older but," the boy's eyes darkened to a storm cloud gray, "she was the one who did not wait."

"You mean …"

The boy raked a hand through his hair, taking a deep, shuddering breath. "Yes, my Lady. My mother died before she could tell me."

"Oh, my…" Dandrane gasped involuntary.

His voice was hollow. "It was years ago. She sickened. Doesn't make it any easier to take."

Dandrane's instinct was to give the boy a hug; he looked like he could use one. Without thinking, she threw her arms around him.

"Ouch!"

Dandrane hastily pulled away. The boy grimaced with pain, clutching at his side.

"It's okay. It doesn't hurt that badly." He closed his eyes, took a deep breath. "My Lady, you are too kind."

Dandrane had done a foolish thing. She should have known better than to embrace him when his entire body was sore. Not to mention that it was inappropriate for her to hug him when she was supposed to reserve her affections for someone else.

"I can tell you're different," said Elric. "I believe that mother would have liked you. And she normally had no use for nobles or knights, except one of course."

Elric suddenly averted his gaze, pivoting his head to stare at the shrubbery just behind them.

"My Lady, if I am not being too bold, may I ask what took you away from this evening's grand event?"

"Um…." Dandrane felt her face turn bright red, as red as her hair. She was glad Elric had looked away from her when he did.

"I'm sorry," he said immediately afterward. "You don't have to answer that."

Could she trust Elric? Based on the nature of his ballads, surely he of all people would understand.

Elric then looked Dandrane's way again. "But if you do tell me, I won't think any less of you. I'll still think you beauteous, wonderful, and a lady."

What was left of Dandrane's walls came crashing down, making her dangerously exposed, but also strangely empowered. She had worked so hard to maintain her masquerade. Because if anyone looked past the lady and saw the girl who listened to forbidden ballads, one who hated the rules by which she was bound, and who wanted to make her own decisions about whom she loved and what she wanted to do with her life, well, they would hate her. But Dandrane didn't have to hide, not from Elric. And she was tired of hiding.

"Will you vow not to tell anyone?"

"I vow."

"I…I don't want to marry Claudin." Dandrane screwed her eyes shut, willing herself not to cry. "My brother arranged it just this week to bring peace between Claudin's father and King Arthur. He didn't bother to tell me until last night. Claudin seems pleased, as if I was a tourney prize he had just won. But I don't feel a thing for him."

"You could, perhaps, learn to love him," Elric offered.

Dandrane let out a humorless laugh. "I don't want to have to learn to love someone. I always thought that it would just happen. That I would meet someone, and just know that I'm supposed to be with that person. Sounds like one of your ballads, does it not?"

"It does," said Elric. "Maybe because that's how I always hoped it would happen with me. A beautiful maiden, a moonlit garden, a chance meeting."

For the next six months, Dandrane wondered what might have happened but for …

There was a rustling in the bushes surrounding the garden, as if someone had been hiding there, listening to the conversation of the two young people. Then, from another direction …

"Dandrane! Dandrane!"

Dandrane cursed under her breath. That voice belonged to the last person she wanted to see. She felt the walls build up around her again. The woman inside her struggled to stand her ground; the proper lady she had been taught to be fought to take her place.

"Claudin's coming! Elric, you must go." The crunch of grass was deafening in the still of the night, the prince's footsteps were creeping closer and closer.

"I know." Elric sighed. "I wish we had more time…"

And with a parting glance he was gone, dissipating like an apparition. Elric the Minstrel. The beautiful young man with the ocean gray eyes.

Dandrane thought about the minstrel from time to time. Sometimes she dreamed about meeting him again - except his face would not be all bruised up - and he would take her away on all sorts of adventures.

But since she only saw him when she was asleep or daydreaming she began to wonder if he even existed. She doubted if she'd actually have the daring to run off with him. It seemed romantic when reading or dreaming about it, but it was another thing to take such a leap of faith in real life.

"Dandrane. Dandrane!" It was Claudin's voice, pulling her out of her reverie. "You're crying."

"What?" Dandrane brushed her eyes with the back of her hand; they were, to her embarrassment, wet.

"I have a present for you, a pre-wedding gift. I was going to wait until we arrived at the castle, but I think you could use it now."

Claudin reached into the pocket of his tunic and handed Dandrane a rectangular velvet box. Dandrane reluctantly removed the lid to reveal a dolphin necklace made of pure gold and incrusted with precious gems.

"It's pretty." Dandrane's heart ached. When Claudin clasped the chain around her slender neck it felt as heavy as lead.

Since they had parted at Yule, Claudin had sent Dandrane tokens of his love – sweets, fine wines, oils, perfumes, and various items of jewelry. Hardly a fortnight went by that a messenger did not arrive at her mother's keep bearing some token of his esteem. She gave most of these presents away. Just then, Dandrane recognized the emerald brooch that pinned Sine's cloak as the same one Claudin had sent her three months ago, and prayed he wouldn't notice.

I hate this, Dandrane groaned inwardly. *I hate lying. I should have said something the night Percival told me about the betrothal. I should have said something this morning before we all left the keep.*

Why am I such a coward?

Of course, Dandrane knew the answer. She feared upsetting Claudin, not to mention her brother. She feared that her refusal would could cause a diplomatic rift, maybe even lead to war between the two kings.

Just because I don't love Claudin doesn't mean I bear ill will against his county. I want peace among our nations, between all nations, but why is a forced marriage considered a solution? Could not Arthur and Claudas have come to an agreement between themselves without dragging me and Claudin into it?

She would have loved to have asked her brother that. She wished she had.

But she hadn't. It was simply easier to give in and agree to the marriage. That way, everyone would be happy and the countries would be united. Back then she had tried to convince herself she could sacrifice her own wellbeing for the greater good. Now the wedding was less than a month away, and she had serious doubts.

Dandrane wanted to do the right thing. Though, to be honest, she didn't know what the right thing was. There was the right thing for everyone else and there was the right thing for herself. Dandrane didn't believe in marrying without love, yet she was engaged to Claudin. Dandrane also knew it was wrong to have feelings for someone else when you were engaged, yet she had developed feelings for Elric. Dandrane felt herself being split in two. A war raged within her. Her head and heart were entangled in a fearsome battle, each one struggling to gain the advantage.

Just then the carriage came to an abrupt halt. Dandrane and Claudin were nearly thrown out of their seats. Sine flew out of her seat and crashed into Claudin.

"Ouch!" Claudin yelped.

Sine gasped. "Sir Claudin, I am sorry."

"It's all right," he said. "I've suffered stronger blows in tournaments" he said with a smile. "I'll survive."

Bending down to pick the manuscript off the floor, Sine said, "I wonder why we stopped. We can't be at the castle yet. I hope nothing happened to the coach."

A sudden impulse came over Dandrane. "I'll go out to see what's going on," she volunteered. "Stall him," she mouthed to Sine, as she swung open the door. Thinking *What am I doing* and realizing it was what proper ladies did not do, she hopped out of the carriage and went to investigate, relived to be free of Claudin, however briefly.

It did not take long for Dandrane to discover the cause of all the commotion - a young man kneeling in the middle of the road. His head was down, his hands moving frantically to collect the rolls of parchment scattered about the cobblestone road. An empty pouch lay nearby.

"Let me help you with that." Dandrane bent and picked up the pouch. She knelt next the young man and began to help him replace his scrolls. He cocked his head to the side as he reached out to take his pouch, and a jolt shot up her arm as if she had just touched a bolt of lightning.

Because she *knew* him. The gaze of his eyes was just as intense now as they were that night in the garden. He was Elric the minstrel, of that there was no question.

Dandrane quickly shifted her gaze downward to the pile of fallen parchment. She and Elric gathered up the rest of the rolls in silence. She could not make eye contact; she didn't trust herself to speak. Her cheeks felt uncomfortably warn. The one thing Dandrane hated about having red hair, she blushed way too easily.

Once Elric had all his ballads stowed safely in his pouch, he and Dandrane rose to their feet.

"Thank you, Lady Dandrane," said Elric, giving a slight bow.

"You're welcome, Elric." Dandrane smiled in inspire of herself. She *was* glad Elric was there, even if he made her life more complicated. "And you really should be more careful," she teased. "Every time I see you, you're either getting pounded or you're about to be pounded. What happened this time?"

"Bandits, I fear. They thought my pouch contained more than my poor songs. When they found that it did not, they took their disappointment out on me."

"I am glad you are not hurt." Dandrane glanced toward her coach. This was her moment, the chance to decide between her duty and her heart. Regretfully she said to Elric, "I really must be going. Please take care of yourself now."

It was with an effort that Dandrane turned her back on the minstrel. She dashed back to the carriage just as Claudin was stepping out.

"It is all right, Claudin, All is well. We can go!" Dandrane pushed Claudin inside, and slammed the door shut.

"What was that all about?" Claudin asked Dandrane as the coach jolted into motion.

Dandrane shrugged. "Some young man dropped some papers into the road," she replied, hoping to sound casual. "I helped him picked them up."

Again she chided herself for what she deemed her cowardice. If she'd been an ordinary maiden, she might have asked Elric to accompany her to a tavern. She could have had a perfectly nice meal with someone whose company she enjoyed. But she was a lady, sister to a knight, and it was her fate to ride to Camelot and marry a king's son, because that's what duty required.

"You called that young man by name. How do you know him?" Claudin asked in a voice partway between suspicion and curiosity.

Dandrane sighed. For once, she decided to tell the truth. Well, as much of the truth as she could. "I met him at our betrothal party. Remember when I had to leave the Great Hall because I had a headache and needed some air?"

Claudin's eyes narrowed as he nodded slowly as Dandrane continued.

"He just happened to be in the garden when I was there. We spoke briefly."

"Yes, I remember. A minstrel I was told. I believe his name was Elric."

Claudin knew, Dandrane realized. He had known all along. But how? The rustling in the bushes, it must have one of the King's men set to watch her.

"You were spying on me," she said in accusation. "It was your man in the bushes. No matter. He would have told you that I did nothing improper. Our meeting was by chance."

"Man in the bushes?" Claudin seemed puzzled. "But I had no ..."

"If you do not trust me why did you agree to marry me?"

"I had no man in the bushes, my lady. And I did not know that you were not alone until I came upon in the garden. I heard you call him by name and send him off, as a lady should. I later asked about him and to my surprise discovered that he was a famous, or rather notorious bard, one with much talent but best known for his scandalous songs. Odd to have met him on the road to Camelot."

Dandrane felt anger rush through her. "Odd?" she said, almost shouting. How dare he make such accusations about her? "Are you accusing me of arranging an assignation? Is your jealousy such that you have lost reason? If you find me so untrustworthy, maybe we should call the engagement off."

Dandrane turned her head to the window, resuming her survey of the countryside.

"My Lady ... Dandrane..." Her name hung like fog in the air. "Forgive me. I had no intent on questioning your honor or trustworthiness. I perhaps overreacted in remarking on a simple coincidence."

Dandrane calmed as quickly as she had gotten angry. Still she wondered at her reaction. "Claudin, believe me, you have nothing to worry about on my part. I would never betray you."

And she would not. She had given her word, or rather, her brother had given it for her. But she felt bound by it. *And it is not as if I will ever see Elric again*, she told herself. Still, that was what she had thought after the first time they had met. But both times they had met by chance. What were the odds of a third encounter?

Best change the subject. "I'm wearing the earrings you sent me," she said.

"Ah. You *are* wearing them. They look stunning on you."

Claudin had sent them a few weeks ago, along with the letter informing her of his coming to escort her to Camelot. Dandrane had only put on the sapphire studs that morning because her mother had insisted. "It will please Claudin to see you wear them," she'd said, "And they bring out your eyes." Just then Dandrane was glad she had taken her mother's advice.

"I just want you to know," said Claudin, "that you're very special to me. And I would not have us parted for anything."

He said this in all seriousness, Dandrane knew. She let out a long, deep sigh, realizing the fine prison in which she found herself. Her only consoling thought was, if she ever had children, she would never put them in such a situation. They could marry whomever they wanted, whether they were noble or not, or not marry at all. She wasn't one to underestimate the power of choice.

And maybe she hadn't fully giving up hers. Dandrane remembered the last words Elric said at their first meeting, "I wish we had more time."

We do have time, Dandrane told herself. *I'm not married yet.*

Dandrane briefly glanced at Sine, who had resumed her quiet reading of *The Court Painter.*

I have to be brave, she decided. *Like the lady in the ballad who made her own choice.*

Suddenly Dandrane sensed a plan taking shape. It would be risky, but with luck it just might work. In that moment her head and her heart stopped fighting. And her heart had won.

"Claudin," she said, feigning a yawn, "we have traveled far today. Could we rest at the next town and perhaps continue in the morning?"

"An excellent idea, my Lady." The knight shouted instructions to the driver.

Dandrane did not know the name of the town in which they stopped. Nor the name of the inn at which they stayed. If Claudin had told her she did not hear him, so busy was she in planning her escape from him. The town would have a tavern, and taverns had minstrels. With luck, she would find Elric there, and together they would run off on a life of love and adventure. And if she did not find him, then she would seek adventure on her own.

"I do not think this wise, my Lady."

Dandrane refused to listen to her companion. "Wise or not, it is what I have decided on, Sine. Now I have written a note for Claudin. It absolves you of all blame. Perhaps he will marry you instead. The last service I require of you is that you change clothes with me. A lady leaving this inn will be noticed. A servant will not be."

So it was that dressed in Sine's dress and cloak Dandrane left the inn unnoticed. Once outside in the cool evening air, she realized that she had no idea of how to find a tavern. She had just decided to walk through the town and listen for sounds of revelry when …

"I knew if I waited you would come to me."

Elric stepped out of the shadows.

She rushed into his embrace. He kissed her and she lost all reason. She did not question how he had known where she would be. To be in his arms was all she wanted, and she would do anything - anything at all - to be with him.

"Can you ride?" he asked. She was the daughter and sister of knights, of course she could. "I have horses waiting. Come with me now, and by the time Claudin knows you are gone we will be far away from him."

Again she agreed without question. Before long, she and the minstrel were mounted and on their way out of the village.

This was what she wanted. To be riding free in the open air, her true love beside her.

True love? the sensible part of her asked. *You barely know him and yet you are giving up everything for him.*

Not caring about being sensible, Dandrane continued riding until …

There were riders up ahead blocking the road. There were enough of them to keep the pair from going around them. Looking back, Dandrane saw more riders approaching. In the moon's light she saw that Claudin was at their head.

If nothing else, she thought, *at least the engagement is off.*

Forced to dismount, the men-at-arms treated her gently. Elric they treated not as gently, but did him no real harm. They waited in silence for Claudin to arrive.

"This time," the knight said to her, "I *was* watching you. I sent a guard outside the inn, in case there was yet another coincidence." Before Dandrane could protest, Claudin added. "It was not that I distrusted you, my lady, but rather the minstrel. I feared he was tracking you for some reason. It seems I was correct."

"Claudin, I can explain …"

"No doubt you can, my Lady. But please be silent while I speak to the minstrel."

Claudin approached Elric. Speaking loudly enough for Dandrane to hear he said, "You are the minstrel Elric?"

"I am, Sir Knight."

"You have a certain reputation and a considerable talent. I have heard your tunes and they are quite good. Perhaps you could sing us one now."

"My lord, I do not think this the time or the place."

"Not even to save your life?"

Dandrane gasped. Would Claudin really kill Elric? And if so, what would become of her?

"Fetch your harp, minstrel, and play us a tune. Perhaps *The Deceived Bride.* But wait, where is your harp? I do not see it in your hand, nor is it on your horse, nor was it with you on the road today." Claudin drew his sword, placed it against the so-called minstrel's chest. "Assume your true form, or die in this one."

To Dandrane's amazement, the one with whom she was running off began to change from a young man to an older one.

"Eliavres, I believe. And you would have used your magic to ruin this lady as you did Ysave." Claudin's sword slashed twice leaving deep cuts on the wizard's cheeks. "This sword was blessed by the Lady of the Lake, and again in Jerusalem. The marks it gave you cannot be disguised, and all will now know you for what you are. Get you gone, and be thankful it is ill luck to slay a wizard."

Eliavres departed on foot, for Claudin would not permit him to take his horse. When he was gone, the knight turned to Dandrane.

"How did you know?" she asked.

"I suspected, my Lady. After your first meeting I made inquiries about Elric and learned that he had set out for Eire to learn from its bards. I thought it unlikely that he would have returned so soon. So while it was he you met the first time, it was likely not him this time. You were bewitched, my Lady. No fault can lie with you."

From deep inside her, Dandrane found the courage to say, "I was not entirely bewitched, my Lord. Had it truly been Elric I would have gone with him." Trying not to see the hurt on Claudin's face she continued. "I do not love you, nor do I think I will come to love you."

She waited for a reply, any reply, form Claudin's anger to his sorrow. But he just stood there, silent in his disbelief. Not wishing to lose her newly found courage, Dandrane continued.

"You could force me to honor the agreement you made with my brother. I know I have little say in this matter. But I am asking you as a true knight to free me from my brother's promise."

Claudin thought for a moment then said, "I will not be Mark to your Isolde even if you were to stray only in your heart. And I would be a poor knight to force a lady to do anything against her will. Yet …"

"Claudin, you once swore that you would give me anything. If you would be true to your word then give me my freedom."

"To do what?"

"To follow my dream, to seek out the true Elric."

Again Claudin was quiet, then looked hard at her and she could see in his eyes that he had come to a decision.

"Mount your horse, my Lady. We ride back to the inn. Tomorrow we set out."

Dandrane's heart fell, but then Claudin continued, "Me for Camelot where I shall have to tell a tale worthy of a bard to explain all this. You, my Lady, you who may perhaps have the courage of a knight, to the west coast to take ship for Eire along with your companion and some men-at-arms to protect you on your journey. May you find your dream. But should you not, return to me and there will be no questions."

The next day Dandrane went west with Sine, away from Tintagel, away from the tower of duty, in quest of a dream.

And should I not find it, she thought, *I will not return to Claudin. I will simply find another.*

The Power in Unity

David Lee Summers

"Ambrosius had married Arthur's own sister, who had borne unto him Gawain and Mordred, he did reinstate in the Dukedom of Lothian and of the other provinces thereby that had appertained unto him aforetime." Geoffrey of Monmouth, *The History of the Kings of Britain*, Book IX, Chapter 9.

People had been disappearing from the township of Nuevo Santa Fe on the planet Sufiro and Sheriff Manuel Raton intended to put a stop to it. He patrolled the streets in his hover car. Only the hum of its propulsors kept him company. Tracking down the kidnappers would be much easier if he could use nano-surveillance drones, but the ores in the valley's surrounding mountains blocked the signals and the strong winds swept them out of town, never to be heard from again, rendering them not just useless, but an expensive loss.

It's not that he liked the drones. They compromised privacy, but he had vowed to use any means necessary to protect these people. He owed it to them.

He scanned the houses. A few were modern plascrete structures, but most were local materials such as adobe or even wood from the nearby pine forests. New Granada attracted those who had lost everything and hoped to start over -- people like his family when they settled the planet.

He turned a corner and saw a carryhover parked in front of Hoshi Matsumoto's house. The man repaired farm equipment and didn't own a carryhover. Raton tapped his vehicle's accelerator, then killed the propulsors, drifting by Matsumoto's house in silence. The carryhover's cargo area stood open and empty, as though someone had made a delivery, but the porch lights were off, Matsumoto's door was closed, and no deliverymen were in sight -- and it was after midnight.

Raton allowed the hover to drift to the next block before applying the brakes and letting his vehicle settle on the ground. He hopped out and strode back to Matsumoto's house. He knocked. When no one answered, he tried the door and found it unlocked. Drawing his hepler pistol, he entered. All appeared neat and orderly. A light shone beside a chair and a book lay face down on an end table. He peered through a door into the kitchen, then turned on his flashlight and crept down the darkened hall to a bedroom at the back of the house.

He pushed open the door and the hairs on the back of his neck stood on end. Hoshi Matsumoto lay trussed up on the bed like a calf, silent and still. Dead or tranqued, Raton couldn't tell.

"Empty your hands and reach for the sky." The cold voice came from the shadows at his right.

He shifted his gaze just enough to see a pistol. Raton dropped his weapon and the flashlight, then raised his hands.

Someone jumped on him from the left, grabbed his arms and pulled them down behind his back. Raton closed his hand into a ball and pressed a control stud in his palm, sending a stun pulse through his sleeves, knocking the assailant who held him backwards.

Raton dove for the floor as the gunman in the shadows fired, scorching the floor inches from his head. He grabbed his hepler and flashlight and aimed into the shadows. The shooter had vanished. Footsteps echoed from the hall.

The sheriff rolled over and checked the stunned man -- out cold, at least for the time being. He leapt to his feet and ran after the other suspect. As he reached the yard, the carryhover pulled away, setting the neighborhood dogs barking. Raton ran to the street, hoping he could see a license plate on the retreating carryhover. Even if he couldn't make it out, perhaps his bodycam would catch an image.

The carryhover turned a corner and disappeared from view. He considered giving chase, but he needed to check on Mr. Matsumoto and he wasn't sure how long his assailant would remain unconscious.

He jogged through the house, rolled his attacker over and zip-tied his hands together, then stood and checked on Mr. Matsumoto. The repairman had a steady pulse and his chest rose and fell as though in a deep sleep. Only tranqued, as he had hoped.

Raton reached for his radio and called in medical and police backup. While waiting, the sheriff knelt down and found his assailant had a wallet.

Raton scanned the man's ID with his compupad. A weight settled in the pit of his stomach. Mr. Gordon Lassiter was an employee of the Stone-Raton Corporation on the continent of Tejo, halfway around the planet.

Raton had long suspected the company his father founded had been making huge profits by hiring cheap labor from Nuevo Santa Fe and other cities on the continent of New Granada. This suggested they weren't merely hiring people for unfair wages, but actually abducting them to work as slaves.

The revelation couldn't have come at a worse time. The next day, he planned to meet with the planet's most powerful woman, Mary Hill, Governor of Tejo. The Earth Alliance taxed both continents excessively and she wanted to present a united front as she demanded Earth's council reduce Sufiro's tax burden.

Raton rubbed his hand through his hair. When he'd been a boy, Mary Hill had been like an aunt. She taught him to repair hover cars and how to play both chess and poker. In the process, she taught Raton how to read people.

Raton left Tejo because a man named Sam Stone murdered his father in order to grab sole ownership of the Stone-Raton Corporation. Instead of seeking justice, Mary Hill turned a blind eye on the crime, afraid prosecution would destroy not just the corporation but Tejo itself. Raton couldn't live there after that and left.

Now he knew the Stone-Raton Corporation had taken another step against people he cared about.

The assailant -- Lassiter -- began to stir and Raton resisted the urge to kick him.

Sirens broke upon the sheriff's consciousness. He heaved a sigh and went out to meet them. He could think more about his meeting with Mary Hill once Lassiter was safely locked up and the paramedics had tended to Mr. Matsumoto.

> "Howbeit, [Arthur] sent word unto the Emperors through their ambassadors that in no wise would he pay the tribute, nor would go to Rome for the sake of obeying their decree, but rather for the sake of demanding from them what they had by judicial sentence decreed to demand from him." Geoffrey of Monmouth, *The History of the Kings of Britain*, Book IX, Chapter 20.

Mary Hill scanned the surrounding countryside as her hover limo carried her through the pass into Nuevo Santa Fe. She had things to discuss with Manuel Raton that wouldn't be prudent over a hololink. No matter how secure the connection, there were people who could listen in. It seemed quaint to travel overland, but the same ores and winds that interfered with Raton's nano-drones prohibited air and space travel into the valley. Unfortunately the pass made the possibility of ambush seem all too likely in light of the botched personnel extraction.

She tried to brush her fears aside. In over a decade, Raton had not sought revenge for his father's death. Why start now?

"Troubled?"

Mary blinked and looked over at the creature sitting next to her in the back of the hover limo. Var Gwenyu came from a small, phase-locked planet orbiting Proxima Centauri, the smallest star in the Alpha Centauri system. From a distance, a Centauran might pass for human. They had a head, stood upright on limbs, and had a trunk with another set of limbs. They had two tentacles for each human arm or leg, giving them a total of eight limbs -- like an octopus.

Var spread languidly on the seat. When Mary first saw the Proxima Centauran, she thought him hideous, but her feelings changed as she grew to know Var. A warmth filled her belly and her cheeks flushed.

"Just letting my imagination run away with me." Mary chuckled and slid closer to Var.

She tended to think of Var as male, but Centaurans had no strict gender. Each individual carried both eggs and sperm. Centaurans could not fertilize themselves, and it would be a bad idea even if they could. Mated Centaurans sometimes picked one individual to be mother for life. Other couples took turns.

"You seem unduly worried about this meeting." Var draped a tentacle around Mary's shoulder. "Manuel Raton must agree Earth's taxation is egregious. Allying with you is the best way to put an end to it."

Mary sighed, uncertain whether Manuel could be counted on to view the situation as logically as Var. Earth had been taxing Sufiro heavily even though the planet had one resource no other Earth colony possessed -- the mineral Erdonium. The mineral had a crystal structure that made it both strong and malleable, and uniquely suited for building space vessels that traveled at super-light speeds. Until Sufiro, the only worlds with Erdonium were those close to their stars like Mercury or the hot side of Proxima Centauri. The problem was that all of Sufiro's Erdonium was in Tejo and a single continent had no sway over Earth's senate.

New Granada had no single government. She needed the continent united and allied with Tejo to give her power to negotiate. Manuel Raton was popular and could make that happen. "My relationship with Manuel Raton is … complicated," said Mary at last.

"More complicated than our relationship?"

Mary laughed. "Our relationship is good and … interesting, but it's hardly complicated."

Var came to Sufiro representing Galactic Erdonium. They bought the third largest stock share in the Stone-Raton mines, making them part owners. In that way, Var was like a prince, sanctioning the work of the upstart humans who mined a resource they had never before controlled.

"Something beyond the political and financial ramifications of this meeting troubles you." His tentacle worked its way down the front of Mary's blouse.

She slapped at it playfully and it retreated.

On Earth, Mary Hill had sold used hover cars. She used her ability to read people and to help her make the best deals. A person who bought a hover from Mary always went away happy, even when she sold a vehicle for well over its value.

When she arrived on Sufiro, Mary turned her skills to politics. She'd joined the expedition with the Stones and the Ratons that found the Erdonium. She let them control the company while she controlled the continent. Now she hoped to unite a world.

The hover limo cleared the pass and Mary noted Nuevo Santa Fe's ramshackle houses. She settled in a town like this on Sufiro and remembered the struggle for shelter and food. Personnel extraction was not slavery. The Stone-Raton Corporation gave people a good place to live and good food to eat. To her mind, that made a better life than scraping by in a rude dwelling with no amenities.

Var's tentacle returned and flicked over her nipple. She turned and smiled. Meeting Var was nothing like love at first sight. Rather, she resented the off-world corporation's meddling. Over time, Var made deals, maneuvered, and bluffed people in ways that made her take a second look at this alien.

And she warmed up to Var's appearance -- mollusks could be cute, right? His warm, brown eyes melted her heart and he could adjust his muscle tension to be firm in all the right places while still being soft and cuddly.

"I've known Manuel Raton since he was a boy." Mary put her hand on Var's chest and felt his heart beating. "Our relationship hasn't always been an easy one."

"Ah," Var imitated a human nod -- difficult since Centaurans didn't really have necks. "You refer to his father's death."

Centaurans weren't telepathic -- no race in the galaxy was -- but they could be extraordinarily empathic.

"You were not involved. He can be made to see that." Var spoke softly, reassuring her.

"I hope that's true."

She snuggled into him, while one of his lower tentacles worked its way up her skirt and she lost herself in his caress. She lost track of time, but came back to her senses when the chauffeur cleared his throat, holding the door open.

Mary Hill affixed a stern expression, buttoned her blouse, straightened her skirt, and walked into the Nuevo Santa Fe Sheriff's Office.

> "When Arthur learned that they were upon the march, he made over the charge of defending Britain unto his nephew Mordred and his Queen Guenevere..." Geoffrey of Monmouth, *The History of the Kings of Britain*, Book X, Chapter 2.

Manuel Raton displayed a hologram of Gordon Lassiter, the man he'd captured while on patrol. He then pulled up the scan of the carryhover he'd watched speed away from the crime scene. He enhanced the image of the license plate and ground his teeth -- a rental from New Des Moines, the spaceport town to the south.

He looked up as Chief Deputy Li Chang knocked and poked her head around the door. "Mary Hill and Var Gwenyu to see you, Sheriff."

Raton frowned but nodded. "Show them in."

Mary Hill wore a broad smile as she entered the room. She looked much as he remembered her -- about five-foot-five with short hair. Although he'd seen her graying hair in holovids, her face looked much craggier in person than he expected. She opened her arms, as though expecting an embrace. "Manuel, it's been so long."

"Mary, we have a problem." He inclined his head toward the hologram of Lassiter. "People have been mysteriously disappearing for years and I think they're being taken to work in Tejan mines." The sheriff dropped into a chair without approaching her. "I know you want to find a way to put our difficult past behind us, but this has got to stop."

Mary Hill's smile only faltered a little as she clasped her hands in front of her. "It's possible Stone-Raton mines have … overreached, but your best chance at bringing a case like this to trial is by joining with me rather than opposing me."

Raton narrowed his gaze and decided he would listen to her argument. He indicated Mary and Var should sit. "The Stone-Raton mines and the Tejan government are virtually inseparable," said the sheriff. "Joining you would be like an admission that kidnapping New Granadans was okay."

Mary shook her head. "If we're united, then under Earth Alliance law you can prosecute --" her eyes darted to the hologram "-- Mr. Lassiter and file suit against the Stone-Raton Corporation for damages. If we're not united, then you're like an independent world. You could declare war, but how far would that get you against Tejo, much less the Earth Alliance?"

Raton took a deep breath and let it out slowly. "Look, I know why you've come to me. I'm sheriff of New Granada's largest township. To make the unification deal you're proposing stick, I'd have to get the backing of the other townships, effectively running for the presidency." *Which would get me out of your hair*. He left that last part unspoken.

Var Gwenyu leaned forward. "That power would put you in a position to seek justice." Raton felt himself drawn into the alien's seductive brown-eyed gaze.

"Your people are being taxed into poverty," pressed Mary, yanking Raton from his reverie. "I need you on my side if we're ever going to get Earth to take us seriously and negotiate in good faith with us. It's the only way we'll make things better on Sufiro."

Raton frowned and folded his arms. He knew he was being manipulated. Despite that, he didn't see how the people who'd elected him would fail to benefit. He also had to admit that he kind of liked the idea of running for a presidential office. He could do far more good than he could as sheriff. He could deal with Hill as an equal and he would be in a better position to expose Stone-Raton Corporation's policy of kidnapping New Granadans.

"All right, what do we need to do to make this work?"

"The first thing you need to do is hold off prosecuting Gordon Lassiter."

Raton's brow furrowed, not liking her opening hand, but he had his own card to play. "I'll consider it, if you'll promise to get the Stone-Raton Corporation to end the kidnappings."

"But the summer coming on, at which

> time he designed to march unto Rome, he had begun to climb the passes of the mountains, when message was brought him that his nephew Mordred, unto whom he had committed the charge of Britain, had tyrannously and traitorously set the crown of the kingdom upon his own head, and had linked him in unhallowed union with Guenevere the Queen in despite of her former marriage." Geoffrey of Monmouth, *The History of the Kings of Britain*, Book X, Chapter 13.

Two weeks later, Manuel Raton sat at home sipping tea. A team of friends and advisors had just departed. All were behind the idea of him running for the presidency of New Granada. As sheriff, Raton could investigate Lassiter's ties to the Stone-Raton Corporation, but even if he found ties, what could he do?

The investigation could continue while he ran for president. If the investigation bore fruit, the high office would give him more power to end the abduction of New Granadans and bring those already taken back home. They had discussed ideas and worked out strategies. Although he knew he needed to get some sleep, his thoughts buzzed with possibilities.

The door chime startled him. He turned his head, expecting to see a misplaced coat or a forgotten compupad. With neither in evidence, he shrugged and walked to the door.

When he answered, he shuffled back a step or two, surprised to see the Centauran, Var Gwenyu. The alien wore a shimmery, form-fitting one-piece suit that accentuated his -- no her, definitely her -- curves.

"What brings you here?" stammered Raton. "With Mary Hill on her way to Earth, I thought you would be busy in Tejo."

Var gently pushed Raton back inside and closed the door behind her. "We're being manipulated, you and I."

Raton frowned. "I know. I'm being careful."

"Not careful enough," said Var. "Like you, I believed Mary Hill was working to make things better on this world, but I have discovered evidence that she's only working to make things better for Tejo and the Stone-Raton Corporation."

Raton pursed his lips and nodded. He gestured for Var to sit and offered a drink. She took a glass of wine. "What have you discovered?"

"When I came here with President Hill, she seemed nervous. It made me suspicious." Var took a sip of wine, as though to steady her nerves. "I started looking into Earth law. As you know from the incident with Gordon Lassiter, Stone-Raton Corporation has been quietly engaged in a policy of personnel extraction, grabbing workers from New Granada. It's illegal, but the corporation gets away with it because New Granada has no unified government to pose a challenge."

Raton shook his head. "Mary -- Ms. Hill -- has kept her word. The kidnappings have stopped."

"She's biding her time. She discovered an old clause in the Earth Alliance laws not invoked for over a century and mostly forgotten. If New Granada is part of the Alliance, then any industry deemed necessary for military success can conscript people openly in time of war."

The sheriff dropped onto the couch next to Var. "She wants to institute forced conscription to fill the mines?" He poured a glass of wine for himself and took a gulp. "Of course, there would have to be a war."

"In a galaxy as big as ours, there's always a war somewhere."

Raton set the glass down and put his face in his hands. "What else have you learned?"

"In time of war, the possessions of any non-humans may be confiscated without compensation. My corporation is a major stockholder in the Stone-Raton mines. She could use her new position as leader of an Alliance world to have me ejected and my ownings seized. My company would lose not only its profits, but its initial investment."

Raton looked up. "Surely the Alpha Centauran Hegemony wouldn't stand for that."

Var snorted a laugh that would have been cute if not for the suppressed bitterness. "What would they do? Declare war? There's always war somewhere." Two of Var's tentacles inched behind Raton and began massaging the tension from his shoulders.

"She wanted me to hold off prosecuting Lassiter. She said it was to foster a spirit of amity. Is there something else?"

"His credentials are fake. Gordon Lassiter is not an employee of the Stone-Raton Corporation -- or at least not a traditional employee."

"What do you mean?"

"He's a mercenary from Prospero. Corporations don't hire mercenaries. Governments do. The truth of his identity would prove collusion between the government and the Stone-Raton Corporation. The fact that Tejo has been hiring mercenaries from a world outside the Earth Alliance would threaten Mary Hill's plans."

Raton nodded slowly. Mercenaries explained how Mary could stop the kidnappings so quickly. She was the one paying their salaries. He picked up the glass of wine and settled back into Var's warm embrace. He expected her to be squishy and cold like an octopus, but she was warm and firm like a woman. It had been too long since he'd lost himself in a woman's embrace.

"How did you learn that Lassiter was a mercenary? Surely those aren't files Mary leaves open on her computer."

"She has called a name at the height of ecstasy -- the name of a former lover, I believe -- Morgan. Knowing that, the password was not hard to decrypt."

Raton decided he didn't want to know more just yet and took another sip of wine.

> "When this was reported unto Queen Guenevere, she was forthwith smitten with despair and fled from York unto Caerleon, where she purposed thenceforth to lead a chaste life amongst the nuns, and did take the veil of their order in the church of Julius the Martyr." Geoffrey of Monmouth, *The History of the Kings of Britain*, Book XI, Chapter 1.

Mary Hill's yacht, the *Prydwen*, jumped into normal space at a way station at Tau Ceti. One more jump and they'd reach Earth. Her compupad pinged as messages came in from the way station. She picked up the pad. About halfway down the list of messages, she saw one from Var. The Centauran was so good to her. She hated that Var would probably lose his position after she seized Galactic Erdonium's stock, but she suspected Var would forgive her.

Her mouth fell open as she read Var's letter. "With regret," wrote Var, "I must return home so I may work to assure Galactic Erdonium's interests."

Mary snorted. If her plans succeeded, there was nothing Var could do to protect Galactic Erdonium's stocks, short of full scale war, and there was no way the Confederation would allow that to happen.

She poured herself a glass of brandy to calm her nerves. Everything she did was for Tejo and for Sufiro. On Earth she'd only owned a small business. She'd risen to a planet's leadership and was determined to give back and make life better for everyone on the planet.

She turned her attention to the news feed. She took a sip of brandy, but spit it out when she read that Manuel Raton had brought charges against Gordon Lassiter.

She set the brandy snifter down with a thunk. She never had any animosity toward Manuel and honestly thought of him as a prodigal son. His talents were wasted as sheriff of a small town on the far side of the galaxy. She wanted to see him succeed.

Yes, she wanted to make the biggest profit she could from the Erdonium and yes, that meant she would have to conscript people to work the mines, but that gave them a better life. Why couldn't Manuel see that?

Mary blinked, grabbed the brandy snifter and downed another gulp. Manuel putting Lassiter on trial could unravel her plans. She kept Lassiter in place as a peace offering, a show of trust. If Manuel learned the truth about Lassiter, it would destroy her negotiations with the Earth Alliance. Lassiter would have to be extracted.

The problem was, she couldn't risk sending instructions over the hyperspace links. She'd have to go back. She looked at the date displayed on her compupad. It was only a day before her meeting on Earth.

She strode forward into the yacht's cockpit. The pilot looked up and nodded. "Ma'am, we'll be ready to make the final jump to Earth in about four hours."

"How long would it take it go back to Sufiro and return to this point?"

The pilot's brow furrowed and he frowned. He punched data into his computer, then double checked the results. "I'd allow four days round trip."

Hill performed a few mental calculations, thought about the discrete preparations she could make ahead of time. "Get me Senator Costello."

"Yes, ma'am," said the pilot.

By the time she returned to the executive cabin, the senator's hologram sat in an empty chair, waiting to speak with her. "I'm looking forward to our meeting tomorrow," he said.

"I'm sorry, Senator, but I'm going to have to ask to reschedule. Something's come up and I need to return to Sufiro."

Senator Costello looked down and shook his head, as though disappointed. "I'm sorry to hear that, Ms. Hill. I'm afraid the hearing time is locked in. We can't change things at this late date."

"Oh?" Mary arched her eyebrows as though shocked. "I'm so sorry to hear that. I fear we may have to increase our export duties on Erdonium shipments going out to the Earth Alliance. If it proves too much, I'm sure I can find other buyers. Alpha Coma Berenices has expressed interest."

Senator Costello blanched. "How long do you need?"

"Oh, not long," she said. "Do you think you can reschedule our meeting for next week?"

He looked at an unseen display to his left and frowned, but nodded. "It'll be difficult, but I think we can make that work."

"Delighted to hear it and I'm very sorry to have created this inconvenience."

Mary terminated the connection, then allowed her mouth to tick up slightly. At least she still had a little power over Earth. Now, she just needed to reign in Manuel.

> "And after much of the day had been spent on this wise, Arthur at last, with one battalion wherein were six thousand six hundred and sixty-six men, made a charge upon the company wherein he knew Mordred to be, and hewing a path with their swords, cut clean through it and inflicted a most grievous slaughter." Geoffrey of Monmouth, *The History of the Kings of Britain*, Book XI, Chapter 2.

The old pirate captain living in Southern New Granada alerted Manuel that *Prydwen* had returned much earlier than expected. Mary Hill hadn't had time to go to Earth, negotiate, and return. The premature return only meant one thing. She had come back to extract Gordon Lassiter from his holding cell.

Manuel could see no reason for Hill to procrastinate. She would strike as soon as she could muster forces, travel around the world, and come to Nuevo Santa Fe. Given the number of disappearances he'd been investigating, Raton guessed Hill had plenty of mercenaries to draw on. He expected her to make her play in the pre-dawn hours the next day. The only advantage he had was the geography-driven weather which kept spaceships from landing in his town. That meant any attack would come overland through the pass.

He gathered his deputies and filled them in on the situation. Two would guard Lassiter's holding cell. The rest would spread out through the pass. "When possible, I want you to stun them. Take them alive, if possible," ordered Manuel.

"Stun them?" Schulze's brow wrinkled. "Why?" The big man shrugged.

"The more mercenaries we capture, the more it builds our case." Manuel studied his deputies' faces and nodded. "Any other questions?"

They shook their heads. "Go get some sleep and we'll meet back here at midnight."

As the deputies departed, Manuel fell back into his chair. He'd tried to talk Var into staying. Var could fight for her people better from a position of power on Sufiro than from a faraway corporate office. Manuel wondered if she'd used intimacy to manipulate him, or if there had been genuine feeling. A tear trickled down his cheek as he wondered whether or not he would ever see Var Gwenyu again.

The sheriff shook off the tears and went back to a cot he kept in a dark corner of the office. There, he fell into a restless slumber until the first of his deputies -- reliable, mountain-like Schultze -- returned. Soon, the rest of the team had assembled. They poured over the map one more time, checked their equipment and moved out.

Raton drove out to the pass with his chief deputy, Li Chang. The quiet woman chewed her thumbnail as her eyes roved the rocks of the pass, illuminated only by starlight. Raton and Chang left the hover car near a crook in the river that ran through the pass and hiked up a gully to get a better view of the road. A chill breeze prompted Raton to pull up his collar.

As Raton took a position behind a boulder, Schultze's voice came over his compupad. "I see something moving, but can't make it out. I think they're in stealth suits."

The Tejans had enough money to afford the expensive camouflage. Optical sensors on the suit transmitted images from one side of the suit to the other. If the person wearing the stealth suit stood absolutely still, it was almost impossible to see them.

A moment later, a pair of bright flashes flared up from Schultze's position. Raton spat a curse as he peered up over the rock and tried to distinguish the silhouettes of his people from those of the spindly trees that clung tenaciously to the sandy soil.

The sheriff tapped his compupad and spoke to Schultze's partner. "Jones, what do you see?"

There was no answer. A moment later, another flash appeared from the same direction. "Got one," growled Susan Jones, "but not before they vaporized Schultze. I'm going to subdue him before he wakes up."

Raton waited for several tense minutes while waiting for Jones's report. A fireball erupted from her position. Apparently the mercenary had been wired. Raton wondered if he knew he'd been made into a human bomb to keep Mary Hill's secrets.

The sheriff tapped the compupad, broadcasting to all his deputies. "Until further notice, don't approach fallen suspects. My capture order is rescinded."

Raton scanned the terrain with a pair of binoculars. Wind blew through the pass, setting the thin grass rustling. His hair blew into his eyes and he shivered. He blew in his hands to warm them, then scurried around the boulder, trying to get a better view.

Another set of flashes erupted in the distance followed by a third set. No reports followed either one.

"I think I see something," called Li Chang, about twenty yards in front of him.

Raton turned her direction. She stood and aimed, but a hepler beam knocked her backwards, sprawled across a rocky outcropping. Her open eyes glared at Raton in silent accusation.

The sheriff crept through the brush toward her position. A shimmering form bobbed near a cluster of rocks just ahead. Raton took aim and squeezed the trigger. The figure dropped down, flattening the tall grass.

The sheriff scrambled up the slope toward the person, who pulled themselves to their feet. Apparently he'd only struck a glancing blow. Up close, he could make out the figure's female form. He covered her with his hepler pistol. She stood upright and pulled the hood from her suit -- Mary Hill.

She lifted her hepler pistol and aimed it at Raton. "Manuel, why are you doing this? Don't you see we could work together and make Sufiro great? Don't you see the potential wealth? Work with me Manuel. There's power in unity." Her chin quivered and her hepler pistol trembled.

Manuel nudged the gun's power to maximum with his thumb. "Power for whom?"

The Valley of No Return

Edward J. McFadden III

"And so, perhaps, the truth winds somewhere between the road to Glastonbury, Isle of the Priests, and the road to Avalon, lost forever in the mists of the Summer Sea."

— *Marion Zimmer Bradley, The Mists of Avalon*

An Expected Chance Meeting

White smoke leaked from the dragon's mouth, its piercing red eyes shifting back and forth like searchlights. Jimmy was half in the bag and almost believed the eyes hunted for him. The beast's great jaws opened with a roar and fire scorched the gray rocks and lit the night sky. Flames reflected in the lake before him, and the heat of the serpent's breath pushed across the water.

Castle ramparts stood tall in the background, lit in blue and red, and a lone figure clad in gray-blue robes stood on the far shore of the lake holding a staff of gold. Another stream of fire erupted from the dragon's mouth as it swept its head in a wide arc, spreading flames. Jimmy Paige, who had been born Morgan Pendleton, wanted to step away from the heat, but held his ground. Screams and cheers rose in a tumult, but he didn't take his eyes off the huge reptile.

The animatronic dragon outside the Excalibur Hotel and Casino in Las Vegas looked more realistic at night, but now with the spectacle done for an hour there'd be a run on the prime casino chairs and he'd have to hightail it to the MGM Grand or New York, New York. He couldn't hit the Excalibur's main casino because Abigale would be there and he didn't want her to see him yet. Tonight was his last night of fun before he had to go to work, and work is what Abigale Janson would be.

The crowd dispersed fast, and Jimmy suppressed a chuckle. Many of the women wore medieval costumes, and the men period battle dress or court clothes. The Excalibur was hosting an Avalon Quest role playing game convention. He still couldn't believe grownups did this kind of thing. Sure, he understood kids doing it, but forty-year-old men? It sometimes made him question his place in this crazy world. He scraped for everything he had, and these numb-nuts danced around pretending to be fools, but then he remembered why he was in Vegas. Plenty of goats. Easy marks.

He went to the MGM and planted himself at a hundred-dollar table of Texas Hold'em and preceded to lose four grand before an hour had past. He hit his stride after about six scotches, but had to take a break when two women complained to the dealer that he was harassing them. Apparently telling a woman she had a great rack and killer ass wasn't appropriate anymore. PC bullshit.

He stumbled out onto the strip and stared across the street at the gray castle with blue and red ramparts. As a castle the thing looked pitiful, but he had to admit the dinner jousting show wasn't bad. He stood on the sidewalk and people flowed around him as though he were a rock in a stream; unyielding, hard, and unmovable. A blonde with big ruby lips and inflated breasts stopped next to him and looked him up and down, obviously unimpressed. Her heels were stilts, her blouse slit to her bellybutton, and her skirt was so short Jimmy thought he glimpsed the landing strip.

"Need a date, sweetie?" Her voice gravel and smoke.

He turned up his nose and looked away in disgust. He wouldn't spend his hard earned winnings on an old bald tire. Good thing he was a character actor and had extensive experience playing a drunk. It was his specialty. The world spun as millions of lights lit the disco ball that is Las Vegas at night. A warm breeze carried the scent of rot and hibiscus, and Jimmy felt the pull of sleep. Time to get some rest, review his notes, and get his game face on.

The next day Jimmy sat in on an afternoon Avalon Quest panel, though he didn't understand what the hell they were talking about. Points for this, deduct points for that, arguments about whether traditional rules should be used, or video game rules, and which version. From what Jimmy could gather, the old timers liked the traditional Dungeons and Dragons format, while the young bucks preferred the iPad and cellphone apps, which were similar to Pokémon Go and let the gamer interact with their physical environment while playing Avalon Quest.

He didn't take his eyes off Abigale as she left the panel and planted herself in front of a slot machine in the Excalibur's main casino. She glanced around several times as though she sensed him watching her. A master of reflective surfaces, Jimmy could stare at a goat for hours and they wouldn't notice because he'd never look directly at them.

Jimmy wore tight jeans and a white Fabio pirate shirt, which he'd carefully selected after thirty seconds of research on the internet. He'd taken off his snake skin boots because Abigale was a member of PETA, and they'd been replaced with sandals. He had his hair pulled back in a ponytail and wore blue tinted steampunk glasses. Not his usual look.

Abigale's slot machine trumpeted, and she wiggled up and down on her stool. She wore a purple and white sundress that hid her weight well, but her plastic sandals broke the illusion. A tangled coil of long blonde hair sat atop her head, and a pencil stuck from the mound like a pitchfork from a pile of hay. Even Abigale's smile looked broken. Half her face sagged, and the other lifted, her face confused and out of sync.

Time to make the approach.

"My lady," Jimmy said. He swept his right hand across his chest with a flourish as he bent the knee. Abigale giggled. "My handle is Lan. May I buy my lady some refreshment?"

Abigale giggled again and her jowls jiggled.

"Lan? For Lancelot?" she said.

"Yes, my lady." The name was a risk because Lancelot wasn't part of the original King Arthur legends but was added later. This might cause purists to question him, but he'd be OK because all Arthur related ethos were fair game in Avalon Quest.

"My handle is Gwen." She stared at him expectantly. "For Guinevere."

"Fate, then, has brought us together," Jimmy said. Fate, internet research, and preparation.

He'd get Abigale to buy his ticket to London, then to Paris, and during their travels he'd milk her bank accounts and credit cards, get her email password, Social Security number, every valuable piece of data that made Abigale Janson who she was. Then when her bank account was dry and her credit cards maxed, he'd give her the slip in Paimpont Forest next to the pile of rocks they called Merlin's Grave.

Did that make him a shit? Yup. When he left Abigale crying, he'd slink off and meet a few colleagues in Paris for a nice six month run of The Down-On-His-Luck American, one of his favorite cons. After he'd eaten all the cheese he could handle and gotten drunk on every French wine, he'd blow on to the next town. Abigale would be fine. She was a resourceful girl. She'd get home, and she'd have a valuable lesson as a memory of her real Avalon quest.

Ignorance is Bliss

Abigale let her head sink into the pillow as Jimmy rolled off her. They lay on the sweat-soaked sheets, panting. He was the first guy she'd been with since high school, and she hadn't worked out so hard since a gym incident several years back that put her in the hospital with a treadmill burn across her face. Even though he did much of the work, she was exhausted. They'd been holed up in her room for three days, and she was missing the convention and hadn't seen her Avalon Quest friends.

The convention and Vegas were an attempt at having a life that didn't involve work or serving someone else's needs, and this time she'd been lucky. Jimmy seemed like a wonderful man, though she hardly knew him. Despite this, they'd already established an undeniable connection. They liked all the same things, and he had a thing for women her size. He appeared honest and open, and though she understood their relationship was nothing more than a ripple in his sea, she'd become determined to enjoy every minute. But she wasn't stupid. She understood why she and others like her gravitated to large scale social simulations like Avalon Quest. AQ let her escape a real world that didn't treat her very well. In AQ she was Guinevere. In real life she was nothing. No man. No house. Barely a car. She'd socked away a few bucks for the future, but recently that future seemed to recede into the distance.

"Camelot isn't built on magic, but on people, on their faith," Jimmy said.

"Merlin to Arthur on the Camelot TV show," she said as she kissed his neck. "You know your stuff."

"In more ways than one."

"Do you ever wish you could go to Avalon? Live there away from all this," she said.

"Every day and there are those who think it's possible," Jimmy said.

"Who thinks it's possible?"

"Historians, grail theorists, and half of the people in this hotel," he said. "Camelot and Avalon are based on real places and real events. Avalon can be found. Of that I have no doubts. How? That I don't know."

"You really believe," she said. "I wish I could."

"I see your cross. You go to church? Believe in a god you've never seen? A god that left no evidence he existed. Why is believing in Avalon any different from that? I'd argue Avalon has significantly more evidence to prove its existence," he said.

"The Vatican might have something to say about that."

"They always do," he said. "You up for room service?"

Jimmy got up and reached for his pants. He'd pulled out his credit card several times when they'd called for food and booze, but she'd insisted on paying. He was her guest and based on their conversations she knew he had little money. As he pulled his jeans off a chair back something flew from a pocket and sailed across the room. A gold chain with an elaborate medallion hanging from it landed on the carpet next to the bed. She stared at it a moment, then looked to Jimmy.

"An old family heirloom," he said, rushing forward and plucking it off the floor and stuffing it back into his jeans. Silence filled the room, this new unknown testing their sprouting relationship. He'd talk about it when he was ready. He'd already told her so much about his life she wondered how a piece of jewelry could make him so uncomfortable.

"I didn't steal it if that's what you're thinking," he said.

"I wasn't thinking that."

He said nothing.

"I admit I'm curious," she said.

"It's my most valuable possession. Nobody knows I have it. If I show you, you can't tell a soul. Nobody. Agreed?"

She nodded, and he brought out the chain, a large flat pendant hanging from it. Abigale reached out and cupped the medallion made of clear stone, studying its smooth surface. Gold lines and gems of red and blue marked the flat surface. It looked like a crude map. On the back two lions faced each other, their mighty wings splayed open.

"Someone in your family had this?" Abigale asked.

"No, that's my cover story."

"Why did you lie?"

"Because the truth is crazy," he said.

"So where *did* you get it?"

"At an estate sale. It's very valuable. Relics of Avalon always are," he said.

"Avalon," she said. Her heart raced, and sweat rolled down her back.

"Allegedly the medallion shows the way to Avalon, but it doesn't say where to start," he said. "So it's not much use."

"Are you sure it's real? Has it been carbon dated?" She loved a good fantasy as much as the next girl, but she wouldn't be made the fool.

"There's a guy in London, Phineas. Works at Oxford in the Archology department. I sent him pictures, and he says he needs to see it himself. Hold it in his hands. I think the medallion shows a map of *Val sans Retour*."

"The Valley of No Return?" she said. *Val sans Retour* was legendary in the Avalon Quest community. It was known as an enchanted land where the powerful sorceress Morgan le Fay imprisoned her lovers.

"So the prophets say, and somewhere therein lies a gateway to Avalon," he said.

Abigale's stomach burned as nausea seeped through her, and her head throbbed. This couldn't be possible, but what did she have to lose? This could be her adventure. She'd dreamed of going to Narnia as a child, and now this gorgeous man wanted to help her find Avalon. Why should she pass it up? To that, the rational portion of her brain said something didn't add up, but Abigale kicked reason to the curb. "We should go see Phineas," she said.

"That would take money I don't have," Jimmy said.

"I've got money," she said. "Twenty-three thousand four hundred and eighty-six clams. No idea how many pounds that converts to."

"How much could two tickets to London be? Thousand? Two, tops," Jimmy said.

"Each," she said.

"Like I said, I don't have the cash. It might be a wild goose chase, anyway. I can't find anything on the Net about this thing. For all I know it's costume jewelry made by a ten-year-old Korean kid in Busan."

"What's the worst that can happen? We spend a few days together in London instead of Vegas?" Abigale said.

"Still, I'm not comfortable with you paying for me. We've just meet, and I'm sure you took a long time to save that much money."

"I insist."

"I'll pay you back."

She leaned across him and grabbed her laptop. Ten minutes later she had them booked on a morning flight to London. Thankfully, she always carried her passport in case she needed a second form of official photo ID.

Jimmy kissed her shoulders and watched as she typed.

The Convincer

Jimmy couldn't believe his good fortune. The trusting butter face had already unknowingly revealed her credit card pin and bank account number, and when she'd gone to the bathroom on the plane he went through her carryon and discovered a small piece of paper tucked into a fold in her makeup case containing all her passcodes. Once he had her email information, he'd dig into her family, and by the time their little quest crashed and burned he'd have everything he needed to strip her, and those she loved, clean of every liquid asset they had, as well as leaving a debt behind like a steaming turd.

They'd landed at Heathrow without incident, and as they headed to the hotel, she hung on him and kissed his neck. Once powder-puffs got a taste, they became ravenous. An Everest of a woman, climbing Abigale multiple times a day was wearing on him. He tried to get his occasional partner, Stubby Nellrow, to meet them as soon as they arrived so they could skip stopping at the hotel, but Stubby claimed to be tied up in a card game and wouldn't be able to meet them until dinner. Jimmy guessed it had nothing to do with his old friend wanting a free meal. They'd worked together many times and Stubby was experienced at playing a college professor. He had the clothes, and in this case he could utilize his British accent, which was excellent.

Stubby, playing his favorite character Dr. Phineas Neighbors, Professor of Archology at Oxford, would authenticate the pendant and help convince Abigale the map did indeed show the path to Avalon. If Abigale attempted to verify his credentials she would find the name Phineas Neighbors on the faculty list at Oxford. Stubby even looked like the former SAS Captain.

When they got to the hotel, he summited Mt. Abigale, and then they got cleaned up and headed over to the Mayflower Pub in Rotherhithe. Two large wood placards with the pub's name and a large sailing ship on them marked the establishment as the oldest pub on the River Thames. There was outside seating along the river where the original Mayflower ship had been moored. When Abigale questioned him about why they weren't meeting Phineas at his office, he said meetings of this type happened outside the legitimate halls of academia.

Phineas waited alone outside on a bench overlooking the Thames holding a tall glass of dark beer. His friend's cheeks were red, and his nose glowed. It was going to be a long night.

"Doc, this is my friend, Abigale."

He took her hand and kissed it. "A pleasure. Can they get you something?" Phineas asked.

Jimmy looked at Abigale, who shrugged.

"Two of those would work just fine," Jimmy said, pointing at Phineas' beer.

Phineas whistled, waved his hand and lifted two fingers.

The Thames gurgled as it rushed past them, its dark waters reeking of rotten fish. The sun was falling, and a bell tolled in the distance.

"Thank you for agreeing to meet with us. I understand your time is precious," Jimmy said, barely containing his laughter. Stubby hadn't graduated high school, and couldn't spell Thames, but when it came to bullshit, he was a master.

"Think nothing of it. There isn't much I won't do for a free supper.

Plus, I'm interested in seeing this artifact myself," Phineas said.

"You're an expert in the Arthur legends?" Abigale asked.

This line of questioning worried Jimmy. Stubby had studied-up for his part, but he didn't know a fraction of what Abigale did.

"I study antiquities of all types, but Avalon doesn't exist from the scientific community's perspective, so I keep those interests to myself. That's why we're here instead of at Oxford," Phineas said.

Abigale said nothing.

"So, let's see it."

With practiced ease Jimmy pulled out the necklace he'd bought from a street vendor in LA. It was a crude map of an island off Mexico. He handed it over to Phineas, who made a show of accepting it delicately.

"Yes, you can almost feel its history." He examined the pendant closely, turning it over several times in his hand. "This is most certainly Sir Gawain's amulet, given to him by Arthur so he could always find his way home to Avalon."

The barmaid brought their beers and Jimmy and Abigale sat beside Phineas who slammed the rest of his and put the glass down. He held out his open palm, and the medallion lay therein.

"See this large green gemstone here?" Phineas said.

They nodded.

"That is Merlin's grave. It is said if one stands by Merlin's tomb when the mist slithers across the land and the air burns your lungs Avalon will reveal itself by the light of the Moon above the Summer Sea, but only those who are deemed worthy may take the final steps."

"What does the grave look like?" Abigale said.

"Here," Phineas said. He fumbled in his bag and brought forth an iPad, tapped at it for a few seconds, and handed to her. It displayed a picture of a huge boulder broken in two pieces of disproportionate sizes. Sunlight streamed through gap between the stones, which sat within a circle of smaller rocks surrounded by a forest.

"We still don't know what we're supposed to do," Jimmy said. He imitated Brando. No, Pacino.

"But I do," Phineas said.

"Well?" Abigale said. "Are you going to tell us?"

"That information is worth something to you?"

"How much?" Jimmy said.

"Five thousand," Phineas said. "I have an unauthorized dig I need funded."

Jimmy was genuinely appalled. "We'll give you a thousand pounds. Now spit it out."

"*Val sans Retour* can be found in the modern day forest of Paimpont in northern France. Bring the medallion to Merlin's grave when the moon passes across the sky and Avalon will be revealed to you," Phineas said.

He was so good Jimmy almost bought the story. *Almost*. Phineas' bullshit struck a chord with Abigale, though. Her wide eyes and dropped jaw only extenuated her common face, and his chest hurt from holding in laughter.

"Can we eat? I'm starved," Jimmy said.

A Leap of Faith

Abigale was having the time of her life jet-setting around the world. If nothing else, she'd have a great story to tell the ladies back at work. Probably nobody would believe her, and she had to admit the last four days had been unbelievable. She was falling for Jimmy in a major way, but she couldn't shake the feeling he was using her. They acted like they'd been a couple for years, yet all she knew about him was what he'd told her. She'd spent two hours searching the web via her phone looking for any information about Jimmy Paige, and found nothing. Not a single picture. No employment history. Nothing. Like he'd just been born. When she'd Googled her own name, a series of images and links appeared showing her work ID photo, pictures and articles she'd posted on social media, and her ranking and character description in Avalon Quest, the picture of her avatar Guinevere1919 prominently displayed.

What was she really risking? It cost 925,00€ to get them from London to Paris, then another 430,00€ for the car rental, plus $934 to get to London. What was her exposure? If he meant to kidnap or hurt her, he'd had ample opportunity along the way, so her misgivings melted away. Perhaps she'd been lucky for the first time in her life. Maybe Jimmy was exactly what he claimed to be; an out of work carpenter who bounced from job to job, city to city, with no real home base, and who loved playing Avalon Quest and getting lost in his fantasies. Did it matter? If it did, did she care?

They barreled southeast on A11, cutting through the French countryside. Tall, dense trees lined the road, and beyond them fields of grapes and sugar beets stretched in uneven grids to the horizon. The Renault Twingo they'd packed themselves into vibrated and shimmied like it might come apart, but it was cheap and got good gas mileage. When they reached Rennes they'd head east to Paimpont Forest.

The sky turned overcast, the gray of an oncoming storm filling the horizon. They had the windows cracked, and the air smelt of flowers and petrol. The weather was similar to back home in Chicago, where spring had sprung.

"You OK," he said.

"Why do you ask?" Abigale said.

"You haven't said a word in twenty minutes and usually you're Chatty Kathy," Jimmy said.

"Actually, I'm not," she said.

He said nothing.

"I guess that's what's wrong. You act like you know me, but you don't." What she didn't say was that when you do get to know me, you won't want to be around me anymore.

"That's the best part of our relationship," he said. He smiled at her, his perfect teeth and gleaming blue eyes pulling her in. "We don't have all the baggage everyone else does. We can be new people with each other. The people we want to be, free of what the world has foisted upon us."

She loved when he said things like that. To her it sounded like poetry. She smiled. "Thank you. For everything."

He took her hand and kissed it, and as she stared at the road before her energy zapped the tips of her fingers and toes. Life coursed in her veins again. She'd fallen into such a deep rut that emerging from it felt like being reborn.

"Everything is going to change for us now. I'm sure it will," Jimmy said.

"You really think we'll be able to get to Avalon? This has been fun, but I don't believe you actually think this quest is real," she said. "What will change? We'll see Merlin's grave. So what? I still need to be back at work Monday, and you'll still move on to your next fling." She wished she hadn't said it, but her heart ached with imagined betrayal.

He looked crushed and stared at the floor, saying nothing. He reached into his pocket and brought forth the medallion. "Stop the car."

"What?"

"Stop the car." Jimmy opened the passenger door, and air rushed into the go-cart of cart like a hurricane.

Abigale stomped on the brake and pulled the Renault to the shoulder. "What is it?"

Jimmy got out of the car and walked toward the exit ahead. She'd done it again, pushed away someone trying to care for her. This is what she did. She'd go through all the hard parts and then just as smooth seas approached she'd turn on the wave machine. He'd been a perfect gentleman, and loved her in ways no one ever had, and yet she attacked and alienated him. She was self-destructive and had been her entire life despite her attempts at change.

She rolled down the passenger window and inched the car forward along the shoulder. Cars tore past them, punctuated with gaps of silence where an occasional cow or songbird would compete to be heard.

"I'm sorry. Get back in the car. Please," she said. "It's hard for me."

He stopped walking, and she brought the Renault to a halt.

"I meant nothing by it. But…" Words failed her.

"That's why I lied. I told you it was crazy. *You* forced me to tell you," he said.

That was true. "Get in."

He sighed and got back in the car.

"I'm sorry. I really like you, but what do you expect to find?"

"Something amazing," he said.

They drove on in silence, and the hours slipped away. It was 1 PM when they arrived in Paimpont, and everything had shut down for midday meal. They had water, wine, and snacks, though Jimmy had already drank half the wine. They past a building with a red roof and an empty parking lot, then veered left. Forest filled in both sides of the lane, a thin shoulder of patchy grass all that separated the road from the thick vegetation. A flat green field opened on the left.

Abigale pulled over and killed the engine.

"Let's go find Merlin's grave," Jimmy said.

Thunder crackled in the distance, and the day turned gray and hazy. Abigale locked the car and Jimmy tied the bag of food and beverages to his wrist and they headed off into the woods.

The Breath of the Dragon

The guide map Abigale picked up at the petrol station showed two red lines leading from the parking area to Merlin's grave. One followed a gentle path through the forest alongside a river, and the other cut across the rocky crags on the other side of the stream. They'd chosen the easier route, and the hiking wasn't strenuous, though they stopped to rest several times. Abigale panted and sucked air, and Jimmy became concerned. If she died out here, he'd have to call the police and get involved with the details of why they were here. He'd lose his entire score. A score that wasn't big enough to risk jail.

If he didn't call the cops and left her body it would be discovered. They'd identify her and discover Las Vegas was her last known location. Then they'd track her movements via her credit card account and trace their every step. They'd be pictures and videos of them together. All that equaled a lifetime of worry for Jimmy.

"Take a break, Abigale. There's no rush." You human manatee.

Leaves colored the ground bronze, and a faint mist snaked around the thin beech trees. The soothing sound of water rushing over stones echoed over the scant hills and through the forest. Legend said the tree where Morgan le Fay imprisoned Merlin was hidden within these woods along with its secrets, and those who attempted to find it did so at their own peril. Much of the forest had been destroyed by fire in the seventies, and Jimmy saw the great gilded tree commemorating the forests revival at the edge of the wood.

After hiking another mile they came to the Fairy Lake, which lapped against stones that marked its border. The lake stretched into the distance, disappearing into a tangle of oak trees.

"The Lady of the Lake is said to have appeared here, but not for what most people think. This lake has nothing to do with Excalibur," he said. "Vivian comes wither she wills, where the wind…" Jimmy looked away. What the hell was he doing? The ruse was over, and he should slip away and use the car to get to Paris, and along the way make the calls to execute the final fleecing of Abigale Janson. He didn't need to deal with this bullshit any longer.

"Are you OK?" she said.

He said nothing.

"Come on, there's something through the trees ahead."

Jimmy chuckled and followed. A piece of him was curious about the grave after the research he'd done. A clearing opened ahead, and as the day grew darker, the outline of short wooden fence cut through the trees. Fog settled over the forest and the air grew cold. Whispers floated on the breeze, and Jimmy jerked his head around looking for the source of the voices. He pulled a pint of Bastille whiskey from his jacket pocket and took a pull. The velvety brown liquor provided the familiar calming burn, and he closed his eyes and breathed deep.

Mist snaked across the clearing and the broken stone that marked Merlin's grave sat in its center surrounded by smaller stones. A deformed tree that had been pruned incorrectly stuck from the ground behind the largest rock, its broad branches spreading out over the gravestone. A short wooden fence surrounded part of the glade, but there was no plaque or official marking. Abigale stepped forward in a trance, fully embracing the fantasy. In that instant her face looked pretty, then she shifted her weight, and Jimmy saw her cankles and winced.

"What brings thee, traveler?"

Jimmy spun to find a man with a tight gray beard dressed in black robes that billowed around him in the mist. Jimmy blinked, and the man disappeared, but his voice carried in the fog. "Is it Annwan you seek? Paradise of our fathers?"

The man returned. He held a wooden staff with a crystal globe atop it, and his image shimmered in and out of existence. Mist curled around the man's body like a snake, distorting his facial features. Minutes passed, and the man said, "So? Are you ready to own up to your sins? Proclaim yourself clean and free of malice?"

"What's Annwan?" Jimmy said. He sensed Abigale watching him.

"Who are you talking to?" she said.

"I… I don't know," he sputtered.

"Sure you do," the apparition said. "I am Myrddin, but go by many names. You may call me Merlin."

"Merlin," Jimmy repeated.

"Merlin? What about him?" Abigale said.

Then Abigale wasn't there.

Jimmy stood alone in an open field filled with tall grass, and the man who called himself Merlin stood before him. There was no sound, not even the gentle push of the wind.

"Where am I?" Jimmy said.

"The Otherworld, where you must prove yourself true," Merlin said.

"But… I…"

"Only then can you visit the true Annwan," the wizard said.

"But I seek Avalon." Jimmy heard himself say, but he hadn't wanted to speak. This was a con. A joke. What the hell was he saying?

Merlin laughed. "I see. That is why my lady holds Sir Gawain's amulet?"

"Yes."

"Let us see," Merlin said. In a foreign tongue he recited an incantation that chilled Jimmy to the core, and as Merlin spoke thick mists encircled them, whispering and prodding, searching for weakness. Jimmy's head hurt, and it felt like a million fire ants gnawed on his brain, burrowing in and setting up camp.

Images of Jimmy's life replayed in the mist before him. All the cons. All the people he'd stolen from and hurt. They all stared out from the fog, eyes hard and faces angry. The woman from Topeka gave him the finger, and the dwarf he'd pulled the Little Person Lawsuit scam on pounded his miniature fist into his tiny hand. One by one the people he'd robbed turned their backs on him, yet he felt no guilt. Fools and their money and all that rot.

"Did you wrong them?" Merlin asked.

Jimmy considered this. If he told the truth the wizard might kill him, but wouldn't Merlin know if he lied? Jimmy smiled because Merlin couldn't possibly know how he felt about lying.

"Yes," Jimmy said. "I wronged them, though I didn't mean it and I'm sorry." He did, and he wasn't.

"You have answered wrongly, Morgan Pendleton," Merlin said. "Uther's blood has grown sour in you."

Pain pierced Jimmy's chest, and his ribs cracked and burst through his skin. Blood poured from his mouth as the mist engulfed him, the sound of Merlin's laughter rising above the ringing in his ears.

To Come Undone

A gust of wind swirled the mist and Jimmy vanished. Abigale swiped at the fog, trying to clear it away, but it was like soup. A high pitched hum echoed through the forest and got louder and louder until it hurt her ears. Then with an inrush of air the mists were sucked away, and Abigale grew dizzy. The trees spun, and the ground trembled beneath her feet.

Jimmy lay on the ground before her, a tree limb impaled in his chest, blood covered shards of wood sticking from the end of the branch like gristle. Jimmy's bulging eyes were open in death, and blood dripped from his nose and was thick upon his chin. His mouth hung open, his tongue lolling out like a dead slug.

She fell to her knees, and the air rushed from her lungs. Gasping and sucking for breath she tried not to pass out. The world spun, tiny stars firing like a million lightening bugs swarming around her head. Mist engulfed her, and when it cleared a man in black robes stood before her.

Abigale steadied herself as she stared up at the man. If not for the short cropped beard and hooked nose, she thought he looked like a happy Voldemort. What was happening? She looked down at Jimmy's dead form and panic filled her again. Tears leaked from her eyes and her stomach burned.

"Cry not, my love. Rest in the breath of the dragon. Let it soothe you. Calm your angst."

"Merlin?"

He nodded.

"What happened to Jimmy?" she said.

"He got what he deserved," Merlin said.

"Says who? Jimmy was a…"

"Swine. A trickster. A seller of snake oil. A thief. He was robbing you. Playing you for the fool."

Abigale felt faint. She'd known. Even as she mentally railed against what Merlin said she knew he spoke the truth. She had always known, but like an abused person unable to accept their reality Abigale's desire made one final plea. "All this was my idea. I…"

"That's what deceivers do," Merlin said. "He planned to steal everything you have."

"So you killed him?" Abigale said.

"The dragon passes justice on those who enter his domain." Merlin turned away from her. "I do not choose what the dragon does. I am but a servant, as we all are."

Everything faded, the mist dissipating. Abigale saw stars poking through the clouds. Night had fallen. How long had she been standing there? Fear paralyzed her.

"Are you happy with thy self? The life thee leads?" Merlin said.

Abigale hesitated.

"Consider wisely. Much depends on your answer."

Abigale's eyes went wide and her mouth fell open a crack.

"Take your time. I've got eons," Merlin said, as the remaining mist gathered and engulfed him. He vanished from view and then reappeared as this mist spiraled upward.

Abigale wasn't happy with her life. Not even close. She despised herself. Always had. "No," she said. "I'm not happy with myself at all."

"When you've changed that, make your quest again and perhaps the dragon will alter your destiny. May I see the amulet?" Merlin said.

She handed it to him.

Merlin turned it over in his hand, examining it. He looked up at Abigale and smiled, then his face turned dark and she gasped.

A partially destroyed castle floated in the clouds above the trees, many of its ramparts crumbling while others stood tall. Sections of the portcullis gleamed in the starlight, while other parts were rusted and bent.

One side of the great double wooden gate was cracked and hung open, the other pristine and sturdy. Parts of the keep walls had collapsed, leaving piles of broken brick next to portions that stood strong and clean. Large torches marked the castle's highest tower, but Abigale saw the remains of a larger tower, its top gone. Some of the castle windows were lit, and the sounds of merrymaking floated through the open drapery. Darkness deeper than the blackest night filled many of the windows, pale white faces looking out on the clouds.

"Avalon?" Abigale said.

Merlin nodded and gave her back the medallion.

"What happened… I mean, what *is* happening to it?"

"Avalon is but a reflection of your world. What it is, was, and what it can be," he said.

"You mean…" She didn't want to say it for fear of making it real.

The mists returned, swaddling her in a cold embrace. Whispers filled her mind, a thousand voices all pleading for her to do something different. A gust of wind tore through the glad and blew away the clouds and Avalon was gone.

So was Merlin.

Abigale stood alone in the clearing before Merlin's grave, Jimmy's dead body on the ground before her. The night had cleared, the storm gone. Moonlight filled the forest, but there were no signs of Merlin, or Avalon. Like so many before her, she had caught but a fading glimpse, but was unworthy, at least for now, of final passage.

She'd be back someday.

King Arthur in a Yankee Court

Robert E. Waters

Near the River Camlann, 537 AD

Lines of fire streaked the sky, and the men below, marching through the vast, bloody field, looked heavenward in fear of where that fire had come. Their fears were confirmed, as they crested the hill and saw the line of trebuchet hurling balls of flame against the walls behind them. The men had come out from behind the protection of those sturdy walls on the order of their commander, who knew what the appearance of those engines of war meant.

Mordred, usurper of the throne, had arrived.

King Arthur, proudly wearing the crest of the Pendragon upon his breastplate, walked ahead of his men, stepping through a sea of broken bodies, Excalibur held high, his head higher.

"Step firm, lads," he shouted over the balls of fire crashing against the stone walls behind him. "Step firm!"

His courage gave them strength, and they followed him through the trampled, blood-soaked grass, toward Mordred's advancing lines.

Where was the filthy traitor? Arthur wondered. Somewhere down there, amidst those equally traitorous men who had once given their loyalty to the king. Arthur's time in France away from the throne had made Mordred bold and reckless. How dare he raise an army against the king, against his own father?

A wall of arrows met Arthur's army as they martialed forward. Shields were raised to deflect the attack; Arthur felt the punch of a dozen shafts against his shield. He paused to receive the blow, cut off the shafts at the head with his sword, and then moved at the quick-step before another volley could be delivered. A quick step became a trot, and then a rush. Arthur cast his shield aside, raised Excalibur with both hands, and charged into the enemy line.

Walls of men struck one another with a deafening clamor of steel. Arthur hacked his way through man after man, wondering if he knew those he was killing. In the confusion of war, he did not know anymore which of his knights were his, which were Mordred's. Gawain. Geraint. Percival. Lamorak. Galahad. Lancelot. Who was friend? Who was foe?

Did it matter? In his heart, yes, but in his mind, his duty to country and to throne forced his focus forward, toward the center of the battle lines, where Mordred awaited.

And there he was, almost simple and non-descript amidst the push of men, hacking his way forward just like his father. It did not seem to Arthur that Mordred cared whom he stuck down, so long as his sword found flesh and drew blood. It was a weakness of the boy, to disregard life so readily, and Arthur intended to use that weakness against him, if it so pleased God.

Arthur stepped left to deflect a blow from a muddy farm boy with nothing but a spear as protection. The fear in the boy's eyes stayed Arthur's hand. Why kill an innocent boy simply because he happened to pick the wrong side of a fight? Arthur pushed the lad aside and kept moving forward.

Another kill, then another, until it seemed to Arthur that the tide of battle was shifting in his favor. More of his men were around him than the enemy. That was always a good sign. He was winning.

He deflected a sword stroke from his left, pushed the man back, and saw that it was Mordred. Blood caked the boy's face. There was a wildness in his eyes, a maniacal glee of battle that seemed to push him beyond his physical abilities. He was just a boy after all. One of skill, indeed, but a boy nonetheless, and one that had fallen under the spell of that sorceress Morgan le Fay.

"Stand down," Arthur said, holding firm the tiny spot of ground on which he stood. "You have a chance here, my son, to do the right thing. Abdicate the throne, and bring peace back to the realm. If you do, I promise to spare your life."

"The right thing for me to do, Father," Mordred said, "is to take your head."

The threat hurt more than Arthur was willing to admit. The notion that a son would dare kill his father. But Mordred meant it; Arthur could see the sincerity in the mad boy's face. So be it. He had given Mordred chance after chance to change.

"This is the last time that I shall give you quarter, my son. Stand down… or die."

The cackle from Mordred's mouth ran a chill down Arthur's spine. The boy lunged. Arthur deflected the attack, and over and over, their swords met. Thrust. Parry. Thrust… again and again, until both men were spent, exhausted. Arthur could see weakness in Mordred's face, as the boy tried keeping his assault in check. Then Arthur slipped and allowed Mordred to put a gash across his cheek as dead bodies continued to pile around them. Arthur made one last attempt to break Mordred's defense. He pushed the boy backward, and Mordred slipped and fell as his boot heel struck a discarded lobster-tail burgonet.

Arthur advanced, raised Excalibur above his head, howled his defiance, and brought it down toward Mordred's neck.

"Morgan!" Mordred screamed, holding his sword out like a pin as if to pierce Arthur's stomach. "Save me!"

Arthur ignored the boy's pitiful plea to the sorcerer. He swung his sword toward Mordred's head.

There was a flash of yellow light, as brilliant as the sun. Arthur closed his eyes to it, but swung the sword anyway.

When the flash was gone and he opened his eyes, he was no longer near the River Camlann, nor were there dead men on the ground, nor trebuchets, nor spears, pikes, or swords. He was in a room, a tavern perhaps, surrounded by strange people in strange clothing. And the severed head that lay on the wooden floor before him was not Mordred's, nor anyone that King Arthur knew.

The patrons of the tavern looked at him in silence for a moment, and then erupted in screams.

"Bailiff," Judge Williams said. "Call the case."

"The people versus Arthur Pendragon," the bailiff announced, "docket number 353."

"Bailiff, please produce the accused."

King Arthur was brought into the courtroom from the prisoner holding area. His ankles and wrists were bound in chains, and his royal battle gear had been replaced with a non-descript orange jumpsuit. He had been permitted to bathe to wash away all the blood of battle, but he was considered "hostile" and thus an armed officer of the court stood nearby, his odd fire weapon attached to his thick leather belt. Arthur kept his head high and proud as he was brought into the courtroom. His small shuffles made his chains jangle.

He was placed in front of the judge, and his defense lawyer, a man named Hinks whom he had just met but a few hours ago, stood beside him in a shiny black suit. The man smelled like a woman, all sweet with perfume and fancy lye. Arthur considered saying something, but he was interrupted by the judge.

"Who represents the defendant in this matter?" Judge Williams asked.

"Stewart Hinks, your Honor, standing in for the defense."

"Do you wish to waive the reading of the charges of the case?"

"No," Arthur said before his "attorney" had a chance to answer. "I wish to know why I am being held against my will. This flowery-smelling man has made no sense…"

Judge Williams slammed her wooden hammer into her desk. "You are not permitted to speak at this time, sir. This is an arraignment. You will speak if I specifically ask you a question. Do you understand?"

Who was this woman that she should hold so much authority… and over the king no less? This was Morgan le Fay's doing, for sure. The judge was her puppet, and this was all an illusion. It had to be.

Arthur nodded. The judge continued. "I assume, then, from your client's outburst, that you wish to have the charges read."

Hinks sighed and nodded. "Yes, your honor. My client asks that the charges against him be read."

The judge turned to the Assistant District Attorney and said, "Please read the charges, sir."

Hinks had tried to explain to Arthur that this other man, the so-called Assistant District Attorney, would be in charge of trying to convict Arthur of his crime. But Arthur didn't understand a word of it. What crime is it in war to kill a man, especially one as vile as Mordred?

The Assistant District Attorney stepped forward, introduced himself, and then read the charges. "Your honor, in the manner of The People versus Arthur Pendragon, the accused has been charged with first degree murder of one Willis Kingston, on the night of September 15, 2017, in Applebee's Bar and Grill, 234…"

The man went on and on with all the menial details of the charges, including "aggravated assault" of three other patrons in the bar that night who tried to wrest Excalibur from Arthur's hands. Fools, every one! To try to take his sword in the midst of battle. They were easy to drop. And he had searched for Mordred all through the tavern that night, until the sheriff and his minions came and put a lightning bolt through him with some small hand device. That alone was proof that this was all Morgan le Fay's doing.

"Sir," the judge said, "do you understand the charges against you as they have been read?"

Arthur shook his head and refocused on the judge. "Yes, Your

Honor," he said, mimicking the address protocols his lawyer had explained. "But they are false. I did not kill this man that you claim. I was swinging for Mordred's head. This was a trick perpetrated by Morgan le Fay. She is guilty of this crime."

"Morgan…le Fay?" The judge asked, and Arthur could see a tiny smirk on her face. "And you are… Arthur Pendragon? King Arthur?"

Author nodded. "Yes, Your Honor. I am King Arthur, leader of the Knights of the Round Table, and ruler of Camelot."

He heard scattered laughter coming from those in the audience who had come to witness his arraignment. The judge put a stop to it with a light tap of her gavel. "Okay," she said, "that's enough. I take it that your plea, then, will be 'not guilty'?"

"Yes, your honor," Hinks said before Arthur had a chance to answer. "Not guilty by reason of insanity."

"Are you calling me insane, sir?" Arthur leaned away from his lawyer, taken aback. "I resent the implication, and I will have you know that I'm the only sane one in this room…"

"Order!" Judge Williams shouted, hitting her desk again with her gavel. "No more outbursts from you, sir, or I will hold you in contempt of court! Now…"

The judge continued with other tasks, asked other questions to both the defense attorney and the prosecution. Arthur stood there trying to keep his rage in check. If he had Excalibur with him, he'd…

"Bail will be set to one million," the judge finally said after much paper shuffling, "and I am further ordering that the defendant be given a psychological evaluation to determine if he is fit to stand trial. If so, then the case of the People versus Arthur Pendragon will be placed first on the trial docket, November 1, 2017. This arraignment has concluded."

Arthur was confused. "Wait… what did she say about bail? One million? Who has such money? And what is this psycho…psych evaluation she speaks of? I tell you, I am not insane. I am King Arthur, and I demand that my sword be given back to me and that I be allowed to finish with Mordred. You are all being tricked. You are all being manipulated by Morgan le Fay…"

But no one in the courtroom was listening, even his lawyer who was trying to calm him down. The bailiff and the security guard rushed Arthur, took control of him, and pulled him from the courtroom.

In Arthur's mind, everything was falling apart.

Merlin… Merlin… where are you?

No wallet. No social security card. No insurance card. No proof of identity whatsoever. Arthur Pendragon had come into this strange, loud, fast-paced world washed in the blood of his enemies, wearing only his battle armor and a sword, ranting about some deranged kid named Mordred and a witch named Morgan le Fay. If the situation were reversed, if someone from this world (like Judge Williams, for instance), had appeared on the battlefield with her gavel and in her robes, he too might have thought her mad. Arthur wasn't angry that these people did not believe his "wild story" about ladies in lakes, gallant knights of honor and dignity, power-hungry sons, and sorcerers that could kill with a touch. No. He was angry that he was made to waste time talking to a sniveling little cretin named Dr. Justin Bennett, with glass eyes hanging off his nose, scribbling furiously on a pad of parchment and mumbling, "Yes… yes… I see…"

His lawyer told him that there was nothing to fear from the psychological evaluation. The purpose of it being nothing more than to determine if Arthur was competent enough mentally to stand trial. Of course he was. He could have told them that. But they refused to take his word for it, and thus, here he was, being made to suffer through test after test to divine his personality, and cognitive and neurological characteristics. And somehow, when it was all viewed through the professional psychiatric lens of the man before him, his mental health would be established. Rubbish! But, that was how "the game was played," so said his lawyer, and thus Arthur played the game.

In truth, what he hated the most was speaking about Guinevere, about her and Lancelot, how his heart broke every time he thought of them together and how his spirit was crushed at Mordred's deceit. All Arthur ever wanted was to preside over a kind and just kingdom, one of truth and justice. And it had all fallen apart.

"If you had to do it all over again, Mr. Arthur Pendragon, would you?"

The question from the court psychologist surprised him. He'd never asked himself that question; probably because the answer to it was still waiting to be resolved on that battlefield.

"I don't know," he had answered. "Does a man ever get a chance to remake his life?"

The phycologist had no answer, of course. He never did, but surprisingly, he seemed to sympathize. There was a spark of kindness in the little man's eyes that made Arthur smile.

Three days later, Arthur was cleared to stand trial.

As Judge Williams said, the trial began on November 1st, and like at his arraignment, Arthur was hauled into the courtroom. But this time, there were many more citizens in attendance and "video cameras" to capture the proceedings. Though it had been explained to him what it was, he was afraid of television. What sorcery could project such tiny people through the sky and appear anywhere in the world? He wondered what Merlin would think of such a thing. The old man would probably die of heart failure were he to see all the wonders of this imaginary world that Arthur had been ruthlessly thrust into. *Where was Merlin now?* He wondered.

The trial began with the stories of several tavern patrons on the night that Arthur appeared. The sad account from the beheaded man's betrothed had the courtroom and the jury teary-eyed. Arthur himself couldn't deny that the woman was beside herself with grief at the loss of her love, and he sympathized with her, despite still holding to his innocence. When the court was shown security camera footage of Arthur appearing in a flash, and then cutting off Mr. Kingston's head with one stroke, a collective gasp spread across the room.

Okay, fine, I'm guilty. There was no denying it now. The tiny box with tiny people in it told the world the truth. He, Arthur Pendragon, was guilty of killing Willis Kingston in an Applebee's Bar & Grill. Oh, but what a wonderful kill it was!

Arthur couldn't help but marvel at the precision of his strike, the power of it, and the strong, sharp blade of Excalibur. Too bad it wasn't Mordred's head lolling about on the wooden floor afterwards.

His sword now lay before the court enclosed in a thick cardboard box marked *Exhibit A.* Arthur smiled, though he could not see Excalibur. Yet he was sure that Willis Kingston's blood was still in the fuller, dried black. Too bad the jury could not see such a marvelous sword and revel at its power.

His lawyer gave him a grim stare, and Arthur stopped smiling when he saw the jury looking at him as if he were mad.

When will I get the chance to tell my side of the story?

It was a question that rolled around in his mind, as person after person filed into the courtroom and gave their sworn testimony of the despicable, unconscionable thing he had done. By the time the prosecution rested, Arthur himself was convinced of his guilt.

There was no one who would stand for Arthur, save for himself. At first, his lawyer didn't want Arthur to take the stand, afraid that his client might incriminate himself. Hinks had called for a mistrial on the grounds that his client was insane, but since the court psychologist had cleared him to stand trial, Judge Williams ruled against it. And so…

"The defense may call its first witness," Judge Williams said.

Hinks rose, cleared his throat, and said, "The defense calls Arthur Pendragon to the stand."

Arthur stood. His shackles had been removed prior to entering the courtroom, due to the concern that his lawyer raised about their presence being prejudicial. Judge Williams allowed it but with a strict warning that if the accused made any aggressive move towards the exit, towards anyone in attendance, or the sword, they would be slapped right back on. The bailiff escorted him to the stand, and as he was taught, Arthur raised his right hand and swore that his testimony would be the truth, the whole truth, and nothing but the truth… so help him God.

"You may be seated."

Arthur sat and waited for the first question.

"Please state your name for the record," Hinks said, standing at their table.

Arthur cleared his throat. "My name is Arthur Pendragon, king of Camelot and leader of the Knights of the Round Table."

There were more than a few chuckles around the courtroom. Judge Williams used her gavel to bring order, and Hinks started asking his first question. But before he could finish it, a shaft struck him in the back. Then one struck the bailiff. Then one struck the prosecuting attorney.

The courtroom erupted into chaos.

Arthur understood chaos, so he instinctively dropped and rolled until he was secure behind Judge Williams's desk.

This move was a mistake.

Judge Williams flashed a wild smile at Arthur, her eyes now bloodshot and enraged. She pulled a dagger from beneath her robes and tried to stab Arthur in the chest. Another shaft hit her square in the side, and she fell on top of him.

Hands pulled him free.

"Doctor Justin?"

It was the psychologist who had cleared him for trial. "No time to discuss it now," the man said, pulling Arthur away from Judge Williams's bleeding corpse. "We have to go."

Arthur stood and could now see the madness in the courtroom.

Both sides of the argument were fighting each other, and seeming innocents in the audience were now wielding blades and clubs and purses and walking canes and anything else they could get their hands on. Arthur took a second to marvel at the fight. He could not believe what he was seeing.

"Come!" Justin barked. "We have to get you out of here!"

"Wait!" Arthur said, resisting Justin's yank towards the door leading to the prisoner holding area. "I go nowhere without my sword."

There it lay, ignored, still enclosed in the cardboard box. Arthur dodged an attempt by a juror to take him down. He grabbed Excalibur through a hail of arrow and gunfire, then slipped back behind the judge's desk. "There's a devil to pay!"

"Indeed," said Justin, "and there'll be Merlin to pay if we don't get you out of here."

"Merlin?" The name brought joy to Arthur's beating heart. "I knew he'd rescue me."

"Yeah," Justin said, rolling his eyes. "He's doing all the heavy lifting. Come, there's no time to spare."

The fight to the prisoner holding area was savage. The prosecuting attorney, though wounded by an arrow, put up a strong defense of the doorway, as men and women under his command tried to halt Arthur's exodus. But men and women loyal to Justin's desire to get the king out fought just as forcefully, hacking and hammering their way towards the door, until the assistant DA went down with a bullet to the head. Arthur wielded Excalibur in his own defense, though it was still in the cardboard box and served more to bludgeon his foes than to kill them. That was enough, however, as with his help, the doorway defense collapsed, and he and Justin were able to escape through the holding area, down a long corridor, through an "Exit" door, and into the street of the city where an *Uber* driver waited.

Justin pulled a pistol on the poor driver and handed the boy a scratch of paper. "Take us here. Now!"

"Man, I just do this for extra money. I don't want to get invol…"

"Drive!"

All manner of foul verbiage came from the driver's mouth, but he pulled away from the curve and sped up as Justin kept his pistol trained on the boy's temple.

Arthur righted himself, took a deep breath, and freed *Excalibur* from the box. He smiled for the first time in a long while. What a marvelous sword! "Now, will you explain to me, young man, who you are, and what is going on?"

Justin kept his pistol trained on the driver and his eyes out the back window, but he took a deep breath and said, "My real name is John Albert Sydney Bennett, and I work for Merlin. We have to get you back to where you came through time, at the bar. There, Merlin will take you back to Camlann where you may finish the job."

"Who were all those people fighting in court?"

"Men and women loyal to both you and to Mordred," Justin cum John said. "The time is grim, my King. Since your disappearance, Camelot has fallen into darkness."

Arthur grunted. "I haven't been gone that long." He laid Excalibur over his lap.

"No, you don't understand. Time moves differently here than it does in our world. Here it has been but a few months. There, it has been years, and Camelot has suffered for it. You must go back to the battle, and you must kill Mordred."

Arthur considered. "I don't know."

John Albert was perplexed. "What do you mean, my Lord?"

"I mean… perhaps I shouldn't go back."

"I, I don't understand."

Arthur raised his arms as if he were preaching. "Look at this place. This city. This… world. I do not belong here, true. It would be the honorable thing to do to return to Camelot, to return to my people. But for what purpose?"

The expression on John Albert's face shifted between shock and confusion. "They are your people, and Camelot is your kingdom. It must be saved from Mordred and that ghastly witch…"

Arthur shrugged. "Why? Whether I sit on the throne or that despicable son of mine does, what does it matter, if this is the end result? Me, a king, being tried for murder and being judged by my peers: commoners sitting in judgement of a king and deciding if what I have done is a crime. Is that not the essence of Camelot? Is this not the end result that I have fought for all my life?"

John Albert seemed to consider that question. His eyes darted back and forth between the *Uber* driver and the back window. Finally, he shook his head. "No, my king, that argument is insufficient. If it is true, then all the more reason to return and do your duty. Let the future play out as it may; you are not the king of the future. Your charge is to the people of your kingdom, to keep them safe from tyrants like Mordred and Morgan le Fay. They are not living the *ideal* of Camelot that you have imparted to us all, and as long as that is the world *they* live in, Camelot is dead, both here and there. Go back, my king, and save your people. Save Camelot."

Arthur sighed and laid his head back. What to do… John Albert had a point. *I do not belong in this world. I should go back.* But maybe Arthur wasn't the person to save Camelot. Perhaps, years later, after Mordred died of old age, someone else would come along and take up the challenge that he, King Arthur, refused to take. If so, then his intransigence would leave hundreds, thousands to suffer at the hands of Mordred, of Morgan le Fay, and his legacy, his legend, would be nothing but a cautionary tale of a man… what? Too afraid? Too old? Too stubborn to do what was best, what was knightly? No, he had to go back. As much as he wanted to see the trial of a king be played out, regardless of the result, he had to go back. In the end, there was only one reason to do so that trumped all others: Merlin was holding open the door… and who was brave enough to piss off Merlin?

Arthur sat up straight, nodded. "Okay, let us go."

The back window was shattered by a bullet from a car in pursuit. John Albert returned fire while Arthur tried to protect the screaming driver from errant shots. Now police cars were in pursuit, and it looked as if the chase would come to a crashing end as a SWAT van moved to intercept, but the *Uber* driver swerved through oncoming traffic like a pro, and then ducked into an alley, where he sped up, spun to the right, and plowed his car into a pile of trash.

"Now get out!" The driver screamed. "Applebee's is a block on the right!"

Arthur grabbed Excalibur, opened the door, and gave the driver's shoulder a gentle pat. "Thank you, good sir. You're a credit to your profession."

Sirens blared everywhere, but their brisk jog to the bar and grill was uneventful. Arthur kept low as they made their way down the street. John Albert kept his hand on the king's back to help guide him forward, his pistol up and again fully loaded.

They reached the bar, and John Albert swung the door open, then cleared a path forward by throwing two shots into the ceiling. Patrons screamed and hit the floor.

"Must you be so dramatic?" Arthur asked, shielding his head from falling plaster.

"We have no time to waste," John Albert said, pushing a patron out of the way. "You have…" he looked at his watch "…thirty seconds. Now move!"

Before him and up near the bar, Arthur could see a shimmering line, like a clear gap. It undulated in place, hovering there in mid-air, like the waving arms of a dancer. It was pleasant to look at, and for a moment, he was captivated by its motion. Then John Albert pushed him forward, and Arthur reacted, reaffirming his grip on Excalibur and then moving up to the shimmer.

"What do I do now?" Arthur asked as he stared into a darkness that began to form in the middle of the shimmer. He thought he could see moving figures in the darkness.

"Raise your sword," John Albert said, "and when I tell you to, bring it down to strike a blow like you did that evening."

Yes, Arthur remembered now. He raised Excalibur high above his head. The tip nearly scraped the ceiling of the bar. Arthur held the hilt tight with both hands and waited.

Their pursuers had now reached the bar. They burst in, and John Albert began to empty his clip in their direction.

"Now?" Arthur asked.

"Wait!" More shots.

"NOW?" Arthur screamed.

Several shots, then, "NOW!"

Arthur gritted his teeth, took a step forward towards the shimmering gap, and swung his sword.

Behind him, John Albert took a shot in the gut. The impact of the shot drove him into Arthur's back and pushed the king through the gap.

Near the River Camlann, 537 AD

King Arthur fell forward through the time gap and felt the sting of Mordred's blade pierce his stomach as he swung Excalibur toward the boy's throat. The sword did its duty, slicing through meat and skin and bone. Mordred gurgled his last breath as Arthur fell at his son's side.

He dropped Excalibur and reached for the bleeding wound in his stomach. There was no one to save him. The chaos of battle raged around him, though it looked as though Mordred's men, now realizing their leader's death, were falling back. Arthur smiled through the pain and nodded.

His death did not matter. He had come back through time and had done his duty, like a man, like a king. And the future would play out in time. Not perfect, of course, for no future ever was. But at least now his own people would not suffer at the hands of the madman dead at his side. Their lives might not be perfect, and they might suffer from time to time regardless. But King Arthur was content. He had seen the future. He had seen a glimpse of Camelot, the idea of Camelot, playing out in a small, musty courtroom. And he was content.

Arthur rolled over, closed his eyes, and died.

Farewell. I am going a long way
With these thou sees — if indeed I go
(For all my mind is clouded with a doubt) —
To the island-valley of Avalon;
Where falls not hail, or rain, or any snow,
Nor ever wind blows loudly; but it lies
Deep-meadowed, happy, fair with orchard lawns
And bowery hollows crowned with summer sea,
Where I will heal me of my grievous wound.
Alfred, Lord Tennyson, the Idylls of the King

Here Lies Arthur, the Once and Future King
Thomas Malory, Le Morte d'Arthur

The Round Table

MICHAEL A. BLACK is the author of 29 books, the majority of which are in the mystery and thriller genres, although he has written in sci-fi, western, horror, and sports genres as well. A retired police officer with over 30 years' experience, he has done everything from patrol to investigating homicides to conducting numerous SWAT operations. Black was awarded the Cook County Medal of Merit in 2010. He is also the author of over 100 short stories and articles, and has written two novels with television star, Richard Belzer (*Homicide, Law & Order SVU*). Black is currently writing the Executioner series under the name Don Pendleton. His latest novel is *Blood Trails*.

D.C. (DEB) BROD is the author of the "Getting Even" caper series: *Getting Sassy*, *Getting Lucky*, and *Getting Taken*, and five mysteries in the Quint McCauley private detective series. Her short stories appear in numerous anthologies. She blogs on the writing life with two other writers. "3 Writers in a Café Every Friday" is featured on the *Chicago Tribune's* ChicagoNow.com site. She's currently is at work on a sequel to Heartstone, a contemporary Arthurian thriller. Deb lives in St. Charles, IL. For more information (and photos of her cats!) visit www.dcbrod.com.

AUSTIN S. CAMACHO is the author of six novels about Washington DC-based private eye Hannibal Jones, five in the Stark and O'Brien international adventure-thriller series, and the detective novel, Beyond Blue. His short stories have been featured in several anthologies including *Dying in a Winter Wonderland* – an Independent Mystery Booksellers Association Top Ten Bestseller for 2008. He is featured in the Edgar nominated African American Mystery Writers: A Historical and Thematic Study by Frankie Y. Bailey.

DAVE CASE retired from the Chicago Police Department in July 2017, having spent more than 31 years in the field. His highly-regarded novel, *Out of Cabrini*, reflected his many years working in that particular housing complex. He received many decorations for his meritorious service. Dave has a Master's from Northwestern University in Creative Writing, as well as numerous short stories and articles published. His fiction clearly exhibits his experience on the street and captures the intensity and ferocity of conflict only as one who has been there can.

RUSS COLCHAMIRO is the author of the rollicking space adventure, *Crossline*, the hilarious sci-fi backpacking series *Finders Keepers*, *Genius de Milo*, and *Astropalooza*, and is editor of the new anthology, *Love, Murder & Mayhem*, all with *Crazy 8 Press*. Russ lives in New Jersey with his wife, two children, and crazy dog, Simon. Russ has contributed to several other anthologies, and is now writing a top-secret project and a *Finders Keepers* spin-off series featuring his hard-boiled private eye Angela Hardwicke. For more on Russ' works, visit www.russcolchamiro.com, and follow him on Facebook, Twitter and Instagram @AuthorDudeRuss.

JOHN L. FRENCH is a crime scene supervisor with the Baltimore Police Department Crime Laboratory. As a break from the realities of his job he writes science fiction, pulp, horror, fantasy and, of course, crime fiction. His books include *The Devil of Harbor City*, *The Nightmare Strikes*, *Past Sins*, *Monsters Among Us*, *The Last Redhead*, and (with Patrick Thomas) *Rites of Passage*. He is the editor of *Mermaids 13: Tales from the Sea*; *Bad Cop, No Donut* (which features tales of police behaving badly) and *To Hell in a Fast Car* (which features stories of everyone else behaving badly).

JOHN G. HARTNESS is a teller of tales, a righter of wrong, defender of ladies' virtues, and some people call him Maurice, for he speaks of the pompatus of love. He is also the award-winning author of the urban fantasy series *The Black Knight Chronicles*, the Bubba the Monster Hunter comedic horror series, the Quincy Harker, Demon Hunter dark fantasy series, and many other projects. He is also a cast member of the role-playing podcast *Authors & Dragons*, where a group of comedy, fantasy, and horror writers play *Pathfinder*. Very poorly.

In 2016, John teamed up with a pair of other publishing industry ne'er-do-wells and founded Falstaff Books, a small press dedicated to publishing the best of genre fiction's "misfit toys."

In his copious free time John enjoys long walks on the beach, rescuing kittens from trees, and playing *Magic: the Gathering*.

EDWARD J. MCFADDEN III juggles a full-time career as a university administrator and teacher, with his writing aspirations. His novel *AWAKE* was recently published by Severed Press and his short story Doorways in Time appeared in *Shadows & Reflections*, a Roger Zelazny tribute anthology with an introduction by George R.R. Martin. His first published novel, *The Black Death of Babylon*, was published by Post Mortem Press. Ed is also the author/editor of: *Our Dying Land, HOAXERS, Anywhere But Here, Lucky 13, Jigsaw Nation, Deconstructing Tolkien: A Fundamental Analysis of The Lord of the Rings, Time Capsule, Epitaphs* (W/ Tom Piccirilli), and T*he Second Coming*. He lives on Long Island with his wife Dawn, their daughter Samantha, and their mutt Oli.

DIANE RAETZ is the editor-in-chief of Padwolf Publishing. She co-created The Wildsidhe Chronicles YA series and is the co-author of Once More Upon A Time. Diane edited Apocalypse 13 and co-edited the vampire anthology New Blood.

Native Washingtonian **QUINTIN PETERSON** is a retired D.C. police officer who served the public for three decades. He is an artist and critically acclaimed writer who has authored four DC-based crime novels, a book of poetry, and has contributed to eight crime fiction/noir anthologies, including *DC Noir*, edited by George Pelecanos. His short stories are also featured in several magazines. His latest offering is *The Voynich Gambit*, the sequel to *Guarding Shakespeare*, a noir mystery thriller about a plot to heist a priceless artifact from the Folger Shakespeare Memorial Library in Washington, D.C.

HILDY SILVERMAN is the publisher of Space and Time, a five-decade-old magazine featuring fantasy, horror, and science fiction (www.spaceandtimemagazine.com). She is also a short fiction author whose most recent publications include, "The Great Chasm" (2016, co-authored w/ David Silverman, *Altered States of the Union*, Hauman, ed.), "A Scandal in the Bloodline" (2017, *Baker Street Irregulars*, Ventrella & Maberry, eds.), "The Show Killer" (2017, *TV Gods 2: Summer Programming*, Young and Hillman, eds.), and "Invasive Maneuvers" (2017, *Love, Murder and Mayhem*, Colchamiro, ed).

DAVID LEE SUMMERS is the author of eleven novels and numerous short stories and poems. His most recent novels are the global steampunk adventure, *Owl Riders,* and a horror novel set an astronomical observatory, *The Astronomer's Crypt*. His short stories have appeared in such magazines and anthologies as *Cemetery Dance*, *Realms of Fantasy*, and *Straight Outta Tombstone*. He's been nominated for the Science Fiction Poetry Association's Rhysling and Dwarf Stars Awards. When he's not writing, David operates telescopes at Kitt Peak National Observatory. Find David on the web at www.davidleesummers.com.

PATRICK THOMAS is the award-wining author of the beloved Murphy's Lore series and the darkly hilarious Dear Cthulhu advice empire. His more than 35 books include *Fairy with a Gun, By Darkness Cursed, Lore & Dysorder, Dead to Rites, Startenders, As the Gears Turn,* and *Exile and Entrance.* He is the co-author of the Mystic Investigators and the Jack Gardner mysteries. In addition to Camelot 13 he is the co-editor of *New Blood* (with Diane Raetz) and *Hear Them Roar* (with CJ Henderson). His *Soul for Hire* story "Act of Contrition" has been made into a short film. Visit him online at www.patthomas.net.

For the past 23 years, **ROBERT E WATERS** has served in the gaming industry, first as a Managing Editor at The Avalon Hill Game Company, and then as a producer, designer, and writer for several computer game studios. He is currently a designer at Breakaway LTD. His first published novel was "The Wayward Eight" (2014) for the tabletop game Wild West Exodus. His second novel, "The Cross of Saint Boniface," an historical fantasy set in the 16th century, is available now on Amazon. Robert has been publishing fiction professionally since 2003, with his first sale to Weird Tales, "The Assassin's Retirement Party." Since then, he has sold over 45 stories to various online and print magazines and anthologies, including stories to Padwolf Publishing (the "13" anthology series), The Black Library (Games Workshop), Dragon Moon Press, Marietta Publishing, Dark Quest Books, Mundania Press, Nth Degree/Nth Zine, Cloud Imperium Games, Winged Hussar Press, Zmok Publishing, and the online magazine The Grantville Gazette, which publishes stories set in Baen Book's best-selling alternate history series, 1632/Ring of Fire. Robert has also put his editorial skills to task by co-editing the anthology Fantastic Futures 13 (Padwolf Publishing) which features science fiction and fantasy stories about Earth's potential future. From time to time, he also writes short fiction reviews for Tangent Online. He also served for seven years as an assistant editor for Weird Tales. Robert is currently living in Baltimore, Maryland with his wife Beth, their son Jason, their cat Buzz, and a menagerie of tropical fish who like to play among the ruins of a sunken Spanish Galleon. His website can be found at www.roberternestwaters.com.

SUSANNE WOLF had her first short story published when she was 12. Her other publication credits include work in *Anthology of Short Stories by Young Americans, A Celebration of Young Poets,* and the *York Review.* Susanne has a BA in English Literary Studies from York College of Pennsylvania, as well as minors in Fine Art and Creative Writing. She currently resides in Baltimore, MD with her husband David, where is she currently working on several young adult novels.

DANIEL HORNE is an artist whose career spans more than three decades. His art has graced almost 500 book covers from *The Hardy Boys* to the *Dungeons and Dragons* game books and all points in-between. This masterful illustrator had done gaming work for Iron Crown Enterprises, West End Games, Alderac Entertainment Group, and Troll Lord Games, illustrated cards for Magic The Gathering and provided the art for the packaging for many of the Batman toys of the 1990s. Daniel has illustrated children's books including *Young Merlin* which won the Children's Choice award for best illustrated book. His comic work includes cards and covers ranging from Spider-man to Vamprella. Daniel has done covers for magazines including *Dragon, Amazing Stories*, and *Dungeon* as well as a back cover for *Heavy Metal.* Daniel did the portrait of the murdered mother in Guillermo Del Toro's movie *Crimson Peak.* Daniel's work is included in the book Masters of Dragonlance Art and his painting "Arcadia" was chosen as the cover of prestigious fantasy art annual *SPECTRUM 9.* His historical portraits are carried in art galleys and have been part of museum shows. He is currently working on a young adult project. Visit his website at www.danielhornestudios.com to learn more.

TALES FROM THE SEA
MERMAIDS
13
Edited by
John L. French

APOCALYPSE
13
THIRTEEN FANTASTICAL
TALES FOR THE END OF DAYS
DEFCON 1
... WARNING...
ANTHOLOGY
MISSLE LAUNCH
EDITED BY
DIANE RAETZ

WHAT WILL THE FUTURE HOLD FOR EARTH?
FANTASTIC
13
FUTURES
ANTHOLOGY
EDITED BY
ROBERT E. WATERS
JAMES R. STRATTON

EDITED BY EDWARD J. MCFADDEN III
LUCKY
13
Thirteen Tales of
Crime & Mayhem
Good or bad, it runs out eventually.
It's all just a matter of luck.
FEATURING
Trent Zelazny
Jessica McHugh
Matt Schairiti
Sarah A. Hoyt
Brady Allen
Danielle Ackley-McPhail
Patrick Thomas
Robert E. Waters
G. Elmer Munson
Diane Raetz
Georgina Morales
John L. French
Michael Laimo

CPSIA information can be obtained
at www.ICGtesting.com
Printed in the USA
LVHW03s2301220818
587768LV00006B/914/P

9 781890 096779